Prologue 1

Chapter 1 – The assignment 11

Chapter 2 - Interview 27

Chapter 3 – A curious lead 44

Chapter 4 – I smell a rat 60

Chapter 5 – On a mission 76

Chapter 6 – Close call 93

Chapter 7 – Just missed 110

Chapter 8 – Being watched 126

Chapter 9 – So sorry 142

Chapter 10 – Revelations 159

Chapter 11 – Unexpected ally 176

Chapter 12 – Not what we thought 192

Chapter 13 – Now we know 212

Epilogue 222

Area 91
A Thriller by Alex Ryan
©2023 by Alex Ryan
All Rights Reserved
Print Edition

Edited by Andy Gamache

ISBN: 9798393024543

A secret government research facility with a dubious reputation and speckled past becomes the focus in the investigation of a missing researcher who disappeared in the course of a terrible accident nearly four decades ago. Ace private investigator Bruce Highland is brought in to find his whereabouts, and uncovers a tangled web of corruption, deceit and lies.

More by Alex Ryan
Bruce Highland Series:
The Tenth (2020)
Conrad's Honor (2019)
The Mohnhaupt Protocol (2019)
Deadly Heirloom (2018)
Project Dark Chapter (2018)
Leon's Fire (2017)
The Lambda Tribe (2017)
The Back Door Key (2016)
The Vine Fraternity (2016)
Gauthier's List (2016)
The Man with Three Selves (2015)
The Gatekeepers (2015)

Other Works:
Entrenched (2022)
Rain Unto Death (2017)

This is a work of fiction. Any similarity between real persons and fictional characters is entirely coincidental. Certain historical facts have been modified and altered to suit fictional purposes. This material is copyrighted and may not be reproduced in part or entirety without permission.

http://www.authoralexryan.com
authoralexryan@hotmail.com
https://www.facebook.com/authoralexryan

Prologue
Washington DC, 1984

The Marine escort to the left of Irving Fuller was all business. His gait was so precise it almost seemed as if he was a robot. If it were any other time – at least prior to the past twenty-four hours, he might even try to engage the Marine in conversation. Perhaps even interject a playful dig just to get a reaction. The first time that Fuller walked the halls of the Pentagon, he felt what one could best describe as, belittled. And this is a man that isn't easily belittled. But today, the massive hallways were a blur. He felt as if he were in a trance.

"We're here, sir," the Marine said in a strong, controlling voice reminiscent of a drill instructor.

"Huh? Oh. Right. Thank you, um... corporal?"

"Sergeant, sir. You may proceed inside the conference room. I'll remain here to escort you back."

"Sorry. I'll get it right one of these days. And thank you. I hope I won't be long."

Fuller tugged at his necktie as the door closed behind him. Colonel Reston was seated behind the massive mahogany table, which was entirely too wide for casual greetings. There was a woman dressed in civilian business attire seated next to him. Fuller wasn't expecting anyone else aside from the two at this meeting.

"Hello Dr. Fuller, why don't you come join us on this side so we don't have to scream at each other. Under ordinary circumstances, I would have preferred to meet in my office, but... anyway, this is CIA Officer Karen Risso. She is the lead for the Agency on this project."

Fuller glanced over at the woman and gave a slight nod. "Right."

Reston looked confused. "You know each other?"

"We've met."

The woman cleared her throat and spoke. She was tall, broad shouldered and blonde, somewhat resembling an East German Olympic track and field competitor hopped up on questionable performance enhancing supplements. "Dr. Fuller, ordinarily I would not personally meet with members of the research team, but I want to hear for myself exactly what the situation is."

Fuller pulled a coil bound report from a leather satchel and flopped it in front of Reston. Karen Risso grabbed it and placed her hands over it. "To give you the twenty words or less version, there has been a major incident at the facility, and most of my team are dead as a result."

"Irving, what exactly happened? Can you tell us that?" Reston asked.

"I don't know exactly. But the facility itself is destroyed. Two of my team and I made it out, and they enacted a code black protocol."

Risso shook her head in frustration. "You executed a code black protocol?"

"I authorized it," Reston replied. "The worst has happened, and it's a seal-in-place and containment issue from here on out."

"What is the basis of the authorization?" Risso asked.

Colonel Reston pulled out a small tape recorder. "One of the team members put in a call to the secure emergency line. It's somewhat graphic but it was placed from within the facility as the crisis was unfolding." Reston played the tape.

"Yes, that was Chad Green's voice," Fuller said.

"What about the research documentation?" Risso asked.

"Destroyed."

"The bodies of the deceased?"

"Unrecoverable."

"What about public knowledge? Were emergency services involved?"

"No. It happened very quickly. Base security has not been notified yet. But at some point, some notifications will have to be made."

"Is there any public danger present?"

"Right now, the structure is in containment. But there is a great danger to the public that needs to be addressed."

"What about potential for a breach of national security? Are there sensitive items or documents present within the structure?"

"Well, yes," Fuller choked slightly.

"That is very messy," Risso said. "Do you have a plan of action, Dr. Fuller?"

"Yes, I do. It will take some money. A lot of money. Basically, we fill the structure with concrete and seal everything in place. I'll need an emergency authorization."

"What about the dead personnel? How are they going to be accounted for?"

Fuller looked down for a second. "I don't know. I suppose at some point, law enforcement will need to be notified. Not my area of knowledge though."

Reston crossed his arms and sat silently, as he gazed at a light fixture above. "The project is classified beyond the base commander himself. As long as the incident is contained within the post, and we can keep notification to the local provost marshal, we should be able to contain the situation. They can make an appropriate determination and issue the death notices. In fact, I'll handle that myself. Personally."

"What about documentation? Is my report good enough?" Fuller asked.

"Neither of us has had a chance to read it. But I already know it's probably not going to work. What we need to document are the steps we took to mitigate a severe threat to the environment and public safety stemming from a catastrophic industrial accident, and basically leave it at that."

"I'm not exactly an environmental scientist," Fuller replied.

"Well, you are now. I really don't want to throw any butter bars from the corps of engineers on this if I don't have to. You're a bright guy. You can figure what to say and how to say it."

"Okay."

"Oh, and one more thing. The provost marshal is going to need some documentation of who died in there and his staff will probably want to know who lived, and will likely want to talk to the survivors."

"The staff roster?" Fuller asked.

"Yeah. We'll need a sanitized one. I'll take care of that. How many did you say escaped?"

"Two, in addition to myself."

"Does this report say which two?" Reston asked, pointing to the document under Risso's arms.

"Yes."

"Good, they're coming off the list."

"But uh, they all have base entry passes. Those can be audited."

"Right. Good point." Reston gave the report one further look, then stood up and continued, "I guess that is all I need to know for now. Thank you again for coming in and meeting with us today. The Marine will show you out."

As the Marine guard escorted Fuller away from the conference room, Colonel Reston rubbed his chin, feeling the developing five o'clock shadow. "You know, Karen, I was captain back when this project was originally formulated. It could have ended the goddamn war in 'Nam. We just didn't have the technology to make it work. What a twist of fate. Now it actually happens, and on my watch, and it blows up in my face."

"I was a fresh hire at the Agency when the project started, and I was put on staff as a gopher," Risso replied. "Eventually, I climbed enough steps up the ladder that they had me take it over. Colonel, this is going to end up hurting me more than it hurts you. It's not going to look good on my resume at all."

"Yeah. I remember you. The little blonde girl tagging along with that dickhead Malone during those meetings at Langley. Colonel Popp used to toy with me and tell me that you were checking me out."

"You trying to tell me something, Colonel?"

"Mmm, maybe."

"I'll take that under advisement."

"Well," Reston said. "Since the project is now officially dead, it looks like our working relationship is going to part company. I know there is nothing to celebrate about, but do you want to grab a drink this evening?"

"I think I'll pass on that Colonel, but thanks for the offer. Oh, by the way, I didn't want to say it in front of your man Fuller, but I'm pretty sure my director isn't going to go for his plan as presented either. We need to rethink things a bit and modify it. We need to change it to something a little more protective of our investment."

"Agreed. I'll think about that. Maybe we can discuss that at a later time. Over drinks perhaps."

Risso rolled her eyes. "Might I remind you, Colonel that although I'm willing overlook your innuendos, condescending implications and uninvited advances, you still work for us, and not the other way around."

"All right. Fair enough. I can make things work out."

"Oh, and Colonel, I'll need that tape. It will help me clear that emergency authorization."

"Yes Ma'am." Reston indignantly flipped the tape over to her.

That evening, Karen Risso sat alone in a corner booth in the dark, exclusive DC bar which was largely patronized by high profile executives looking for a discreet place for a romantic tryst, as well as underworld figures looking to conduct business on neutral but safe territory. She compulsively checked her pager, which she had set in silent mode. A dark figure approached and took a seat in the booth beside her.

"How did things with Reston go after I left?" The man asked.

"Fine, Irving. Just fine."

"Good."

The next afternoon, Chad Green was sitting in his small seaside apartment. He seemed to be in limbo and trying to think of what to do. He didn't know who to call. Who to talk to. The government service personnel administration he had dealt with was back in DC. And the conditions of the NDA were very clear and strict. Don't tell anyone anything about what happens or happened inside that compound, or outside of that compound, else face federal prosecution on felony charges. Treason charges. You would think that Dr. Fuller would give direction to return to DC for either reassignment or release from service due to the apparent termination of the project, but he's been gone. His phone goes to voicemail, and nobody at his office seems to be checking his voice mail. It's only been two days since the incident, but payday came and passed yesterday with nobody to hand him a paycheck, and at some point, rent on the small seaside apartment will be due.

He looked over at the surfboard propped against the living room wall. This is Monterey. Surfing doesn't get much better than here. Surfing calms his mind. Surfing takes off the edge. But right now, cutting a clean line through a tube is probably going to be the time Dr. Fuller will call him to inform him of his status and next steps.

He nervously paced across the shag carpet. The whole team was dead, save for Dr. Fuller and Sarah Lock. He badly wanted to call Sarah, but he didn't have her number and didn't know where she lived. He didn't work directly with her, or otherwise associate with her outside of work, and team associations outside of work were actively discouraged to begin with. The contact list was still in the compound and probably destroyed, and the only other person that would have it was Dr. Fuller. The last instruction he received, was stay home and await instructions, and for god's sake do not go back to the site or even enter the post. Then his phone rang.

"Hello?" Chad said nervously.

"Chad?"

"Yes, Dr. Fuller?"

"Listen, we need to meet. As you might imagine, we're in closeout mode."

"Are you alone?"

"No. I'm with Sarah Lock right now."

"Are you at the site?"

"No. Stay away from it. I have to drop off a report to the base commander, and after that it's off limits to all of us. Can you meet us at the Cliff House at three o'clock?"

"I guess, where is it?"

"It's on Del Monte by the wharf... I don't have the address, but it's in the phone book."

"I'll find it."

"Oh Chad, and one more thing. I have an uneasy feeling. A real uneasy feeling. Just watch your back, okay?"

"Yeah. Sure thing."

Just watch your back, okay? Dr. Fuller isn't one to either joke around or play drama queen. If he pulls a line out of a classic gangster movie, he's dead serious. He pulled into the parking lot of the Cliff House. From the looks of it, it seemed to be an iconic local establishment probably known best for its seafood, and the prices are probably commensurate with its exclusivity, reputation and Dr. Fuller's expense allotment. He scanned the area for Dr. Fuller's red Chrysler LeBaron. A convertible Chrysler

LeBaron. A sports car for old men that feel they should be seen in a Lincoln Continental or Buick Regal, rather than an actual sports car. There was no sign of it, or Sarah's yellow piece of crap Escort for that matter.

He was a little bit spooked by Dr. Fuller's comment. He nervously entered through the large, heavy glass front entry door, and took a seat by the bar. He was still a few minutes early. But the team culture was 'show up ten minutes before your report time or you're late' so he was a little surprised that they were not there yet, and he had a clear view of all the tables, as he took a seat at the bar.

"What can I get for you?" The bartender asked.

Chad was a scientist, not a cop, or a spook, or a thug, but he was an avid reader of action-adventure novels, and frequently channels his inner Walter Mitty. He didn't anticipate that one. He should have. This is no time to get wasted, and he isn't much of a drinker to begin with. But you can't just sit there at the bar and say you're waiting for some people to arrive. No, you've got to blend in and pretend you belong there. Maybe it's paranoia, but his watch was starting to close in on three o'clock, and no sign of Dr. Fuller either walking through the door, or even driving into the parking lot. "I'll have a beer."

"I got a couple featured local microbreweries on tap. One is a golden…"

"I'll just have a… a Budweiser. Yeah."

"Sure thing."

The grizzled looking bartender smiled, poured the beer and pushed it towards Chad. "There you go. A Bud, for a bud. That will be a buck sixty please."

Three-thirty came and went. Still no sign of either Dr. Fuller or Sarah. "You got a phone I can use?" Chad asked.

"Yeah, as long as it's a local call." The bartender handed him a cordless handset from behind the bar.

Chad tried twice to call Dr. Fuller at his office, but like before, both calls went directly to voicemail. The second time he started to leave a message stating that he was waiting at the Cliff House, and decided against leaving it. It was pointless. Dr. Fuller knew damn well he was supposed to be at the Cliff House. "Hey, um, excuse me," he said to the bartender, "there isn't another Cliff House around here is there?"

"Nope. This is the only one."

That beer went down too easy. He stopped at a convenience store on the way back and picked up a six pack of Miller, sat down on the couch, and turned on the television to the local news station.

Earlier today, at approximately two-forty in the afternoon, a fatal vehicle accident, apparently caused by road rage, claimed the lives of a man and a woman on highway 101 in Sand City. The victims were in a red 1982 Chrysler LeBaron convertible. Names have been withheld pending notification of the families. Police have no leads on the offending party. Any witnesses are urged to call...

Chad's jaw dropped. Road rage accident? Not hardly. It was pretty clear who the occupants were. He now felt that he had a giant target printed on his back. What now? Go to the police? And tell them what?

Shortly after he switched the television off, his telephone rang, causing him to flinch and crush the aluminum can, sending a shower of foam all over the couch. "Hello?"

"Mr. Green?"

"Yes?"

"I want you to listen to me carefully. Sometime tonight, two men are going to show up at your place while you are asleep. Their intention is to break in, and then kill you, probably by strangulation, and then stage your apartment to look as if it were a robbery that went bad. And if they are unsuccessful, they will keep trying, and trying, and trying, and they will not stop until they are successful."

"What? Why? Who is this?"

"Don't worry about who I am. But if you don't want to end up like your two friends, I would disappear if I were you."

"Wh...why didn't you warn them?"

"I did."

Chapter 1 – The assignment
Modern Day

The fog had burned off, revealing a very large tree covered hill. A small coastal mountain, if you want to call it – at least it looks that way if you're standing at its base and looking up. Melanie Green parked her Honda Accord next to a pair of antiquated steel water tanks. It was as far up the hill as she could drive. She tugged at her tan, convertible hiking pants and started a journey up a rocky, overgrown path that would have once been a vehicle roadway.

All that remained was a marker. A plain concrete pedestal roughly eighteen inches high under a grove of trees. She had made that pilgrimage nearly every year, since 1995, when the military installation at Fort Ord was closed and the land opened to the public. Most of it anyway. There were still some environmental hot spots, and technically this was one of them but you wouldn't know it unless you were there at the time, or knew someone that was.

Melanie's thin, angular features and straight, shoulder length red hair loomed over the pedestal. In years past, sometimes she would find flowers laying on the pedestal. But they would never stay there. Any remnants of visitor presence would have been removed prior to the next year. She had yet to cross paths with any of the other families, but then again, pinning down the exact date was a little bit tough to do.

A large, old man wearing a sweater and a flat cap, smoking a large cigar emerged from the trail a few minutes later. "Pardon my intrusion," he said with a faint Scottish accent suggestive that he had lived in the United States for most of his life. He approached the pedestal, smiled and made a quick sign of the cross.

Melanie was intrigued. This was a remote area, and not a place to encounter strangers with ill intent. But he didn't appear to be threatening in any way other than his large physical presence. She blushed slightly, not sure of how to react. "Are you... one of... them? I mean the families?"

"No. I'm not. My name is Roland Macleod. I'm a retired Army colonel in the MP corps. I was actually the provost marshal on this base when the incident happened."

"Provost marshal?" Melanie replied.

"Yes, the commanding military law enforcement officer. Responsible for keeping law and order on the base."

"What happened? I never did get an explanation of what happened to my brother, other than he perished in a terrible accident."

"You would think I would be in a position to tell you. But I'm not. I know very little of what happened myself. The research project which went on here was so highly classified that nobody had access to it other than the research team itself. Even us. There was apparently an environmental holocaust that occurred in the structure underneath us, and it was sealed up. It's a bit of an obscure local legend. They call it Area 91."

Melanie extended her hand. "Well, I guess it's nice to finally be able to connect with someone that was actually there. Melanie Green by the way."

MacLeod shook her hand and took a step back as if he was in deep thought.

"Is everything okay?" Melanie asked.

"Sure." He stood for a few moments in silence. "If I may ask, who was your brother?"

"His name was Chad Green."

Immediately, Macleod's eyebrows raised. "Chad Green?"

"You knew him?"

"Not exactly, but your brother did not perish in that compound."

"What?"

"No, there were three survivors. There was the program director, a secretary, and your brother, Chad Green."

"We were told he was dead."

"Oh no – or at least he was still alive after the incident. The reason why we know so little about what happened, is because the survivors all died or disappeared. The program manager and the secretary were both killed in a freak car accident the evening after the incident was reported. The head man, Irving Fuller gave a brief statement when the incident was reported but we never got the opportunity to talk to him in detail. He reported three survivors, himself, a woman, and your brother, Chad Green."

"We have heard absolutely nothing from him since then. Are you positive he survived?"

"We wanted to talk to Chad Green, but we couldn't find him. Being military police, and he was a civilian employee living off post, we had no authority to go off post and detain him for interview. So, we reached out to the local police, and they weren't really interested since he wasn't accused of a crime. So, we asked CID to take a look. They do have authority over civilians in connection with federal activities. They were able to gain access to his apartment, and they reported that it appeared as if he left in a hurry. They canvassed the neighbors, and one reported seeing him load up his car late at night, and drive off. From there it appeared as if he disappeared off the earth."

"So, he could still be alive?"

"He could be, yes."

"Was there some sort of cover up then?"

"I don't know about that."

"I see, but did you still like, investigate?"

"Investigate what? The determination was that the incident was an accident, and there was no evidence to suggest that there was criminal activity involved. All we could do is exercise due diligence, and we did."

"Has anybody ever thought to go down there and take a look?"

"The site was declared an extreme safety hazard, and was completely backfilled with concrete. So, that would pretty much be impossible at this point in time. It was deemed too hazardous to even retrieve the bodies."

"What brings you here?" Melanie asked.

"The same thing that brings you here. I feel a sadness about what happened, and sometimes come here on the anniversary to pay respect."

East Sacramento is your typical older, exclusive neighborhood on the urban fringes of the capital of the State of California, and home to Bruce Highland, licensed private investigator. Bruce isn't your typical gumshoe detective; he was a former US Army military intelligence agent. More accurately, a warrant officer with special agent status. He's uniquely the kind of guy that you call when you want to investigate something or someone in the government that the government does not want investigated. He specializes in high level, high stakes investigations, such as large insurance claims and corporate espionage. And yes, also the occasional cheating spouse call if his workload happens to be very low.

He's military in appearance, with fit, chiseled features, and close-cropped brown hair. With his bio, you might think he's some sort of action-oriented superhero, but he's not. He's just a regular guy, who tends to get involved with irregular activities. He runs his private investigation business out of his home. If you want to get a hold of him, you might find him grilling a steak in his back yard, pumping iron at the gym early morning, cycling in the heart of wine country, or hanging out at his favorite pub, the Crop & Saddle.

Flashy movie detectives drive flashy red Ferraris and lead flashy lives. Real life detectives do not drive flashy cars or lead flashy lives, at least if they want to be effective. Bruce was busy washing his somewhat starting-to-show-its-age Nissan Altima in the driveway of his home. It's not so much that he enjoys hand washing his non-descript old person's car that stands out as much as a grasshopper in an overgrown lawn, but it gives him an excuse to hang out in the front without looking overly creepy. Out of the corner of his eye, he spotted an older model Mercedes sedan drive slowly, scanning the homes. She appeared to be looking for a specific address, and stopped briefly in front of Bruce's home, looked somewhat confused, and started to drive off. Then she stopped, double checked her phone, and backed up, stopping in front of the driveway.

"Can I help you?" Bruce said, wringing out a washcloth.

"I don't know if I'm in the right place. I'm looking for a business called Highland Investigations," the woman said.

"Well, you're at the right place. Did you call?"

"I tried to, but it just went to voice mail. And since I was in the area anyway, I thought I might walk in. I was kind of expecting to see an office."

Bruce dried his hands and retrieved his cell phone from inside the garage. "I'll be damned. I guess you did call. Someone did anyway. I had my phone in silent mode. I don't normally meet my clients here, but since you're already here, what can I do for you?"

"I would like to look in to possibly hiring you."

"Well, okay. Why don't you come inside." Bruce led her to a wooden kitchen table, and motioned for her to take a seat. "How did you find me?"

"You were recommended by Rick Harris."

"Rick Harris, as in Detective Rick Harris in Redwood City?"

"Yes. He's a friend of my aunt's."

"And you are?"

"Melanie Green."

"All right Melanie, how can I help you?"

"In 1984, my brother Chad Green was working on some sort of secret military research project in the Fort Ord Army base. There was some kind of accident, and almost the whole team died as a result. We were notified by the government that he had died, and we were presented with a death certificate. Well, I had a chance meeting with a retired colonel who was some sort of MP commander at the time, and he remembered the incident. And he told me that Chad had not in fact died in that accident, and that he appears to have fled the area."

Bruce held up his hand, as if to motion her to stop, and mentally processed what she was telling him for a couple minutes. "Okay, let me get this straight. You have officially been notified of your brother's death over... let me see, what, close to forty years ago. And you have neither heard from nor seen your brother since. And some guy claiming to be an MP colonel, that you by chance ran into, is telling you otherwise?"

Melanie looked up at the ceiling briefly. "Okay, it sounds a little crazy. But yes."

"So, what do you want from me?"

"I want you to find my brother."

Bruce sat in silence for a moment. "Look, I'm going to be honest with you. Even if this so-called colonel is on the up and up, which, by the way I seriously doubt, the likelihood of finding someone that has been missing that long is not very likely."

"I understand that."

"Not that I want to push away work, but I hate spinning wheels and budget on long shots that are unlikely to pan out. I'm not exactly the cheapest kid on the block."

"I understand that too. But that won't be a problem. My uncle is a wealthy man, and he's agreed to fund an investigation."

Bruce sighed. "Okay, what do you know about this... secret research program?"

"Nothing. Chad was very tight-lipped about it. He didn't even say exactly where it was. I started poking around down there in Monterey in search of answers around 1994. Some of the locals knew where the site was. It was a big underground bunker near the top of a hill inside Fort Ord. They referred to it as 'Area 91.' I went out there almost every year since, on the anniversary of the incident, as they call it, to sort of pay homage. I understand it is a gravesite to most of the team."

"So where did you meet said colonel?"

"Two weeks ago, at the site itself. He introduced himself. He was a large man. Old. He looked like that guy that played a Russian submarine captain, and even had a Scottish accent. His name was um... Roland. Roland Macleod."

Bruce hastily scribbled down some notes on a pad of paper. "I'll tell you what. Two things, okay. I'll check out this Roland Macleod, and this... Area 91. If they both check out, then we can go from there. Secondly, my normal rate is eight hundred a day plus expenses, and this could take months with no guarantee of success. Do the math."

Melanie scowled. "That's a lot."

"At the risk of sounding immodest, I'm pretty good at what I do. If you removed the time element and tin foil hat component, I would say I can normally wrap up a missing person's investigation in a matter of days. If I can't wrap it up within a couple weeks, it's usually not worth pursuing further."

"I can work with that."

"All right. Give me some contact information, and I'll get back to you."

Bruce bid her farewell, and watched her drive off. Damn, the water spots. He cursed himself for not drying his car properly. Just then, a large elderly lady in hair curlers and a bath robe ambled on by.

"Well, well, well, Bruce; that was a mighty cute looking girl that just left. It's about time you've found someone."

"Very funny Blanche. She was here to talk to me about a case."

Blanche did have a point. Blanche had a hell of a point. Bruce cracked open a beer. It was too soon to even think about exploring that option. She did have those piercing blue eyes.

He settled down in front of his computer with a mantra. Find a reason to dismiss Melanie Green's wild claims.

A cursory Internet search revealed little about Roland Macleod other than an individual by that name resided in Salinas, which was right next door to Monterey, and he fell into the right age bracket. A more in-depth look using his privileged PI and LEO accessible databases revealed that Roland Macleod was in fact a former Army colonel, and was in fact the provost marshal at Fort Ord during the time period. He was the son of a Scottish born British consulate official, last assigned in New York City, became a naturalized citizen at the age of eighteen, and was accepted at West Point a year later. A stock photo taken at his retirement for a news article revealed that he fit the general description of that which Melanie gave.

There was little information available on Area 91, other than a few dated news articles citing hearsay accounts of some secret area on Fort Ord named Area 91, as well as a couple accounts in local tabloids claiming that it was a secret UFO base reputed to harbor space aliens. There were certainly no official records pertaining to any type of secret facility located within the confines of the base. Granted, Melanie's story seemed pretty wild, with some details, which, if true, hinted at some sort of possible government cover up. But, Bruce had seen wilder and stranger.

And then there was the third thing. The one that Bruce did not allude to, and that was Melanie herself. Melanie

Green was born in Canton, Ohio, the youngest of three siblings. Chad Green was the middle brother, and Hazel Green was the older sister. All three attended Cornell University. Melanie graduated with a degree in chemistry. The other two siblings' academic tracks were unspecified. Melanie's current address was listed in Redwood City, California. Chad's last known address was in Reston, Virginia. This was obviously not consistent with an assignment in Monterey, but temporary residences don't always show up in personal databases. That said, he was a real person, with no history extending past 1984. Which meant that more than likely, he died in 1984.

Bruce dug a little further. His last employer was the federal government. He held a GS 10 paygrade, which would correspond to a mid-level technical or supervisory position. That in fact could jibe with a super-secret military research project, particularly if his last known was in Reston. But it could also mean he was a GSA manager at a supply warehouse.

Bruce was trying to find a way to eliminate taking on Melanie's case, but as he got into it, it seemed to become apparent that at least a second look might be warranted. He was starting to encroach on research efforts he wouldn't ordinarily do until there was a signed contract in place. Still, it's damned hard to live that far off the grid. Again, Bruce thought, he's probably dead. But, if so, Melanie, and the family, would still want to know what happened to him, right?

You would think that some event, so catastrophic as to claim several lives, would at least have a mention in the local newspaper, even if it is on base. But there was no mention of such. Then Bruce had a thought. Melanie mentioned two team members killed in a freak car accident. She attended visits of 'Area 91' on specific anniversary dates. By conjecture, Bruce narrowed the date range back to a week forward and week past this anniversary date.

June 6, 1984. That was a Wednesday. There were three fatal automobile accidents during that two-week period. One of them was on that date. There were two individuals involved: A man named Irving Fuller, the driver, and a woman named Sarah Lock. They were killed in a hit and run crash on Highway 101. Irving Fuller was a professor, and a leading researcher in the field of bioengineering. And he held a very high-level GS position, with a last known permanent address in Arlington, Virginia. Sarah Lock was a local, with a lower GS level commensurate with a secretary or clerk of some sort.

Bruce decided to sleep on it. He remained unconvinced that he would be able to determine the whereabouts or fate of Chad Green. But so far, the pieces of Melanie's account of what happened seemed to fit.

For Bruce, the one mind-clearing event of the day is the daily morning gym routine. It was a ritual that He very rarely misses, and then only for drastic reasons. It's a timed event. He arrives at zero-dark thirty, does his prescribed weight routine appropriate for the day of the week. He then settles into an hour-long cardio session, usually focusing his attention on a true crime segment airing on the hour on the television, unless there is a co-joiner on an adjacent machine who is present to engage in conversation. And of course, what was the topic of the true crime program for today? The unsolved disappearance of a young law school student.

The one thing about clients willing to pay your extravagant billing rate for premium service, is that they get premium service. You go to them. Redwood City is a pretty good haul from Sacramento, and the Bay Area traffic makes it a very unpalatable drive during the commute hours. Not hour, but hours. But as fortune had it, Melanie has one of those jobs where she can spend two days a week working from home, affording a late morning visit.

Melanie's appearance suggested that her apartment would be clean, neat, and arranged almost to the point of OCD. It was. And her apartment itself suggested another, completely irrelevant point. She was single. Bruce kicked himself mentally for making the observation. He was neither in the market, nor was he on the market.

He was still relieved that she was single with no outwardly apparent boyfriend (or girlfriend) as those generally affect the client-investigator relationship in a negative way. Husbands and boyfriends generally view private investigators, particularly strong male private investigators, as outsiders interfering with internal affairs at best, and as competitors at worst. And the dynamic doesn't get much better if the roles are reversed – it's the husband or boyfriend that hires the investigator. The wife or girlfriend still feels put out, justifiably or not.

"Can I offer you something to drink? Water? Tea? Sparkling water?" Melanie asked. She was dressed in gym tights, and a light sweat jacket. Who dresses up to show up for work in front of their home computer?

"You mean like those canned zero calorie fizzy water things?" Bruce replied.

She smiled. "Lemon or Elderberry Passionfruit Essence?"

"How fancy. I'll try the Elderberry stuff."

Melanie returned with two glasses of sparkling water over ice. "So obviously you didn't drive all the way over here to just tell me you aren't interested in the case."

"Actually, I almost decided to fly here to save time, but you don't live very close to a suitable airport. Anyway, I wouldn't say I'm one hundred percent committed, but so far everything you've told me more or less checks out, so I suppose it's worth further exploration. That would of course be on your dime."

"Of course. So, what is the first step you are going to take?"

"For starters, I want to talk to this Roland Macleod. I mean I've verified he is a real person, but I want to talk to him face to face to get an idea if he's being straight up."

"And then?"

"I'm going to need to spend some time. Probably a couple days, checking out some of the local resources. A lot of times, newspapers from back then have fiche records of news articles that never make it to the online digital world. Secondly, this was an old military post and some of the workers and even military personnel themselves may still be around. VFW halls and Rotary Clubs are good places to canvas."

"And after that?"

"Well, barring leads dug up from those sources, and information from family and friends – which, I suspect you have already exhausted, it could stop there."

"So, when are you going to start?"

Bruce sipped his water. "This stuff is actually pretty good. Oh, when am I going to start? Usually, in most missing persons cases, time is of the essence. The first twenty-four hours is the most critical. In this case, the first twenty-four hours has passed. In fact, the first twenty-four years have passed. So, from an investigative standpoint, it doesn't much matter if I start now, or in a week, or in a month." Bruce could read visible discontent on her face. "But I have an easy schedule presently, so I'll start tomorrow."

The visible discontent from Melanie's face disappeared. "I want to go with you."

Bruce was taken aback. "As a general rule, I don't like to involve clients with field investigative work or subject interviews."

"Okay, but, for example, how will you know that the Roland Macleod you are talking to is the same one I talked with?"

"Oh, I can get a good sense of that without requiring your presence."

"What... what about... I might know something about something he mentions in an interview."

"Forgive my ignorance, but unless you've left out a substantial bit of information when you last talked to me, you don't seem to know much at all."

Melanie scowled. "What ever happened to the customer is always right?"

"That old adage doesn't apply here. You don't take your car to the mechanic if you're able and willing to fix it yourself."

"Look, don't take this the wrong way, Mr. Highland, but we are paying you a lot of money for this effort. And it's not like we don't trust you or anything, but the family would feel a lot better if they could see progress being made. You're the one that makes the rules, right?"

"Yeah, you're right. It's not a hard and fast rule. But it's a rule for two reasons. One is client protection, and the other is frankly, and don't take this the wrong way, but I can generally cover more ground on my own."

"Do you really think you're going to run into bad guys, at least at this stage of the investigation? And as to your second point, or more correctly, your assertion, I'll stay out of your way. I promise."

Bruce took a deep breath. "Okay. I'll tell you what. You can go along with me for the initial interview with Roland Macleod. After that, I'm sending you on a cab ride home, and I'm going to start hitting the old folks' hangouts."

Melanie beamed. "Okay. That works. When do we leave?"

"Tomorrow, if I can get something set up with Macleod. You didn't get his number, did you?"

"No, I didn't think to. Sorry."

"Don't apologize to me, I just wanted to ask first. It's not going to be very hard for me to figure out."

"All right. Just let me know."

"Righto. I've got some forms for you to fill out. Just email them to me when you're done."

"What's your email?"

"It's on the forms."

Melanie scanned the forms. "Oh. Right. Oh... and Mr. Highland, one more thing."

Bruce rolled his eyes. "You can call me Bruce. I only get called Mr. Highland when I'm in trouble."

"Fair enough. I just want to make sure that this arrangement is strictly professional. If you know what I mean."

"I think I know what you mean, and see, that's the other reason why I don't like to involve clients directly in investigations. Things get misconstrued. Intentions get misread. No, I assure you that I absolutely, strictly do not mix personal and professional venues."

"Good. Then we both have the same understanding."

A Rubik's Cube was all the rage back in the 1980's. Dr. Sherpov thought it would be good therapy. Elena Yakut seemed to have a penchant for riddles and puzzles. The scars have mostly healed, and therapy slowly returned her tall, svelte figure and her long blonde hair had mostly grown back.

"How are you doing Elena? The staff says you have made remarkable progress."

She held the plastic square toy in her hand and stared out the window. The trees in St. Petersburg were now in full bloom. The harsh Russian winter was finally over. It had been exceptionally long and cold. She turned and spoke. "Doctor, I have been having these strange dreams lately. Dreams of being in places that I've never been to."

"Mystical places? Magical places?"

"No. California."

"You watch a lot of television and internet videos, no?"

"Yes."

"Of course. Elena, your dreams are your subconscious trying to speak to you. You feel trapped. You seek escape. But just know that we are all trying to help you here."

"That makes sense."

"Elena, I have to tell you something. I have been reassigned to a facility in Moscow. You are going to have a new doctor. His name is Jakob Katz. He will take over my duties. He is a very good psychiatrist."

Elena sat in silence, seemingly unfazed, as she stroked the white terrycloth robe. Sherpov walked out of the room, and traveled down three flights of stairs and across the hallway to his office. As expected, sharply on the hour, there was a knock at his door.

"Come in," Sherpov announced.

In walked a man with somewhat darkish, weathered skin and a straight black beard. "Doctor Sherpov, I am Jakob Katz."

"Yes, we spoke on the phone. I trust you have had an opportunity to meet with the director?"

"Yes, he has informed me of my duties."

"Very well. I would like to brief you on one of our special charges. Elena Yakut."

"Elena Yakut. The name sounds familiar."

"She was one of the three survivors of Aeroflot flight 7230. She was in terrible condition when she came to us. She has been making very good progress. But the problem is, she has no memory of anything prior to her awakening at the medical facility. Not even her own name. And this is after three years."

Katz ran his fingers through his beard. "That is a very unusual case. Usually, there are some memories."

"Another thing has been bothering me, and I wish I could stay longer to sort it out. She has started speaking English lately. The friends and family of Elena claim that she does not speak English."

"What are you saying? Do you mean to imply that she is actually someone else?"

"There are explanations for it. Television. The internet. She possibly could have picked up some English but that is difficult for a middle-aged adult to do under the best of conditions."

"That could be it yes," Katz replied.

"It's not just one thing. It is small things. Like for example, earlier today, she told me she had been having dreams of being in the United States. California."

"Again, sometimes with traumatic brain injuries, a clean slate means the conscious may be more easily populated with images and languages. I've seen it before."

"Perhaps," Sherpov replied. "You know, when the crash happened, most of the bodies were burned beyond recognition. Beyond identification. The other two survivors were positively identified through personal documents and dental records. Elena had none of that available when she was recovered. Do you know how they identified her? They went through the flight manifest, and the security camera footage at St. Petersburg, and visually identified her that way."

"But, what about her friends and relatives?"

"None have visited her since shortly after the crash. They did identify her visually as well but she was in very bad shape at the time and looks quite different today. And... and, she knows how to speak, how to eat, how to bathe, how to solve complex puzzles, how to read, yet, she cannot recall her own name. I think, Dr. Katz, it is because she has been assigned the name Elena Yakut and conditioned to it, blocking memories of her birth name."

"All distinct possibilities, doctor. All distinct possibilities."

Chapter 2 - Interview

The swaying of the car on the twisting roads made it difficult for Melanie to read a small paperback novel she had brought with her to pass the time, so she finally gave up and put it back in her purse. "What time are we meeting with Mr. Macleod?"

"Ten. At a coffee house in downtown Salinas," Bruce replied. "It's kind of an awkward time. Too late for breakfast, and too early for lunch. If you want, we can stop to grab a bite to eat. We have time."

"I'm good."

"What's your day job, Melanie?"

"I'm a lab chemist. I analyze water samples."

"Huh. It seems like that is one job that can't be easily done at home."

"Well, I split my time. Sometimes I'm in the lab, running the mass spectrometers and gas chromatographs, which I obviously have to be physically there for, and sometimes I do quality assurance, which does not require me to be physically present at the lab."

"I see. Sounds pretty interesting."

"It's kind of boring, to tell the truth. I'm sure your job is a lot more adventurous and exciting."

Bruce chuckled. "That's a common misconception. It's mostly boring, academic and monotonous. Stakeouts are usually as exciting as they get, and trust me, they are about as exciting as watching paint dry. If your days are action packed and adventurous, you're doing it wrong. That said, it does have its moments."

"How did you become a private investigator?"

"My career as an Army intelligence officer came to an end when I brought down a general for espionage. And it just seemed to be like a logical thing to do."

"Wow, so you were a spy?"

"No, I was a warrant officer in the military intelligence corps. We busted spies. My assignment was in West Germany, cold war era."

"Did you run around with a gun, like the CIA guys?"

"We carried sidearms for personal protection, yes. And we were considered to be federal agents, those of us with special agent status. And by the way, CIA agents generally don't carry guns. Another big misconception. And they don't spy. Most are analysts and program managers. Even the field agents don't spy. They recruit and manage spies."

The Coffee Tree was a large, rustic building with oak barrels for tables and wooden chairs. It more resembled some sort of trendy brew pub. And it was virtually deserted. Which, was probably why Macleod chose it as a place to meet. Macleod could be seen sitting at a corner table at the far end of the room, reading a newspaper. He glanced up at Melanie and Bruce as they approached, and motioned for them to take a seat.

"I'm kind of use to seeing coffee houses packed with people," Melanie said.

Macleod smiled. "Cross the hill from Monterey to Salinas, and it's like being on another continent. This is the home of farmers and migrant workers. Not hipsters and yuppies. But they do make a quite nice breakfast croissant."

"Bruce Highland," Bruce said extending his arm.

"Ahh yes, Mr. Highland. You have a rather impressive bio. Former military intelligence, and ties with the Agency."

"I see you did your homework," Bruce replied.

"Due diligence. I'm a cop. Or was a cop. Once a cop, always a cop." Macleod's Scottish drogue became slightly thicker. "So, tell me, Mr. Highland, am I correct in presuming that you are engaged in an effort to locate Miss Green's long-lost brother?"

"That's right. Can you tell me what exactly happened starting from the time of this accident back in 1984?"

"Well, there is some dispute over when the incident, as we called it, actually occurred. Our office got a call mid-morning of June 6th, it was a Wednesday. A man that identified himself as Irving Fuller had driven over to our station, and asked to speak with the man in charge. The duty sergeant called me from my office, where I was informed that there had been a bad accident at the research facility popularly known to us as 'Area 91,' and that the facility had been sealed due to a severe public danger threat. We were further informed that ten members of the research team had perished inside, and three members escaped including Fuller himself. We responded to the perimeter of the site and called in emergency services, where it was determined that they were not needed. We asked for Irving Fuller to give a detailed statement. He said he would, but he first had to attend to securing the site for safety reasons, and that an environmental determination had been made to backfill the underground vault structure with concrete, to stabilize the hazard."

"What kind of... hazard was this?"

"He didn't say. The environmental report that was issued at a later time stated that the hazard was chemical in nature but that the details were classified."

"Who prepared this report?"

"He did."

"So, he prepared and certified his own environmental report?"

"That's correct."

"That sounds pretty irregular and suspicious." Bruce rubbed his chin.

"It may well be, but it wasn't a matter for the Provost Marshal's office. Anyway, Mr. Fuller had made arrangements for construction equipment and crews to be brought to the site for emergency containment work. He agreed to come back to the post with the other two surviving team members so detailed statements could be taken, but he never made it. Both himself and a secretary, Sarah Lock, were killed in a vehicle accident on the way. And at that time, the third surviving team member, Chad Green, could not be located."

"Did you take steps to locate him?"

"Yes, we did. We had a roster of the research team members with contact information. We were the ones, after all, who issued their base entry passes, and attempted to call him on the listed phone number. Local authorities were contacted for assistance, but they deemed the request to be of insufficient priority to expedite in a timely fashion. We contacted CID to locate him the following day, since they have authority off post over civilians. Their investigation found that he was observed leaving his apartment late at night, in an apparent haste."

"Huh," Bruce said. "I'm just thinking out loud here. And Melanie, please remain objective as we need to consider all possibilities, but do you think it's possible that Chad Green could have been responsible for causing the accident – possibly as a sabotage effort, killed two witnesses, and fled?"

"What are you implying, Bruce?" Melanie asked in a strained voice.

Macleod held up his hand in a motion to calm Melanie. "Actually, that was the first thing that occurred to me. But there are a couple problems with that. First, Irving Fuller was very adamant that it was strictly an accident. Secondly, I was not convinced that the incident actually occurred on the 6th when Fuller had reported it. I believed it could have actually happened two days earlier."

"What made you believe that?"

"You see, when we issue temporary base passes to civilian employees, their visits actually had to be logged in, both coming and going. It was the base commander's policy. With the exception of Fuller, Green and Lock, nobody else had logged an exit or entrance since Monday morning on the 4th. That anomaly was discovered too late to ask Fuller for an explanation."

"What about the bodies inside the vault?"

"Like I told Miss Green previously, it was deemed too much of a risk to public safety to remove them and they were sealed inside with concrete, along with everything else."

"What about death notifications?"

"The base medical officer was informed of the situation, issued a roster of the deceased individuals along with a statement of the circumstances. He issued the death certificates, and subsequently notified the Office of Personnel Management."

"But what about my brother? I have his death certificate," Melanie said.

"I can't answer that one," Macleod said. "But I assure you it didn't come from the base medical officer. I had to account for all of them personally."

"What about for Fuller and Lock?" Bruce asked.

"That incident occurred off post. Presumably the county coroner would have issued the death certificates. But we would not have been involved."

Bruce stretched out his back. "So, what's your best guess? I mean why do you think Chad Green split, and do you think the deaths of Irving Fuller and Sarah Lock were coincidental?"

"My gut feeling?" Macleod said. "I think someone targeted all of them as witnesses, or perhaps a potential security leak, but I don't have a shred of evidence to suggest either of our suggested scenarios."

"Had any further attempts been made to locate Chad Green?"

"We requested that CID take a look at financials and passport activity. Mr. Green emptied his entire bank account into a cashier's check the following day, and the trail ended there. But that's not a crime. He was never a suspect in a criminal investigation."

"What about his passport?" Melanie asked. "He never left the country?"

"Well, he didn't go to any place that had incoming passport control like Canada or Europe. Hell, you can drive right into Mexico with no passport," Macleod said. Bruce nodded in agreement.

"So, he could be anyplace then," Melanie replied.

"I don't want to get your hopes up, Miss Green, you need to understand that it's hard as hell to live anyplace in complete anonymity."

"Agreed," Bruce said. "A lot of things can happen over all of those years, and if you're in a foreign country hiding out, especially a third world country, and you pass away, it's unlikely anyone would ever know." Bruce sensed that the interview session was drawing to an end, judging by Macleod's body language. "So tell me, you seem to be rather candid about what happened. Usually, you guys are pretty tight lipped, you know, operational security and all that. Why are you so forthcoming?"

Macleod turned slightly red. "I'm a cop, Mr. Highland. I don't like being lied to. I just report what I see and what I find. I don't know if there is any kind of cover up going on here, but if there is, I'm not going to stand in the way of it being exposed."

"Have you ever wanted to know if there was a cover up?" Bruce asked.

"Even if it was my fight, and it's not, there isn't a shred of evidence to go on. Now if there is nothing further, I have an appointment with my gardener I would like to keep."

"So, what do you think?" Melanie asked as she closed the passenger door of the Altima behind her.

"Oh, I think he's being straight up. At least I don't think he's covering anything up. But at face value, the way things were handled, going by his account, it seems pretty irregular to me. The problem is, we're still not even one inch closer to being on the trail of your brother, and so far, he was our best shot. You still want to continue on with this investigation?" Bruce asked.

"Yes. I mean we're barely a day into it, right?"

"Okay, well, let's find you a cab, or rideshare, and I will...."

"I want to come."

"Remember our...."

"I want to come."

"Now we had this disc...."

"Do you even know where the site is? You know you need to visit the location just to get a feel for things, don't you?"

"Are you always so insistent?"

Melanie displayed a slight air of disgust as she stared at the gaudy sign. The Starlight Motel looked like the type of establishment that would rent rooms by the hour, and not by the night. "Bruce, this place looks totally sleazy. Are you seriously going to book a couple rooms here?"

"Well, my rate is eight hundred plus expenses. I usually try to keep expenses down on food and lodging, unless there is a compelling investigative reason to do otherwise. But if you want to go someplace nicer, I'm not going to argue with you."

With Macleod's interview out of the way, and two rooms at the much nicer Crabtree Inn booked, Bruce drove Melanie to the local American Legion Hall. "Are we... welcome in this place?" Melanie asked.

"I'm actually a Legion member, so yes," Bruce replied.

"I never pegged you as the kind of person that hangs around old people day drinking and swapping war stories," Melanie said as she giggled.

"I'm not, but this organization falls in the category of those I belong to so that I can use them as an investigative tool. I can't count how many times I've gotten useful information on a case by talking to these people. So, here's our cover story. We're both investigative reporters, and we're doing a segment on Area 91 and the former Fort Ord army base. And were looking for people that either worked there or were stationed there in the early to mid-1980's."

It took roughly two beers, and one brisket sandwich each before they were directed to a gentleman named Earl Hightower. Normally Earl comes in on Thursday nights but Norm Franks texted him and persuaded him to come down to the hall. It's not like he had work to do that day.

Earl looked like a fairly engaging individual when he sat down at the bar. He looked approvingly at Melanie. "Understand you folks are looking for some background on Area 91?"

Bruce nudged Melanie. "That's right," she replied. "What was your function?"

"Utility operator. Worked on the base from '79 until it closed in '94, then two more years on the remaining Presidio. Used to make rounds at the water tanks up on the hill. Area 91 was some kind of underground bunker or something like that. None of us knew about it until they unearthed it in '82, moved some people in and declared it strictly off limits to all except those assigned there. In fact, nobody was even allowed on the hill itself except base security and the utility operators."

"Did you know what was going on there?" Melanie asked.

"No. I mean there were a lot of rumors. Secret alien research. Development of new kinds of nuclear weapons. You name it."

"What did it look like?"

"They posted a sentry on the access road, so you couldn't get close enough to see what was going on. And at the time they had a fence around the perimeter. And it was electrified."

"Some kind of accident happened in June of 1984. Do you remember any of that?"

"Yeah, like it was yesterday, but we didn't really know about any accident at the time. That story only circulated through the rumor mill. It was never made public. But I remember that over a two-day period, they moved some heavy equipment up there. A dozer and an excavator, and hauled a couple truckloads of debris away the first day. Then they sent a concrete truck up there, did some more earth work, then left."

"Wait," Bruce said. "You said a concrete truck. Do you mean, one concrete truck?"

"I only saw one."

"Could there have been others?"

"Not unless they reopened the site in the middle of the night. The crews up there were working day shift, and I was at the tank site from sunup to quitting time because we had a rehab project going on for those tanks at the time."

"Huh. Okay."

"Yeah, well anyway, so, after they were done, the fence was taken down, and that was that. You could go up there, and tell they had stripped some things on the ground and backfilled the side of the hill."

"So, you worked for base public works then, right?"

"That is correct. As a civilian employee."

"So, they probably had records. Building plans, things like that, right?"

"Yeah, they had a plan room. That's where they kept the original copies of the utility maps. They were all hand drawn ink on Mylar back then."

"So, you said the Area 91 structure was unearthed in 1982. Somebody obviously knew about it. Do you know if any plans of it existed?"

"Nope, but I didn't have access to that stuff anyway. I mean I assume it's still there. The public works office is on the Presidio grounds."

"Who would have had access at the time?"

"Let me see... okay, so, '82... Major Richards. Tom Richards. He was the public works officer at the time."

"I wonder if they kept all that stuff," Bruce retorted.

"Well, there was another major, Phillip Cox. He was the public works officer when the base closed in '94. He might know. Couldn't tell you where either one of them is now." Earl's cell phone vibrated, and he pulled it out and unlocked it. "Dang it, listen, nice chatting with you folks but I gotta go."

"Thank you very much for your time," Bruce replied. He started to get up, and turned his attention to the bartender. "Oh, one more thing. If you wouldn't mind asking around, I'd love to talk with people that were on base during '82 to '85 or thereabouts. Here's my card."

It was as if a light rain had fallen on the hillside as the morning fog started to dissipate. Getting permission to enter the Presidio at the gate was like pulling teeth. Melanie usually was able to pull it off in the past with a wink and a nod, but Bruce was forced to go through more proper channels. Bruce surveyed the rough, overgrown path leading to the small clearing in the trees, in the middle of which was the concrete slab. "So this is the place, huh."

"This is it." Melanie stepped up on to the slab.

"So where is this vault?"

"I would assume below us. They said it was underground."

"Who is 'they'?"

"Some old lady that worked at the local library when I started checking into this several years ago."

Bruce stepped back, and eyed the embankment behind the site. "Hmm. I wonder why they would do that."

"Do what?"

"Well, a lot of these old underground bunkers you see a lot on the California coast, were actually built by knocking off the top or side of a hill, building the structure, and then backfilling the hill back over it, rather than excavating and pouring."

"Well, I certainly don't know."

"There's nothing marked here at all, to warn of any kind of hazard. But then I guess if it was backfilled with solid concrete, why bother."

"So does seeing this place add anything useful?" Melanie asked.

"Not really." No sooner than Bruce spoke, than the sun broke through the clouds, and he caught a glimpse of something shiny in the corner of his eye. It up in a tree. He looked at it, and the shimmering disappeared. He turned his attention back to the rocky hillside, and there was the shimmering again. He turned again and stared up at the tree. It appeared to be coming from behind the crook of two large, high branches. He tore through the dense underbrush obstructing the tree, and forced his way back around it. He was surprised to find another slightly less overgrown foot path, or perhaps it was an animal path, arriving from another location. "Hey Melanie. Come back here. Check this out."

Running up the backside of the tree was a thick, rubber clad cable. It disappeared behind some branches. At the bottom of the tree, it was threaded through the thick brush just out of sight of the narrow trail.

They followed the trail, which terminated at a cyclone fence, this was actually the backside of a water tank structure. Which, was inexplicable as the brush was entirely too thick against the fence to access the trail from the front of the tank site. But there was a cut in the fence, where it could be pushed away and a man could walk through the opening. The cable continued a short distance to the rear of the utility site, and disappeared into a downturned conduit from an electrical junction box.

"What's going on here, Bruce?" Melanie said with a confused look.

"Somebody is running power all the way up to that tree just outside of the site clearing. I'm ninety nine percent sure it's a video surveillance camera, probably with a proximity alarm. Don't get any closer to that fence than we already are. That site's got surveillance cameras of its own. They all do."

"Why would they put a camera up at the site?"

"I don't know. But when we get back, completely ignore that tree. Pretend it doesn't exist. I suspect whoever is watching, probably knows they have been made by now. But if they haven't, let's not give them confirmation." Bruce drove away from the utility tank site down the narrow, rutted dirt road, expecting at any time to see some black Tahoes or Explorers coming out of the woodwork to tail them.

Why exactly would someone bring power all the way from the water tanks to the Area 91 site? It would have had power of its own. The most logical explanation is that the site was gutted in 1984. But why surveil the site? Nobody says you can't go there. No sign says stay out. Probably because 'do not enter' signs are an obvious invitation to enter. Don't promote. Don't advertise. It is after all an environmental hazard. Maybe that is the reason. Just maybe.

Melanie swirled a glass of red wine and poked at her baked flounder as the surf crashed onto the beach nearby. "You know, it seems like this is turning into an investigation of Area 91 more than a search for my brother."

"Well, right now it is the only lead we have. By the way, you really should have gone for the filet. It's pretty good."

"Hmm. This is a little bit dry. But I'm trying to cut back on red meat."

"I'm just thinking out loud. So, we have this underground structure that is obviously large enough to accommodate thirteen people, and their stuff reasonably comfortably, given they went there daily for a two-year period. You would have to have concrete trucks cycling through nonstop for a day or two in order to fill it in. Our man Earl was fairly adamant there was only one. Remember, Macleod stated that the structure was backfilled with concrete, and it was in a report."

"Why would they say it was filled with concrete if it wasn't?" Melanie asked.

"To discourage people from trying to get in. That might explain the surveillance camera as well."

"I don't know Bruce; think maybe you're starting to get a case of the tinfoil hat syndrome?" Melanie said with a chuckle.

Bruce sighed. "I think I'm going to play a card that I really don't want to play."

"What's that?"

"Oh, I have a friend."

High above the massive parking lot of the CIA's McLean, Virginia headquarters, in the newer complex referred to as the 'New Headquarters Building' sits senior program manager Nielson's corner office. He plays point for projects that he could never tell you about, because if he did, he would have to have someone kill you. Or more likely he would be terminated and prosecuted for mishandling classified information. Nielson really has no life. He tells his staffers he can't have outside relationships with women because of his work and requirement for confidentiality. If that were actually true, then twenty-one thousand other Agency employees would be in the same boat, and most are probably finding ways to make it work. More to the point, he's a tallish, lanky geek of a man who wears slightly rumpled polyester suits. In his defense, he argues that they are in fact Montgomery Ward's top of the line polyester suits – polyester blend suits at that. Of course, the rebuttal to that argument is that Montgomery Ward closed all of its remaining stores for good in 2001. Although they reemerged as an online only retailer, they still apparently don't sell polyester blend suits.

Define a friend. A friend is someone that you associate with on a regular basis outside of whatever setting you primarily know them from. A coworker is not a friend. A coworker is a coworker. If you play racquetball with your coworker in the morning before work, he's still a coworker. If you go on weekend fishing trips with him, then he's a friend. If you're banging your coworker on the side, well, then she is a friend. An extra special friend. Nielson doesn't really have much in the way of friends, extra special or otherwise. The closest thing he does have to a friend is the guy he always calls when he's in a jam, and that can fix problems for him. Small problems are mutually fixed by trading favors. Big problems are fixed by payment via the Agency's massive and untraceable discretionary fund. That go-to man has experience working with, and for, the Agency. That man is Bruce Highland.

Nielson stared blankly at the small plastic basketball hoop stuck to the wall with suction cups above the metal waste bin. After hours, when he isn't looking, janitors will routinely empty the waste bin all over the floor, replace the bin and take photos with their cell phones so they can later post creative memes to social media when they leave the site. The ring of his public cell phone jarred him into a state of full consciousness.

"Nielson speaking."

"Oh, this is Nielson? Well gosh darn it, I was trying to call Miles. I know this is Nielson speaking. You do this to me every time!" Bruce Highland chided.

"Hi Bruce. What do you want this time?"

"Oh, so that's how it is. It's always 'Bruce wants something' and not 'hey Nielson, let's grab some drinks at the gentleman's club and burn off a few stacks of five-dollar bills.'"

"Something tells me that you are not in the DC area right now, waiting in a bar with a wad of fives and a rocket in your pocket."

"Okay you're right. Do you know anything about a project related to a place called 'Area 91' in the former Fort Ord base in the mid-80's?"

"Nope. Haven't a clue."

"Well okay, let me rephrase this, can you check?"

"You do realize that when I check into secret government projects on your behalf, I am technically committing sins that the Pope himself can't atone me for, and it usually blows up in my face, right?"

"Well speaking of sins, remember that girl in Roanoke I set you up with by playing wingman last month? If I remember correctly, that one blew up in her face."

"Okay, okay. I'll poke around a little bit. I'll take an... eekie peekie."

Bruce terminated the call and flagged the waiter down for another glass of wine. "Done."

Melanie glared at him with a cold stare. "Girl? Wingman? Things blowing up in her face? What the hell, Bruce?"

"What do you think I am, a saint?"

Melanie shook her head in disapproval. "Men!" She chugged her wine. "What are you looking at?"

Bruce chuckled. "You have a nice face." Melanie slapped him.

The wine was starting to wear off, as Melanie flipped through the channels of the motel television set, finally landing on an old detective series set in Hawaii with the handsome guy with the mustache who drives a red Ferrari. She wondered what Bruce would look like with a mustache. She wondered what Bruce would look like in a Ferrari. She wondered what she would look like in a Ferrari. She ultimately decided Bruce looks much better without a mustache.

She was about to call it a night when she received a call from her sister. "Hey Hazel, what's up?"

"How's things going with the investigation?" Hazel replied.

"Honestly, not all that great. We're probably one more day here, and if we don't dig up anything solid, we will probably head back."

"We?"

"Oh, yeah. I thought I told you. I came down with Bruce Highland to help out."

"The investigator?"

"Yes."

"Okay. Oh – all right, I've got something here, and you're not going to believe it. Are you sitting down?"

"I'm lying down, what is it?"

"I was going through mom's old stuff just double checking some things, and do you remember the last postcard that Chad sent to mom from Mexico?"

"Not really. I wasn't exactly very old then."

"Okay well I remember it. It was hand dated May 4, 1984, okay, a month before he went missing. And guess what? Nobody bothered to look at the postmark. The postmark was dated January 9, 1985."

"It could be that the postmark is wrong."

"Very highly unlikely. These things are automatic. I think Chad was trying to tell us something."

"What did it say?"

"It says 'I'm alive and doing well. Send my regards to Hazel and Melanie.'"

"Can you take a picture of it and send it to me?"

"Sure."

Chapter 3 – A curious lead

Bruce looked at the photographs of the postcard sent from Ensenada, Mexico. The handwritten date was May 4, 1984. The postmark was indeed January 9, 1985. "I don't know. It is the Mexican postal system. They could have screwed up the date," Bruce said.

"That's what I thought at first," Melanie said. "But it would have been a weird thing for him to say, if he actually sent it on a vacation trip from Mexico prior to his disappearance. It only makes sense if he actually sent it six months later, to let us know he is okay. He probably pre-dated it to throw off anyone that might have intercepted mail to our mother from him. We didn't even catch it until now."

"Wait, what's this?" Bruce said, eyeing the photograph of the picture side of the postcard. "Zoom in on that, right there."

"Oh, wow, what is that?"

"It's called a backstamp. Sometimes a receiving postal office might apply it when they receive a letter. It's dated January 14, 1985. Consistent with transit from Mexico to Northern California during that time period. So, this is legit." Bruce handed the phone back to Melanie and poured himself another cup of coffee from the hotel lobby continental breakfast bar. "But... it doesn't tell us much more than we already knew. That he was still alive when he left Monterey, California in his car."

"But now we know where he went."

"Well, we know where he was on that particular date when he mailed the postcard, but that was nearly forty years ago. The likelihood that he stayed there isn't very. I have to believe that after all this time, whatever issues caused him to flee and disappear, would have gone away a long time ago. Why didn't he come back if he's still alive?

At a very minimum, I would think that he would find a way to reach out and contact you again."

"I wish he had. We really want to know what happened to him."

"I understand. If you want me to keep grinding away at this, the next logical move would be to pay a visit to Ensenada, Mexico, and see if we can find him there. Which, I suspect, will be more of an exercise of ruling out that he isn't there."

"I'm up for it," Melanie said.

"You have to understand, once we get in international territory, the rules of how we get things done change a little bit. We're going to need to bring on a local PI. Over there, connections and local knowledge are far more important than they are here in the US. That's going to result in more expenses."

Melanie rolled her eyes. "It is what it is, I guess. Do you know anybody down there?"

"Actually, I do. I've tracked down more than one man in Ensenada. It's a popular place for aging white guys to hide out."

With the initial trip to Monterey completed, Bruce was back in his Sacramento home and office. He was busy cleaning his carry weapon, a Sig Sauer P226 nine-millimeter semiautomatic pistol. It was the same type as his issue sidearm when he was an MI special agent in Cold War West Germany. The Army ended up adopting the Beretta 92 as the M9 to replace the aging but iconic M1911 service weapon, but frankly, the Sig was a better gun, and MI agents (as well as federal law enforcement agencies) had a little more free choice over what they carried than the rank-and-file military. He just returned from a range session to keep his carry permit current.

With a few of the mundane administrative and domestic tasks out of the way, he settled in to see if he could locate either of the former Fort Ord public works officers. Phil Cox was now a full bird colonel, was still on active-duty status and currently deployed in Poland. Tom Richards was a little bit more elusive, and the commonality of the name didn't help. Regardless, Bruce was able to track him down to an assisted living facility in Reno, Nevada. Old age and senility weren't positive factors in milking information from four decades ago, but on the other hand Reno wasn't all that far away. Bruce was about to dial Melanie on the phone to inform her of his intention to pay Mr. Richards a visit, when he kicked himself and realized that now he was asking for her permission to do his own investigation. Hell no. Bruce almost threw down his cell phone in frustration. Plus, she was starting to get a little bit sensitive about the investigation focusing on Area 91, more than the whereabouts of her brother. She didn't seem to understand that Area 91 may well hold the key behind her brother's seemingly irrational disappearance and disguised communication shortly thereafter.

Phone conversations generally don't work as well as face to face meetings when interviewing subjects. And this goes even more so for the elderly. The Enchanted Gardens was pretty much like your standard 24/7 senior care facility, nestled at the base of the east side of the Sierra mountains. The backdrop could serve as a television commercial setting for a beer commercial featuring Clydesdales, and/or mountainous echoes depicting the hissing of refreshment. A bleach blonde nurse grabbed her white smock and put it on, covered the upper portion of her tight slacks, which had a translucent sheerness bordering on inappropriate. She led Bruce to a day room, where the sole occupant, a bald, wrinkled old man sat in a recliner chair, nursing a boxed juice with a straw.

"Hello Mr. Richards. My name is Bruce Highland. I understand you were a public works officer on the Fort Ord military base in the mid 1980's?"

"Yeah, that's me pal, who's asking?" Richards replied.
"My name is...."
"I know your name! You just said it. What is this in reference to?"
"All right. I'm a private investigator looking into a matter that happened on base in 1984."
"I don't want to talk about it."
Bruce sighed. "You know, I drove a long way. All the way from Sacramento to talk to you. All I want to know, is if you can tell me anything about a facility called Area 91. But, if you don't want to talk, I can't make you."
"What?" Richards said "You want to talk about Area 91? Sure, I'll talk to you about Area 91. I thought you were here about those sexual harassment allegations. All of these women privates claiming I was using rank and position so I could bang them over my drafting table. Thrusting, moaning, climaxing... uhhhhhh."
"No, no. I'm not here about that. I'm sure you were quite the stallion back in the day. So, what's the story with Area 91?"
"Well, you see, back in the 1950's during the start of the cold war, the department of defense decided to construct oh... about a hundred give or take, secure bomb shelters across the country, starting from the East Coast and working west. The function of these were to allow the leadership of local and state government entities to be able to live and function in the event of a nuclear holocaust. They had three models. An 'A' model, a 'B' model and a 'C' model. Most were constructed on military posts or federally owned lands. One such facility, one of the last few to be built, was constructed at Fort Ord near the top of the central hill. It was sequence number 91, and it was an 'A' model, hence the designation 'A 91.' Now over the years, when tales started emerging over the Air Force testing range known as 'Area 51,' that bunker became known as 'Area 91' and local rumors started flying."

"What did it look like?" Bruce asked.

"It was a very heavily constructed concrete bunker, built into the side of the hill. Buried in it actually. It had a heavy, blast-proof door, and three levels. It had never actually been used, or outfitted with furniture or equipment, and at some point, the front had been backfilled to hide its entrance. Well, in, I want to say 1982 I think, we received orders to uncover it, so it could be used for a top-secret research project. Exactly what that project was I don't know, but they needed something big and heavily constructed which could be used for internal containment, and it fit the bill."

"What were they trying to contain?"

"Oh, I don't know, chemicals maybe? Blasts? Biological weapons? Who knows? For whatever reason, something went south two years later, and we got the order to raze the area in front of it, which had some shed structures and whatnot, pour concrete over the entrance to permanently seal it, and then grade over the concrete to completely bury it."

"But there is an environmental report that said the interior was entirely backfilled with concrete?"

"I don't know anything about that. If that was done, we didn't do it."

"Did you have plans of this thing?"

"Oh yeah, we did. But they were confiscated after we completed our work."

"By who?"

"Some top-level brass from the Pentagon."

Bruce frowned. "So, they are probably gone forever."

"Oh, I doubt it. These were cookie cutter plans, for three different models with different sizes and layouts. Every facility had a plan set included in its documentation, and there were about a hundred. Find a set, look at the 'A' model, and you have it."

"Do you know where any other such facilities are?"

"No, just the one. Maps of the others were deliberately excluded from the documentation."

The nurse returned. "All right Thomas, it's time for your medications."

"Blaaaaah... Hey Highland, Nurse Toni over here has one seriously killer ass, why back in the day, I would have bent that over the table and straight went to work at... oh, I think I just strained my groin. Nurse Toni, you think you could rub it out?"

"Shush!" Toni yelled. "Don't believe a word he says Mr. Highland. He tells wild stories all the time."

"I don't know," Bruce replied. "He seems to have some pretty solid judgement from where I'm standing." Bruce received a sharp slap to the face.

Bruce reclined the seat and stretched out. "Well, this is a first. I don't think I've ever been a passenger before in my own car."

"You know, I would have been willing to spring for plane tickets," Melanie replied, as she checked the blind spot leaving the freeway onramp.

"It's an eight-hour drive to the border. If we flew, we'd have to drive to Oakland, park, wait for an hour to board the flight, the flight itself is another two hours, then we get our stuff in San Diego, cab over to some rental agency that will let us take a car into Mexico, that's going to take an hour... by the time all is said and done, we haven't saved much time. If we saved any at all."

"It's refreshing that you didn't try to fight me over coming with you this time."

"You're looking at the reason why I didn't fight you. I can kick back and watch the cows as we drive down the Five. See look, there is one right there."

"What is she like?" Melanie asked.

"What? Who?"

"Your wife."

Bruce sat in a long silence. Melanie kept driving, never breaking her gaze from the road in front of her. "Why do you ask?"

"I guess I'd like to know if I'm going to get along with her, if I ever get to meet her."

"Well, she was killed in a plane accident three years ago, so I don't think that's going to happen."

"I'm sorry. I didn't know."

"She was on her way to visit her family in Russia. She was actually an officer with the Russian GRU before she came to the United States. That's their modern equivalent of the CIA. She was an expert in cryptology. And computers."

"How did you meet her?"

"On a case. I needed help hacking into a computer network in San Francisco. She was recommended."

"How come you never remarried?"

"It's only been three years plus if I have another woman in my life, I want her to be my girlfriend, not my distant roommate mother figure."

"What was her name?"

"Svetlana. Svetlana Petroya."

"You didn't love her?"

"Of course I did."

"That's funny," Melanie said.

"It is? How so?" Bruce asked.

"No, I don't mean as in comedic, but Zane said the same thing to me after we divorced."

"I see. Who is in your life now?"

"I've been seeing a guy named Braydon off and on. But it's not really... serious."

"What's he like?"

"He's attractive enough. But he's... I don't know how to say it. Okay, the kind, sensitive type. Not at all threatening. Which is great, from a girl's standpoint, up until you have to walk with him down a dark street at night, and you realize that if someone tries to attack you, he's probably incapable of offering any defense."

"So, you don't feel safe around him."

"Right."

"Well, I don't know what to say."

"You know, it's June, and this is the first time I've ever seen you without a jacket on. Those jackets you wear make you look ten pounds heavier than you are."

"More like three pounds, if you factor in the weight of the holster."

"You carry a gun? I didn't know that."

"I don't like to advertise it."

"Have you ever had to use it?"

"You mean my carry piece during PI work? Or are you asking if I've whacked anybody?"

"Well, I guess now that you bring it up, both."

"I've had some close calls, but I've never actually had to use it for self-defense in the course of an investigation. Sometimes looking for bad guys puts you in bad places. But as to the other, yes, I have had confirms in the military. A couple I can talk about, and a couple I can't."

"How did that make you feel?"

"It messes with you for a while. But you get over it."

"Obviously you aren't carrying a gun now."

"It's because we are going to Mexico. They are real funny about that. I don't care to end up in a Mexican prison for the rest of my life. Anyway, why the deep conversation?"

"I just want to know who I'm... with." Melanie drove on for several minutes in silence. Then smiled. "You have sort of an accent. I can't really place it. Just a hint."

"Bedoel jy so?" Bruce replied in a thick Afrikaans accent.

"What the hell is that?"

"I'm originally from Southern Africa. I came to the US as a teenager. A few years earlier my home country of

Rhodesia was overthrown and became Zimbabwe, and my parents and sister were massacred during the revolt. I was able to get away. I had to kill a couple rebel soldiers in order to escape."

"Oh my god. Are you serious?"

"Yep. I joined the United States Army so I could get my citizenship easier. In fact, Bruce Highland is not even my birth name."

"What was it?"

"Bryson Heelund."

"Jesus Bruce, you've been through a lot."

"I assure you, nobody is going to kick my ass. Or yours either, if I'm around."

"You know, I'm not actually some lame scaredy-ass chick. I can hold my own if I have to. A guy tried to assault me in a park once. I got away, and broke his nose in the process."

"Never said you were."

Melanie's cell phone rang. Bruce glanced down at the phone sitting on the center console. It was Braydon. She ignored it.

"You can take the call," Bruce said.

Melanie picked up the phone and answered it in a brisk voice. "Yes?" There was a brief indistinct conversation. "Look I'm going to be gone for a few days. We can do that after I get back." There were further murmurs from the phone. "Okay I gotta go. Bye."

"It's probably not my place, but I have to tell you, it sounds like you've already been married to him for five years. If you know what I mean."

"I shouldn't talk smack about him. I probably shouldn't have brought the subject up."

It was Bruce's cell phone that rang this time. "Hey Nielson, what's up? Bruce asked as he answered the phone.

"Can you give me a call back on the secure line?" Nielson replied.

"Sure, give me a minute. Or two. Or four." The 'secure line' was not a physical line, but rather a secure voice app with a pre-shared, time sensitive key. In this case, the word 'Sure' but it could be the last word in the response, or a middle word. Hopefully the NSA jock that might be snooping in would focus on the 124 number sequence first. A few moments later, a beep and a green icon indicated that there was a secure, encrypted connection. "You there Nielson?"

"Yeah. Okay, so this is what I got. A Project Dark Fury, status inactivated, located at Site A 91, address listed as Huckleberry Loop Road, Monterey, California. Site A 91 is listed as overwatch status."

"What's overwatch status?"

"It means that someone has been specifically assigned to monitor and protect it."

"Huh. Really. Do you have a name of that individual?"

"Nope. Blocked at my access level. Same thing with the project details. Somebody really wants to keep this thing secret."

"We have about ten more seconds before we will need to start a new session with a new key. Anything else?"

"Nope. That's all I got." The line went dead and the green icon went dark.

"What was that about?" Melanie asked.

"It would appear as if our Area 91 is being actively monitored by the CIA."

"Your Nielson buddy, he works for them?"

"He's fairly high up in the Agency ranks, actually." Bruce fumbled for a bottle of water. "Oh, and I know this probably sounds cliché and overdramatic, but let's not mention any connection to Area 91 and the Agency, okay? Trust me, our lives will be much happier that way."

"Okay. Sure."

"Hey um, our buddy there, Roland Macleod... did he ever mention why he was at the site when you were there?"

"He said that he also goes there on the anniversary of the incident to pay his respects. Why?"

"Mmm, just curious."

Bruce and Melanie sat at a small table with a Formica top emblazoned with the local Cerveza Ensenada logo. The proprietor, Carlos Mendez joked that when the brewery flopped, he was able to get the tables, bar handles and half the equipment for practically free. After a ten-minute wait, a dark-skinned woman with a rather svelte figure, and some lines on her face entered, and took a seat. She was wearing a set of white track sweats and running shoes. She had dark, curly hair not typical of Mexican ethnicity. Which she wasn't. She was actually from El Salvador but had been in Ensenada for most of her life.

"Hi Bruce," she said, not introducing herself to Melanie.

"Good to see you Ana, this is my client, Melanie Green."

"Ana Martinez." She gave Melanie an icy stare. Then again, she gives everyone an icy stare. In fact, she has a perpetual icy stare.

"Aaaanyway," Bruce said, "We are trying to track down her brother, Chad Green, whose last known whereabouts were here in Ensenada." Bruce looked sheepish. "In 1985."

Ana rolled her eyes, and stared at Bruce with a 'certainly you can't be serious look.'

"I know, I know. I just texted you a picture of him. Back then. Obviously, he's going to look a little different today."

"Two hundred dollars US, and I will take a look. But don't expect much."

Bruce slid a white envelope discreetly across the table under Ana's hand. "Understood."

"What you want me to do if I find him?"

"Just tell me where he is. Don't let him know he's being looked for."

Ana looked disappointed. "Okay." She got up and walked away with a brisk pace.

"Why did she look disappointed when you told her just to tell you where he was?" Melanie asked.

"Because if you needed two hooded men and a van to apprehend someone, she could provide that service too, as an extra charge."

"She really doesn't like me. I could tell."

"I think you're reading too much into it."

"Right," Melanie replied, in an unconvincing tone.

Bruce started to reply to her comment, then decided it was better to just let it go. "Anyway, got any plans to dinner tonight?"

Melanie choked slightly as she repressed a fit of laughter. "We have one car and I'm in a strange, foreign town. I don't think I have much of a choice in the matter."

"This is really good," Melanie said, as she finished the last touches of her lobster.

"It's pretty hard to go wrong in this town, in terms of restaurants. But it is my favorite."

Three men bearing guitars and large sombreros walked into the restaurant and started singing. "Let me guess, somebody is about to get birthday serenaded."

"I would say that's accurate." Bruce said, downing the rest of his beer.

"Oh my god, seriously?" The men proceeded to Melanie's chair, and sung a birthday song for five minutes, and placed a small paper sombrero on her head, and left. "How did you know it was my birthday?"

"I'm a detective, remember?"

A waiter approached with a small German chocolate cake, placed it in front of Melanie, and lit a candle on the top. Her mouth fell open. German chocolate cake was her favorite. "How did you know? Never mind. I forgot. You're a detective."

Back at the motel bar, Melanie finished off her second Bloody Mary, and could see in the mirror behind the liquor shelf that she was still wearing the sombrero. She took a photo of herself through the mirror, and then took a landscape photo with Bruce beside her, and texted that one to her sister.

"Thank you, Bruce."

"No worries."

"What are we going to do tomorrow?"

"Ordinarily I'd say start canvassing the bars where the local American residents frequent, but I think it's better in this case to let Ana do the work. In the outside chance that your brother might be still alive, and might actually be here, it's clear that he doesn't want to be found, and we don't want to spook him."

"I feel like we should make some kind of effort."

"I understand. For what it's worth, I view this trip as a junket, and I'm not going to bill my time while we're here. So, let's do some touring, kick back a little, maybe do some fishing, if you're into that. Somehow, I'm guessing with that pale skin of yours, tanning on the beach isn't your thing."

"You got that right. Plus, it's been foggy the whole time we've been here."

"Welcome to Baja during the summer. Just like up north, you get the marine layer. Anyway, unless you're up for another drink, I'm going to hit the sack."

Melanie started to waver a little bit. "Thank you, Bruce," she said as Bruce kept her from toppling over.

"Oh boy. Come on Melanie, I'm going to walk you to your room."

She started to stumble again, and Bruce caught her. "Here, put your arm around me. We don't have far to go." Bruce fumbled with her door key, walked her to her bed, and set her down.

"Thank you, Bruce." She kissed him on the cheek, and then lay back on the bed. Bruce determined she was out for the count. A minute later, she heard him leave, locking the door behind him. She got up, changed out of her clothes into her night shirt, and climbed under the comforter.

"Elena, how are you?" Dr. Katz asked as he walked into the facility's exercise room wearing a white lab coat and bearing a tablet computer.

"I had a dream last night," Elena replied. "I was wearing a uniform. A military uniform."

"Hmm. Yes, it represents a regimented lifestyle. Such that you have been experiencing here."

"No," Elena said. "I get these images now, even when I am awake. They just come for an instant. Like a flash."

"The uniform?"

"Yes, and other things. Like, tall buildings and steep streets. Very steep streets. We don't have very many places in Russia that have both tall buildings and steep streets."

Katz sat down. "Elena. These memory flashes, they must be a subconscious activity. Like the uniform. You could not have actually been in the military. If you were, your fingerprints would be on file, and they are not. Plus, we know your life history."

A nurse was standing by, making a routine check of the equipment and the status of the water coolers. "Excuse me, doctor, but when you get a chance, can I speak with you at the front desk?" she asked.

"Certainly, Lubya, what is this regarding?"

"I'd rather not say right now."

Dr. Katz and Nurse Lubya stood at the reception desk viewing a computer screen displaying a lobby surveillance video. "Yesterday, Elena Yakut was visited by her mother and her sister. Elena was seated in the lobby. As you can see in the video, two women walk into the lobby, check in with the receptionist, and they walk around a bit, and even sit next to Elena. But she does not recognize them and they do not recognize her. Ten minutes later, Elena leaves, and the two women go back to the reception, argue a bit, and then leave."

"That is very interesting."

Dr. Katz returned to his office, and did a short Internet search on his computer, revealing the telephone number of The Rosaviatsiya also known as The Federal Air Transport Agency, which is the Russian aviation authority. A few minutes later, he dialed the number, and was greeted by the voice of a receptionist who asked how she could direct his call. "I wish to speak with the investigators for the crash of Aeroflot flight 7230."

Secret program or no secret program, it never made sense to Bruce that some team member, some researcher, some scientist, would disappear and completely go off the grid, and live that way for nearly four decades, but the revelation that the Agency was still actively tracking the site lent a small degree of credibility to the proposition. There was still one major question in Bruce's mind. Was Chad Green actually the innocent surviving victim that he is scripted to be, or could he have actually been a perpetrator? Roland Macleod argued for the former. Certainly, being the perp would be a stronger motivation to disappear from society, and possible prosecution. At any rate, something seemed off about Macleod, and Bruce couldn't quite put his finger on what it was.

A boat trip wasn't happening today, given Melanie's condition on waking up. She didn't outright get sick, but she wasn't exactly on the top of her game either. Bruce sat on a wooden beach chair under an umbrella drinking a beer, and watching a local kid help Melanie cast her fishing line into the surf. It was a chilly morning. Forty-five minutes later, she managed to haul in a rather large sea bass, and brought it over to the table, beaming. "Look what I got!"

"Looks good," Bruce said. "Just give it to the kid. They will clean it and cook it, and bring it back to the motel for lunch."

She sat down on the other chair. "Do you remember last night?" she asked.

"Yeah, we had a good time. Well, I think you did too."

"I mean, do you remember how things ended?"

"Well, you were a little wobbly, but you made it back."

Chapter 4 – I smell a rat

Chad Green was beginning to have a problem. He wasn't independently wealthy. Money goes far here in Baja but only so far. He needed to have an income, but nobody would hire him as he didn't speak any significant degree of Spanish, and if he was able to land a job locally where Spanish wasn't a requirement, it wouldn't be cash under the table. He'd have to break back into the grid. And he felt the end was finally coming. Travel twenty-five miles south of Ensenada, and you're in some fairly remote coastal region, with rugged and beautiful terrain. It seemed like the perfect way to go. Drive down the coastal dirt trail roads as far at the aging Corolla would make it, and hurl yourself over a cliff to the rocks below, and become one with the sea.

It was the hills just to the north of Punta San Jose where one could totally disappear and nobody would ever find you amongst the massive washes and ridges leading down to the sea. He started out mid-morning, before the heat set in. He reached the general location of Punta San Jose, which was a small lighthouse settlement, and went off-road from there, deciding to climb and head north versus south to the ocean. Finally, the small Corolla ran out of gas, but it wasn't going to negotiate the increasingly rugged terrain anyway.

He was also out of water, out of money, and out of a resource to turn to. The air started to heat up, and he was starting to feel just a little bit dizzy from dehydration and exposure. He felt like he just wanted to take a seat on a rock, and let nature take its course and die. In search of the perfect place, he climbed atop a ridgeline, and took a seat on a nice flat, red rock, overlooking a valley below. And he saw something shimmering at the bottom. Squinting, he could barely make out the form of a vehicle. It seemed out of place to be in such a remote area.

Having nothing to lose, he traveled down the ridge, and on closer inspection, he discovered there were two vehicles. Both were stationary and looked abandoned. As he approached the vehicles, he could smell the rotting stench of death. There was a hard top Jeep, and a Land Rover. Both were recent models, probably '82 or '83. As he drew closer, he could tell exactly what happened. It was a classic Mexican standoff. It was literally, a classic Mexican standoff. Two bodies in front of the Jeep, and two bodies in front of the Land Rover. All were bearing pistols. The bodies by the Jeep were apparently Mexican nationals, and the bodies by the Land Rover were apparently American nationals. At least they were white guys anyway. Chad was by no means an expert but guessed they had been there for two or three days.

Chad rummaged through the Land Rover and found water, and hastily guzzled it down. He also found, in the back, a large satchel, stuffed with bound US currency in differing amounts. There had to be at least fifty thousand dollars in there, in his estimation. The examination of the Jeep revealed what he was expecting. Cocaine. Not one, or two, or three, but four 'keys,' or kilograms, of what was probably high purity cocaine, with value of around two hundred grand.

With newfound lucidity, Chad viewed the scene as a gift from God himself. The keys were in the ignition of the Land Rover. It started up. Chad shut it off. The keys were also in the Jeep. The battery was dead. Chad searched the two white victims, and recovered their wallets, pocketing their cash and credit cards. He decided that one man, Thomas Mallory, was the one that looked the closest to him and that would be his new identity. After pilfering the victims of the Jeep, and the Jeep itself, he attempted to start the Jeep by letting it roll down hill and popping the clutch. After getting it running, he stripped all the victims of their identities, and piled their bodies in the rear of the Jeep. He deemed it too risky to try to take the cocaine and sell it somehow later, but decided to take it out and leave it on the ground in case he changed his mind.

There was a bigger problem now. What to do with the bodies? At first, he intended to drive the Jeep south and let it roll off a cliff into the ocean. But it was too far of a distance to hike back to the Land Rover. The problem with leaving it was that if the bodies were found and the authorities were somehow able to identify the body of Thomas Mallory, then his new identity would be compromised. Chad decided a good strategy would be to work both vehicles close to the coast by leapfrogging them, alternating driving the Jeep and the Land Rover.

Finally, it was starting to get late in the day when he approached the coastal dirt trail that separated the wilderness from the coastal cliffs. After carefully verifying that there were no other vehicles within sight of the barren terrain, he put the Jeep in neutral, gave it a good push, and sent the Jeep careening down the hillside, launching it off a cliff and into the ocean below. It instantly disappeared under the water, likely never to be seen again. The bodies themselves wouldn't last a week in that environment.

It had been a week since he had assumed his new identity. The first few days were quite rough. He was a nervous wreck. He had nightmares of the dead bodies. Adrenaline and desperation blocked the dreadful stench initially, but once that wore off, the memory of it was tough to bear. But on the upside, there was substantially more cash than he initially assessed – more in line with what would actually have been needed to purchase four kilograms of coke. He was finally starting to settle into a new lifestyle and actually enjoy it. His plan was to go back to the United States, and just start up a new life someplace. Maybe even California, hiding in plain sight. Of course, it was a risky move. What if the border agents didn't buy his identification? What if Thomas Mallory was a wanted drug trafficker? He had some time to work those issues out.

Ensenada was actually turning out to be a nice, pleasant place. But hanging out here had some issues too. What if the drug cartel was looking for Thomas Mallory? He could still be Chad Green if he needed to be. He was always careful to go strictly by first name and not his own and staying at places where cash is welcomed and anonymity accepted.

Nobody needed to remind him that blowing wads of cash after landing a big windfall will not only deplete it, but it would get him noticed. He needed neither of that. He sold the Land Rover in Tijuana and purchased a cheaper Toyota pickup. That would further throw any searchers for Thomas Mallory off track and would probably, in any case take them back to the States, probably Connecticut, per the plates on the Land Rover. It was also cheaper to run and maintain, and stood out less.

He sat at a bar that was somewhat reminiscent of the Cliff House restaurant of a few months ago – the place where Dr. Fuller never did show up for a meeting. It was also empty as well. An attractive girl in her mid-twenties dressed in a blue apron walked up to the bar, and sat down. Although obviously Hispanic, she spoke very good English. Then again most do, around here. "Mind if I join you?" she asked.

"Certainly," Chad replied.

"I just got off shift." She turned her attention to the bartender. "Carlos, can you please pour a beer for me?" She fumbled for change.

"I'll get this," Chad said.

"Okay. Thank you. I've seen you around. You don't look like the rest."

"The rest?"

"Old white men, chasing after local women. You are so young to be here."

"Oh, yeah, I kind of noticed that myself. No, I'm just um... hanging out. That's all."

"My name is Maria."

Chad thought long and hard about how he was going to answer. She started to look puzzled by the delayed response. "Oh, I'm sorry, I got lost in a thought. Tom."

"Pleased to meet you, Mr. Tom." She nursed the beer, as an awkward silence ensured.

Chad was never very confident with women, and this was literally the first time he had been approached by a woman. He reasoned that it would probably not be in his best interest to enter a relationship.

"Well, I guess I will go now, Tom. Maybe see you around."

"Are you interested in dinner later on?"

"I thought that you would never ask. Carlos, can you pour me another beer?"

His reasoning just went into the trash bin.

Ana met with Bruce and Melanie at the same run-down cantina where they had their initial meeting. She was still wearing the same white track suit from two days ago. "Here is what I found. The police have a record of an abandoned car about twenty miles south of here in the hills, registered to a Chad Green, which was found in November of 1984 in a remote area. It had run out of gas. They attempted to locate him but could not find him. They theorized that he may have tried to walk to safety but did not make it. But no body was ever found. And that's all I have. We have run his photograph by many people who lived here back then near the beach side resorts, and it was just too long ago for anyone to remember."

"All right, thank you Ana, that is helpful," Bruce said. "Obviously he didn't die out there, since he mailed a postcard from here in January of 1985. So, I'm sorry Melanie, but I guess the trail ends."

"But there is one more thing that is very interesting," Ana retorted. "On the same day, when the police searched the area, they came across an area in a valley two miles away where there was an apparent crime scene. They found blood, spent shell casings, drag marks, and tire tracks, as well as four kilograms of cocaine, laying in the sand. The police were baffled. It made no sense to them at all. They do not know if there was a connection to the abandoned car."

"Chad never would have been involved in any kind of drug activity," Melanie said.

"I'm sure that was just a coincidence," Bruce replied. "He obviously didn't walk in on a drug deal gone bad." Or did he?

The Monterey trip did yield some useful leads in regards to Area 91, but not Chad Green. The Ensenada trip was also a total bust, but that one curious coincidence still bugged Bruce a little bit. But at the moment, he didn't have anything further to work with. His cell phone rang. He didn't recognize the number. "Highland speaking."

"Yeah, uh, Mr. Highland, I understand you are looking for people working at Fort Ord back in the eighties for some kind of documentary?"

"Oh, yes. That's right."

"Do you like, feature people in your documentaries?"

"Oh sure. We can. And you can remain anonymous too, if you want."

"Yeah, okay, well, my name is Delmar Washington, and I am a retired master sergeant. I was an MP stationed at Fort Ord from eighty-five to eighty-seven."

"Did you know anything about Area 91?"

"Just the rumors. You know, alien spacecraft, all that."

"What about the accident?"

"Just the hearsay. A bunch of people died of a fire or something. I don't know, I wasn't there."

"Hmm... You were an MP. And Colonel Macleod was your commander?"

"Yeah, yeah he was. Strange man."

"Oh, how so?"

"Well... he was in the military police corps, but he spent his entire career in the Pentagon, until he was assigned a rotation at Fort Ord, and even went back to the Pentagon after that was over. I mean, I don't want to speak ill of him, but he really didn't know what he was doing. It was like he was not only commanding an MP unit for the first time, but actually working in an MP unit, for the first time."

"I'll be damned. Interesting."

"Some of the other guys said that he really botched the investigation into the incident at Area 91."

"I thought it was determined to be an accident?"

"It was, but c'mon, man, eleven people died in that accident, as the poh-leese, you at least take a second look to make sure that is what went down."

"Wait... eleven people died in that accident? I thought thirteen total, with thee survivors?"

"No, we was told it was eleven and two."

Macleod, you lying son of a bitch. "That's huge." Bruce said. "Thank you."

The bustle of the sports pub was almost deafening. It was difficult to talk above the screaming of a dozen drunken frat boys. "Yo Braydon, do a shot with us mang!"

"I'll be right over boys, but I gotta take care of some business first," Braydon replied. He turned towards Melanie, and handed her a package. "I got you a present, here you go. I'll be back in a bit."

Melanie's friend Susan was horrified. "What the hell?" Susan said. "This is supposed to be your birthday dinner."

"Yeah well... I wonder what this is." Melanie peeled a piece of scotch tape up, folded the wrapping back and peered inside. "Oh gee, how nice. A set of cheap lingerie that isn't even my size." She put the tape back on and placed the soft package on the table. "Hey Sue, you up for ditching this soon-to-be vomit smelling shithole and grabbing some drinks at a decent place?"

"Sure, but I mean... what about Braydon?"

"If he thinks he's going to see me with that on, or in any other underwear for that matter, he has another thing coming. At least he was smart enough not to write my name on it, that way he can give it to his next girlfriend."

"Are you sure you're good with this?"

"Oh yeah, I'm good. Real good. Let's go."

The soft improv jazz music droned in the background as the two girls took turns taking paired selfies against the backdrop of a neon lit falls bar with blue tinted water flowing downward in waves. "So, what's the story of that picture that you texted me from Ensenada? The one with the guy in it?"

"That's Bruce, the investigator we hired to find my brother. We had just got back from my birthday dinner."

"Wait, let me get this straight, your hired investigator is taking you out for birthday dinners?"

"He even secretly tracked down my sister to ask what my favorite cake was."

"I don't know Melanie; he looks pretty cute. For his... age."

"He's not that much older than me... besides, I'm not even thinking along those lines. But if I was, and I'm not saying I am, he sure beats the hell out of fortyish drunken frat boys."

"Mm hm. I can tell," Sue said mockingly.

"Oh great, now my phone is blowing up with texts from Braydon. Where U at. U mad at me. U high maintenance... ugh. I should have ran and not walked when he showed up."

"Does this Bruce guy know about Braydon?"

"He does. And as far as he knows, I'm at the Jolly Roger celebrating my birthday with Braydon."

"And he's okay with that?"

"Why wouldn't he be? And if he isn't, he's not letting on." Melanie pulled up a series of selfies. "Which one of us do you like best?"

"This one here, you look like you're trying to hold back a fart in the others."

"Okay, sent." Melanie waited a couple minutes. "Well, there we go, Bruce texted back a thumbs up, followed by a 'glad YOU are having a good time.'"

The coincidences were mounting. But one thing troubled Bruce. Why did Macleod lie to his MP staff, and probably to the base medical officer, about Chad Green and tell them he died in the vault, yet freely admit he was alive to both Melanie and Bruce? In fact, why would he even bring up the subject to begin with?

To that end, Bruce decided to circle back to Macleod and play just a little bit dirty. He didn't exactly have a game plan together yet, but decided that an outright confrontation with Macleod laying down the facts was probably a bad idea and a tip of the hand. There was obviously something wrong with him being in the picture. The man spends his entire career at the Pentagon save for one command tour as a provost marshal? Bruce was beginning to suspect that if he were to go back to the Area 91 site and start digging away with a shovel, it might just be Macleod that showed up.

One thing that occurred to Bruce was to bug his house, provoke him somehow and see what he did and who he called. To that end, Bruce did a stakeout on his Salinas house. It wasn't hard to find out where he lived – that information was available through public records. It was fairly obvious that he wasn't home at the time. It was an older, tiny home with no garage even. He decided to do a short recon of the building. Given the man was a cop, and a former Pentagon hamster, he was probably paranoid about security, so there was probably a camera aimed at the door. Bruce donned an oversized sweat jacket and draped the hood over his face, and carried a crowbar. He carried the crowbar not because he actually wanted to break in, but he wanted it to look as if he was there to break in. This is Salinas. Burglaries are common.

There was no outside mailbox, but there was a mail slot in the door. Bruce gingerly approached the front door and peered through the mail slot, and observed roughly two weeks of accumulated mail and advertisements piled up on the floor. Go figure. The sonofabitch doesn't even live here. He uses the house as an expensive postal box and permanent address. There was going to be absolutely nothing in there of evidentiary value. He was only there to retrieve his mail and meet people there if they need to meet him at his home. That answered one question. Why the hell would a retired, high ranking military officer live in a place like Salinas when he could be living in a nice place like Monterey? It's because he was actually living in a nice place in Monterey.

Of course, there are legitimate explanations for why mail might accumulate in a person's home, such as vacations or out of state work assignments. But it had been a matter of days since he had seen Macleod, not weeks. Bruce wasn't sure why Macleod didn't retrieve his mail while he was there in Salinas. He should have expected that Bruce would tail him. He knew Bruce was an investigator and investigators tail people. Macleod was a cop, and cops are paranoid they are being tailed. At any rate, Bruce was becoming increasingly convinced that the guardian assigned to protect Area 91 was in fact Macleod. The pieces were starting to fit.

So where exactly was Macleod living now? Probably just a hop, skip and jump from the site itself. Maybe even on the Presidio, but not necessarily since as retired military he can come and go as he pleases. In fact, since the site is located on the south slope of the hill and the occupied area of the Presidio is to the north of it. A line-of-sight radio transmitter would favor an off-post house in the hills further south, and there are some nice ones nearby.

Bruce is the kind of guy that looks more at home in casual wear and a leather jacket, but he can be sharp looking in a suit as well. Back in his MI days, his normal uniform was an immaculately tailored Italian suit, specially fitted for use with a shoulder holster, changing into plain military combat fatigues when qualifying at the range or doing admin duties on post. Melanie's eyes bulged out when she opened the door of her apartment.

"Wow, Bruce, you sure look nice, but you didn't have to put on a suit just to see me."

Bruce laughed. "Actually, I had a meeting with a client in The City. I figured I'd stop by to brief you on what's been going on with the case so far. We can go grab a drink if you like."

"Alright. I'm up for that. Where would you like to go?"

"How about that place where you sent me the picture of you and your friend?"

Melanie smiled. "Sure. But I'll need to change into something a little more formal than leggings and a tee shirt."

Bruce took a seat on a sofa facing her bedroom door, which happened to be ajar. She wasn't exactly standing in front of it when she changed, but the dresser mirror was strategically in the line of sight of the reflection of her closet. And she took her time. He wondered if she realized that Bruce was getting an eyeful. He tried his hardest not to look. Failing that, he tried his best to be nonchalant about it.

"Hey Bruce?" she said from the bedroom.

"Would you mind zipping me up?"

Oh, hell yeah. "No problem. I'll be right there." It did occur to him that a request to zip her up, just might lead to a request to zip her back down. He tried yet again, unsuccessfully to quash the thought from his mind.

"What do you think?" Melanie asked. "You look like you fit right in."

"Honestly? It's kind of like being in an elevator with bar service. But... but I like it. Mm hm."

"We could go to the sports pub, but we're both overdressed for that."

"Nah, we can sit and talk here."

"So, what do you have?"

"Nothing solid I'm afraid, but I did learn something very interesting. Back in 1984, your brother was officially listed as deceased, a fatality of the accident. The thing about it is, that it was Roland Macleod himself who made that determination, contrary to what he told us."

"That doesn't make any sense. If his story was that he was dead all along, why would he change it later?"

"I don't know. But I also believe Macleod is somehow involved in watching over Area 91. Protecting it for some reason. Whatever is in there, is so important that its worth killing over to maintain silence, and to hunt people down to keep that silence."

"Are you trying to say that he's using us, as in myself, and you, to track him down?"

"I think that's a distinct possibility."

"Why?"

"He's the only one left that knows what the government was doing in Area 91. Or at least the only rogue civilian that is on the loose. Now remember, two other members, Dr. Fuller and a secretary just conveniently died in a car accident right before they were able to prepare detailed statements. I don't believe it was a freak accident for one second, given what I know now. That kind of termination is right out of the Agency's playbook."

"Are you saying we should stop looking for him?" Melanie asked with a dejected look.

"I'm saying that we need to be careful." Bruce motioned for the bartender to pour another beer. "Does this place have food?"

"It does, but judging by the way you eat, you might not be overly happy."

"Oh, you mean like a giant plate with a tiny dab of mashed potatoes over a nickel sized sliver of beef, with a single asparagus balanced on top?"

"Something like that. Why don't we grab a brisket sandwich at the Jolly Roger on the way back?"

"I thought you were trying to cut back on red meat."

"Bruce... we're talking brisket here...."

"Singing to the choir. Hey bartender, can I get the check please?"

The clash of a pool break could be heard as a server placed two massive brisket sandwiches in hoagie rolls on the table. "Wow," Bruce said. "Now that looks good."

"That's the second time tonight I've seen a look like that on your face," Melanie said with a smile.

"Oh, where was... never mind. Probably best not to ask."

"Probably not."

"That kid over there is giving me some strange looks."

"Oh great. I wouldn't exactly call him a kid, other than the way he acts. That's Braydon. But I wouldn't worry about him. He's harmless."

After finishing up at the sports bar, Bruce and Melanie walked across the parking lot to the car, where they were confronted by three young men. "Can I help you gentlemen?" Bruce asked.

"Yeah, I think you can get lost."

"We're about to do that. Move aside."
"I mean alone."
"Guys, just leave us alone," Melanie said. "I mean it."
"You know them?" Bruce asked.
"Braydon's friends."
"Your pal Braydon isn't man enough to take care of his own business?" Bruce said to the trio.

Bruce made a move for the car, with his arm around Melanie's. The apparent leader made a blocking move. "So this is how you want to play it huh? Real bad move." He turned to Melanie. "Please stand back for a minute."

In one swift, lightning speed punch, Bruce cold cocked the leader, sending him sprawling to the pavement. One of the others attempted to place Bruce in an arm lock behind his back, while the other attempted to land a punch to the face. Bruce sent him flying backwards with a high kick to the chin, then performed a judo throw to flip the remaining man to the ground over his head.

Man number 2 recovered, and charged Bruce, who grabbed his head and drove it hard into his knee, breaking the man's nose and incapacitating him. Man number 3 got up and started to stagger towards Bruce. Bruce waved his finger sideways, as if to convey that he really should back off. Man number 2 picked up a large round rock laying on the curb, and attempted to strike Bruce with it. Before he could do so, Bruce landed a sharp kick to his solar plexus, sending him writhing in pain to the ground.

"I'm so sorry about all of that Bruce," Melanie said back at the apartment, wiping off a couple of bloody scrapes to his face with his jacket, pistol and holster draped over the couch.

"No worries. Wasn't the first time, and probably won't be the last."

"And you had a gun the whole time and didn't use it?"

"I didn't feel like doing the paperwork."

Melanie engaged Bruce in an embrace, and their lips met. Then the doorbell rang. Melanie peered out the peephole, then opened the door. "Susie, what are you doing here?"

"I heard about what happened at the Jolly Roger, I just wanted to make sure you were okay." She awkwardly looked at Bruce. "I didn't like… interrupt anything did I?"

"It's all good," Bruce said. "I gotta hit the road anyway."

Anatoly Karkhov pulled up the passenger manifest of Aeroflot Flight 7230. Methodically, he began to run the female passengers through various informational databases, one by one. He was primarily searching for photographs. He started with Elena Yakut, to compare with the photo Dr. Katz forwarded from the institution. He could not find anything. Nothing on the various social media platforms. But he also noticed that Elena Yakut had absolutely no presence outside of the record of her medical treatment and admission to the institution – a strong indication that she was not alive and well someplace else. He was able to rule out by elimination all but two of the deceased on the passenger manifest. Candice Lowe, and Svetlana Petroya.

Why didn't they identify Elena Yakut from her passport photo? Anatoly quickly realized that she was not travelling on a passport, and did not have one. In fact, most passengers on that flight did not. Candice Lowe was traveling on a Canadian passport. Candice Lowe did superficially resemble the photo of Elena Yakut however. Svetlana Petroya was not travelling on a passport either, but she had one. A United States passport. She also held a Russian passport predating the end of the Soviet Union. She superficially resembled the photo of Elena Yakut as well.

Dr. Katz mentioned that Elena primarily spoke Russian, but also could speak English. It is unlikely that the mystery woman named Elena could be a Canadian citizen with an

English name who speaks fluent Russian. Karkhov concluded that Elena Yakut could only be either herself, or Svetlana Petroya.

There was really no evidence so far to suggest that Elena Yakut had been misidentified by the original investigators, but in the spirit of due diligence, Kharkov decided to place an inquiry on Svetlana Petroya with the Russian Embassy in Washington DC, to see if they could investigate her presence in the United States.

Chapter 5 – On a mission

Maya Goldman worked her way down the crowded street lined with open air markets of every description. A car was almost an impediment in the heart of Tel Aviv. She could see Ari Rosenfeld seated at a small table outside a corner café, reading a newspaper and tending to a steeping pot of tea and a bagel. She took a seat on a metal chair across from him and placed her handbag in her lap. He folded the paper and poured a cup. "Tea?" He offered.

"Sure," Maya replied.

Ari poured another cup of tea and placed it in front of her. "Can I get you something to eat? Sandwich? Bagel?"

"No thanks. I'm on a diet."

"Diet? You're always on a diet. You look like skin and bones."

"I don't think you called me all the way out here just to admonish me on my nutritional habits."

"No, I need you to do something for me."

"I thought you were retired? Maya said."

"Retired?" Ari scoffed. "You never retire from the Mossad. I thought they told you that. Okay... let's just say that I've come back from retirement for a bit."

"So, what is going on?"

"In the early 1980s, we were working on a joint secret research project with the Americans. One of our top scholars, a rising star named Daniel Levin was assigned to work on this project. He was chosen because of his expertise in a brand-new field of microbiology. He was the best in the world. Four years later, he and the rest of the research team were all killed in an accident in a research facility in California. You see, Daniel Levin was my charge. I've spent weeks, months, and even years trying to get some answers. And I never got any."

"Okay." Maya wasn't sure where the conversation was going.

"Well fast forward to a week ago. Representatives from our consulate in San Francisco have picked up some chatter over the Internet that someone seems to be investigating the research facility, which has been referred to by the name of Area 91."

"So, what do you want me to do?"

"I want you to go over there and find out what is going on. I want you to try to find some answers."

"Why me?"

"I'm too old for this. You are young and vibrant. You are one of the most promising agents that I have ever mentored."

"I thought I was the only agent you ever mentored."

"Okay technically you're right but that's beside the point."

"That's exciting, Ari. So will I be working with the CIA?"

Ari choked on his bagel. "God no. They are the last people we want to be involved with if we can help it. They will just stonewall us until the end. When we work together, it is a cooperative effort based on a system of mutual distrust. Which, by the way is another reason I want to send you. A veteran agent will only attract attention."

Ari sipped the tea, and winced as if the taste was off. "Having said that, your starting point, your target if you will, is an American private investigator named Bruce Highland. He himself was a former military intelligence agent and has connections with the American intelligence network."

"So how am I going to approach him? What is my cover story?"

"That's something you're going to have to figure out. But I wouldn't stray too far from the truth. You are an Israeli citizen, and you haven't spent much time in the

United States. Maybe Daniel Levin can be a family member and you're there for answers. Before you throw any cards on the table, I would suggest you study him first, and look for a way in. Which – should not be difficult. He is reported to be single," Ari winked.

"You aren't suggesting that I become a Mata Hari, are you?" Maya retorted with a glare.

Ari looked upwards towards a formation of gathering clouds. "Nothing is off the table, but it is an area to be treaded lightly and with care. An involvement of that nature with someone with his intelligence connections can be either very good for us, or very bad for us. Use your judgement."

"What kind of project were they working on?"

"That, my friend, is the sixty-four thousand shekel question. We don't know other than it has a very powerful military application and that we have a stake in it. The end game is to find out what that is, and can we pick off where the Americans left, if it is so worth it. You manage to pull that one off and you're going to go very far in the organization and very fast."

The flight to San Francisco via Tel Aviv and New York was unsettling. It's not that Maya had been warned that she had agreed to sacrifices of both virtue and life for her nation, it was just that the reality started to hit home. But at any rate, she was a rookie agent on her first real assignment. In retrospect it was a softball exercise compared to those of her more experienced cohorts. Such as working with Iranians to crack the ministry of intelligence. Syria. Lebanon. In other words, working with people that actively want to kill you, in places you are likely to be killed.

She was feeling overwhelmed. Her own supervisor was somewhat miffed at the idea of sending her alone, on an international assignment no less. But when Ari Rosenfeld wants a fish sandwich, you deploy a trawler. When Ari says jump, you don't even ask how high, you just start jumping. She looked in the hotel mirror. She didn't really look all that Jewish with her bleach blonde hair. If anything, appearance wise she could fit that stereotypical Jewish American Princess profile. She was anything but a coddled princess, having earned her commission in the IDF as a lieutenant. Appearances can be deceiving. She could be tough as nails when she needed to be.

The Crop & Saddle was an iconic downtown Sacramento British themed pub; one of a handful that expats from the UK would frequent, congregating en masse on Fridays. Any given weekday, after quitting time, a small crowd of regulars could be found playing liar's dice for small pots of cash accumulated from the buy-in of a dice cup. It is also a location where Bruce Highland likes to conduct his business. It is an intrinsically bad idea to conduct client business at your own home, so Bruce prefers to have client meetings anyplace but his home office.

"Hey Bruce," Pieter said as he turned from the register. "Usual today?"

"Pilsner if you have it," Bruce said.

"That's not your usual," Pieter replied.

"It's not my usual, because usually you don't have one on tap."

"Well, you're in luck today. Here you go."

Bruce grabbed his beer, and noticed a nervous looking man with gaunt features, male pattern baldness and small, wire rimmed glasses standing at the bar next to him. "You wouldn't be Mike Smith, would you?"

"I am. Are you Bruce?"

"Yeah, let's grab a seat back here out of the way." Bruce led him back to a corner table and took a seat. "So, what's going on?"

"My daughter Mary is a freshman at UC Davis. She went missing yesterday," Mike said.

"It just so happens I'm running a special right now on missing persons," Bruce said. Mike Smith appeared to be unamused. "Well anyway, I assume the police are investigating her disappearance, yes?"

"They say she's an adult, and it's too soon."

Bruce swirled his beer. "That's typical. Were there signs of abduction or foul play?"

"No, her roommate said that she went out to pick up some things at a convenience store, and she never came back."

"Okay, I'm going to need to have you fill some forms out and read over my rate sheet. And as much information as you can give me on your daughter including recent pictures, current address, known friends, relatives and associates, and last known whereabouts.

Mike Smith glanced over the material and fee schedule. "Consider yourself hired."

"All right. We're going to need to go over some stuff in more detail later. I want to get an initial feel for what the situation is so I can focus in on the right questions to ask." Bruce skimmed over the forms, then looked over at Mike. "Do you have any idea of what happened?"

"I think she was abducted. Why would someone tell their roommate they were going shopping if their intention was to run away? Plus, she just isn't the runaway type."

"All right. Let me digest this, poke around a bit and I'll get back with you."

"Okay." Mike Smith started to leave. "When you find her, just let me know where she is... don't contact her... just in case she did run away."

Bruce eyed him suspiciously. "Sure thing."

Mary Smith. Having such a common name isn't helpful in a search for missing persons. Mary Smith was born and raised in Concord, attended a Catholic girls' school, graduated with honors, and enrolled in UC Davis to pursue a business degree. Nothing in particular stood out to Bruce in terms of background. Boyfriend from high school enlisted in the Air Force and is currently in Italy. She has no known enemies, and resided in an apartment off campus. Her roommate is one... Nelson Falco? Male? Having a male roommate is somewhat of red flag.

All the time Bruce was reviewing the paperwork, he couldn't help but feel like he was being watched. It was like a sixth sense. Try it in a quiet room. Gaze upon the back of a person's head, out of their field of view. They will noticeably become uncomfortable. In his peripheral vision, he could see a small statured blonde girl dressed in ripped jeans and gray wool sweater sitting alone at a table in front of a laptop occasionally glance in his direction.

It probably meant nothing. It's normally Bruce who is observing the girls and not the other way around. He didn't recognize her, but that doesn't mean very much at this place. He decided to switch up the venue, packed up his papers in a briefcase and went back to the bar to hang out.

"Hey Pieter," Bruce said in a low murmur, "Know that girl over there in the corner?"

Pieter glanced over. "Nope. Never seen her before. Like that, huh?"

"Just asking."

Pieter sighed. "It's been what, two years?"

"Three years," Bruce said.

"It's time to move on, bro."

"Yeah well, that's what I thought when Kim Park and I were together."

"What happened there?"

"Same story as always. The honeymoon ended. Reality set in. It just didn't work out. And it didn't help that she knew Svetlana."

"Didn't I see you in here with a hot little redhead last week? That you failed to introduce me to?"

"Melanie? I failed to introduce you, because there were no introductions for there to be made. She's a client."

"Client huh."

"Yes, client. There was nothing more there."

"Bruce, sometimes I think you're the best judge of character I've ever known, and other times you're the worst. I'm telling you man, there was definitely something there. Straight up."

"You think?"

"Oh yeah."

"Anyway, I need to get going," Bruce said. "I'll hit you up later." Bruce exited the Crop & Saddle, climbed inside his Altima, and waited for several minutes, gazing at the front entrance through his rear-view mirror. Nobody else entered or exited. He drove home.

The Israeli consulate kindly forwarded a Cliff Notes version of what was known of the Area 91 incident, and the local folklore that surrounded it. Maya studied it intently. She was still on the fence about how she would approach Bruce Highland. But she also realized that he took notice of her, and it was quickly going to become a shit or get off the pot type of situation. Broach the subject of Daniel Levin? No, that would be too much of a weird coincidence. He just happens to be looking into this Area 91 site, and she just happens to be visiting from Israel to investigate her long lost uncle's death at... drum roll, Area 91. No, that's not going to work.

Bruce Highland was an attractive guy. Thoughts of succumbing to the depths of a cheap whore spy started to become significantly more palatable. The more she thought about it, the more sense it made to become an Area 91 groupie.

Now the question is, what is a credible explanation for her knowledge of Bruce Highland's connection with Area 91? I overheard you mention it in the bar the other day.

Bruce couldn't get the events of the other night off his mind. Never mind that three guys in a bar tried to kick his ass. He was rather proud of himself but honestly, the punks weren't very good fighters. That's easy enough to get over. But the kiss wasn't. What would have happened if Susie didn't randomly show up at a rather inopportune moment? 'Things' wouldn't have stopped at a kiss; he was sure of that.

He hadn't spoken to her since that night. That was two days ago. It was an awkward silence. But the problem was, he genuinely didn't have anything new to report legitimately tied with the investigation. He started to pick up the phone and call her, when an incoming call beat him to the punch. It was from Ana, his subcontract investigator in Ensenada.

"Hello Bruce?" she said in a thick accent.

"What's up, Ana?"

"Somebody else has been in town asking about Chad Green since you left."

"Really? Who?"

"I don't know. But one of my sources said he overheard some people talking about it."

"Do you think you could find out who it was?"

"I asked my source if he could ask those people. He was afraid to do it. But I don't blame him. In this town, you don't tell people that you have been listening in on their conversations."

"Yeah, I guess. Thank you."

Bruce wasted no time in calling Melanie after the conversation with Ana ended. He dialed her number and waited. It rang several times. Finally, she answered. "Hi Bruce."

"Hey Melanie, I have a question for you. Who knew that we were in Ensenada looking for your brother?"

"Well... my sister of course. And my friend Susie, but she just knew I was in Ensenada, not why I was there. Why?"

"Because apparently there has been someone else in Ensenada looking for your brother after we left."

"Wow, that's crazy."

"Nobody else knew you, or we, were in Ensenada?"

"Ohhh. You know what? Dammit, I shared my status on social media. I guess I really screwed up."

"No, you didn't screw up. I didn't see that one coming myself."

"Do you know who it was?" Melanie asked.

"I have a pretty good idea who it probably is. I just didn't know how. But that could explain it."

"Macleod?"

"Most likely. People in the middle of an active investigation don't just randomly take a three-day vacation to Mexico. I'm sure he followed your social media, put two and two together and assumed that was why you were there, probably with me."

"Hey Bruce?"

"Yeah?"

"I'm sorry about the other night."

"Oh, don't worry about that. A good dry cleaning and a press, and the suit was good as new."

"I'm not talking about that."

Bruce sat in silence for several minutes. "Where do you want to go from here, Melanie?"

"That's up to you, Bruce. That's up to you."

"You still want an investigator, right?"

"Of course I do. But I'm not talking about the case."

"The next time we go out for drinks, can we avoid the Jolly Roger?"

"I think I can work with that."

"I have to tell you though, I kind of feel like a line has been crossed."

"Bruce, that ship sailed well before the other night."

The nurse escorted the man in a gray suit carrying a leather briefcase to the office, and knocked on the door. "Excuse me, Dr. Katz, but there is a man here to see you."

"I am very busy. Can you please ask him to come back later with an appointment?"

"That is not going to work," the man said, holding an identification badge in front of him. "I'm with the GRU. Agent Nikolay Sarkov."

"The GRU? What could the GRU possibly want with me?"

Not you, doctor. I am here to see Elena Yakut. Our bureau has been informed that she may be someone else."

"Why would the GRU be interested in this issue?"

"I am afraid I cannot disclose the reason. I will need a private room with her."

The man named Nikolay Sarkov looked Elena up and down and compared it with a file photograph. He then pulled out a fingerprint kit. "Give me your right thumb, please." He examined the thumb print carefully and compared it to a file card. "Your other thumb please." He then carefully compared it to another thumb print on the file card. "The prints do not lie."

"What is the meaning of this?" Elena asked.

"The Rosaviatsiya reopened the case of Aeroflot flight 7230 and re-examined the identification of the victims. They had made a determination that you could have only been one of two passengers on board. When they made an inquiry into your other possible identity with the Russian embassy in America, we were alerted. And they sent me to investigate. Your real name is Svetlana Petroya, and you were a former cryptologic officer with the GRU."

"I don't understand. If my prints were on file, why didn't they discover my identity three years ago?"

"The GRU maintains prints, and nowadays DNA samples, on all of its present and former agents. But those aren't publicly available to civilian law enforcement and investigative agencies."

"That makes a little bit of sense to me. The memories. The uniform. You must understand though that I have a very difficult time remembering anything prior to the crash."

"I do understand that. Now, I am going to tell you something, and I need you to listen very carefully, as your life is going to depend on it. There are those in the GRU, the old guard, the hard liners left over from the Soviet republic, who feel that you have betrayed the people of Russia. My orders were to investigate and determine if you were in fact Svetlana Petroya, and if you were, then my orders were to kill you."

Svetlana turned ashen. "My god. This is actually true? I can't believe this can be happening."

"Well obviously I don't actually intend on doing that or I wouldn't be telling you. But listen to me – as long as you remain in Russia, you must keep on being Elena Yakut. It is my intention to return to my post, and report that you are not in fact Svetlana Petroya so the case can be closed."

"How come you wish to protect me?"

"I don't believe in the old guard. They are relics that need to be purged from the bureau. Yourself and other victims of political assassination do not deserve death. Quite honestly, you should not have returned to Russia. I'm sure that you felt it was safe to return due to the passage of time, but it was not and is not the case. Ironically, it is quite possible that the crash may have, in the end, protected you."

"Where was I before the crash?"

"A few years ago, you resigned your commission with the GRU citing corruption and illegal surveillance of Russian citizens. And – quite rightly so. But not in the opinion of the hard liners. You ended up relocating to the United States, where you became a citizen. At the time of the crash, you resided in the city of Sacramento, in California. You were married to a private investigator named Bruce Highland."

"Bruce. The name keeps popping up in my head. It makes sense."

"I cannot emphasize strongly enough that you need to find a way to leave Russia."

"I think then, I should be able to go to the American consulate and have my identity confirmed and my passport restored?"

"If you must do so, don't do it while you are still in Russia."

"What do you know of this Bruce Highland?"

"Nothing, they just tell me names and locations. But, speaking to you as a person, and not as an agent of the state, I must warn you that personal relationships have likely changed since the crash. This man, and your family, they all think you are dead."

"I understand."

Sarkov returned to Dr. Katz's office. "I have determined that Elena Yakut is not the person that we thought she might be. She indeed is Elena Yakut. I have no further business here." Sarkov slipped out as silently as he slipped in.

"Elena," Dr. Katz said as he walked into the day room. "The man, the GRU agent named Sarkov, has informed me that you are positively in fact Elena Yakut."

"Yes, doctor. I am quickly remembering more of my childhood. And that miserable job I was working on the Lada assembly line. It is all coming back to me."

"Elena... That Mr. Sarkov may be good at being an intelligence agent with a secret bureau, but he is not a very good liar. And neither are you."

"What is the possibility of obtaining a passport for international travel?"

"You were delivered to this facility with a presumed identity and no documentation. And judging by the last interaction with your supposed mother and sister, I doubt very much they are going to personally vouch for you. So, I don't see that happening."

"I need to get out of Russia."

"I do not know what secret you bear, and I will not press you for it. My job is only to ensure that you are ready to live on your own in society before you are released."

"I am ready, doctor."

"Are you? Let's take a drive to the city this afternoon. Let's see how you handle yourself on the outside."

The Mercedes barreled down the divided Izmaylovskiy Prospekt. Dr. Katz pulled into the grocery store parking lot. "You know St. Petersburg?" Dr. Katz asked.

"No. It looks a lot like Moscow. And Kiev. Just another big city."

Dr. Katz parked the car, and they entered the store. "Have a look around. What do you like?"

"Pizza," she said, as they walked down the frozen foods aisle. "But not this frozen pizza. Real pizza. Like you get at a restaurant."

"Well, that is an interesting revelation. If I would have known that, we could have had some delivered from time to time."

"And... and look, American wines. Over here. Napa Valley. I did not ever think you could find these things here."

"For someone that has never been to the United States, you show a surprising amount of interest and knowledge of it."

"I want to see the butcher section." They walked over to the fresh meat department.

"Are you looking for something in particular?"

"Ribs. Pork ribs. And beef... Americans call it 'tri tip.' I don't know the Russian word for it. But I don't see it."

Dr. Katz jotted a few lines in his pocket notebook. "Here is fifteen hundred rubles. Why don't you buy a few things to take back to the facility?"

"I think we have everything there that we need. I would like to get a bottle of that Napa Valley wine, but it costs a little more than fifteen hundred rubles. Maybe two bottles of this Spanish wine. If, that's allowable."

"We have better wine than that back at the facility. I think maybe we can allow an occasional glass at dinner."

"Then these fresh pastries."

"Go ahead and buy them."

They got back to the car. "Doctor?"

"Yes?"

"Would you mind if I drive the car back?"

They sat across from each other at a small table in the staff dining area. It would almost be a romantic dinner if it had not been in an institutional setting. They each had a glass of a French wine from the Bordeaux region. "I had our chef cook up a special meal. I think you have convinced me that you are capable of functioning on your own. But... you still have two problems. One is that you have no official papers, and second is you have no money. The process to get some identification papers is a long one."

"If I can get out of Russia, I can get some identification papers. At an American consulate. But you're right. I still have no money. Maybe I should get a job and work and save up."

"Elena, or whoever are, this is strictly between me and you. But I come from a long line of persecuted Russian Jews, many of whom have great experience and deep networks, and are quite used to smuggling people in and out of the country. I will prepare your repatriation certificate, issue you a government allotment of cash to get you started plus whatever I can get though charity resources, and then you go see this man." Dr. Katz wrote down a name on a piece of paper. "He can help you. He will be expecting you."

"Thank you so much, doctor."

"Who are you?"

"It's best that you not know."

The Maxim Pluralist is a Handymax class crude carrier traveling from St. Petersburg, to Tilbury Docks in England. The approximately seventeen hundred nautical mile journey will take the better part of a week to complete, loping along at the aging ship's top cruising speed of fourteen knots. Once docked, the stowaway, 'unbeknownst to the crew', would depart the ship, remain in the customs detention area until the ship unloaded its cargo of bulk crude and then left. She would then arrive at the customs house, with some cash and no papers whatsoever. At that point, claiming United States citizenship, she would be promptly escorted by British immigration to the United States consulate in London. And with any luck, would walk away with a passport and hopefully minimal admonishment from the British government for the illegal entry.

It wasn't exactly a free ride. Svetlana spent the entire trip tirelessly working a double shift in the ship's galley, washing dishes, peeling potatoes, cleaning, and even cooking. The Filipino crew offered her a berth with as much privacy as they could on a small ship with limited privacy. The First Officer casually hinted that he would be willing to share his small private stateroom; an offer that Svetlana graciously declined. As the end of the journey grew nearer, she was becoming increasingly apprehensive. The realization that she was cast out on her own was starting to sink in. Her world started three years prior, and she had always been taken care of until now.

And then there was the issue of what will happen when she gets to the United States. Can she go to the United States? Can she stay in England? In the worst case, she would get deported back to Russia, but how are they going to take her with no documentation? (Hopefully, they wouldn't.) Who is this Bruce Highland? Fleeting images come and go. Bicycle rides up the Napa Valley hills. Drinking in pubs. Cooking. Does she even still have a home in California? After three years, probably not, and even in the best case, it would probably be a very awkward reintroduction.

Unbeknownst to her, the one, single saving grace, the only solid way to establish her identity, was by virtue of the fact that she possessed a Sacramento County concealed carry permit. As such her fingerprints were on file with the federal AFIS system. She had forgotten about that, or more accurately the memory of such had not yet returned.

Bruce decided to circle back to Mike Smith, and tell him that frankly, he wasn't going to be able to do much. He dialed his cell phone, waited for several rings and got an answer. "Who is this?" A gruff voice asked.

"I'm sorry, I must have a wrong number," Bruce said. "I was looking for Mike Smith."

"Smith huh. What is your business?"

"I'm the private investigator he hired to try to find his missing daughter."

"Daughter huh. This is Detective Sergeant Grant Moss of the Yolo County Sheriff's Department. You might want to turn on the evening news right now."

Bruce flipped on the television news channel.

In breaking news, two men, Mike Grand and Nelson Falco, have been arrested in connection with a sex trafficking ring. One of the victims, Mary Smith, was able to escape from imprisonment to safety and alert authorities...

Bruce was beside himself. That explains a lot.

Chapter 6 – Close call

"Is that the same guy?" DEA agent Diego Chance peered through a small pair of binoculars.

His partner, Alfonso Padilla grabbed the glasses and stared at the male figure standing outside of the front door of the seaside restaurant. "He looks to be the right age."

Thomas Cromwell was from a wealthy family. He attended an Ivy League university, pursuing a law degree. With his father's political clout, he could have well turned out to be a Supreme Court justice. By all accounts, he was brilliant. Like any spoiled rich kid, he drove fancy cars, and indulged in expensive hobbies. And also, like many spoiled, coddled rich kids who felt as though they were above the reach of the law, he developed some less than wholesome habits, like a fondness for cocaine, an illegal drug which peaked usage in the mid 1980's. And it's not like he didn't have money – he did. But he liked making money, the wrong way.

He had a fondness for Mexico. He would travel south of the border to score a few grams of coke, then bring it back to campus to cut, and score a nice healthy profit. It was a game. A few grams turned into a few ounces, and a few ounces led to pounds, and eventually he was wholesaling to the local organized crime families who in turn supplied the street gangs. And then his name eventually came up in a federal RICO investigation. Then he suddenly disappeared.

You would think after some point in time, an old drug investigation would go away if you've kept your nose clean and attended choir practice every Saturday night for nearly forty years, unless you happened to be a named person of interest in a still unsolved homicide of an undercover federal agent.

There were a lot of theories about what happened to Thomas Cromwell. Death and dismemberment is a known occupational hazard in the trade of high-volume narcotics trafficking, and as the case was passed on from investigator to investigator, it was always assumed he met his demise in some underworld activity that went bad for him. But if he did flee and disappear, he would have most likely gone to Mexico.

Over the years, new division chiefs would shake their rattles and cause the investigators to bring up cold cases. They would poke around, search for leads, find some, and investigate them. And of course, there were enough Thomas Cromwells in the world that most of them were going to prove false. But Chance and Padilla genuinely felt that the pieces were fitting on this one. In the original investigation, complete, detailed, real time credit card transaction history was unavailable, however, investigators were able to piece together a string of purchases made by Cromwell at gas stations, starting from his apartment in Connecticut and culminating in San Diego. They surmised that it was not his intention to visit the zoo. Whether or not he was fleeing, or making another drug run was subject to speculation, but he did reportedly leave with a large, unrecovered sum of cash that belonged to the Guisti Family.

The lead came in, ironically, through a social media platform that focuses on business reviews, primarily of 'Bs. La Estrella de Ensenada.' The Star of Ensenada. I started going to this place in the early 1990's. Tom Cromwell really turned it around!

It piqued the interest of Diego Chance who was doing his periodic Internet search for cold case clues. They pop up all the time, as more and more information gets posted to the web. It was worth a few calls to their local counterpart in Ensenada. They were able to determine, indeed, that the proprietor, Tom Cromwell, along with his co-proprietor, Maria Hernandez, purchased the restaurant in 1995. What was the likelihood of that being the right Thomas Cromwell? Not very. By all accounts, Thomas Cromwell was insistent, to the point of anger that he be referred to as Thomas, and not Tom. And of course, this was ten years after he originally disappeared. If nothing else, it would be a nice junket for Chance and Padilla, at the DEA's time and expense.

Diego Chance was a thin, clean shaven angular man of Portuguese descent, and Alfonso Padilla on the other hand was a short round man with dark skin and a thick black bushy mustache. They were basically the Latin version of Laurel and Hardy. And the gaudy tropical print shirts that even first-time tourist considered tacky, didn't help to tone down that image.

"Well, what do we do now?" Padilla asked.

"Let's just go ask him some questions. See how he responds."

The two agents made their way to the bar. It wasn't quite ten o'clock yet so there were just a handful of brunch customers seated at two tables on the floor. "Bar open yet?" Padilla asked. They were both pleased that it was the man they believed to be the owner, Tom Cromwell, who was playing bartender.

"This is Ensenada. If the door is open, the bar is open. What can I get for you gentlemen?"

"Oh, just a couple iced teas," Chance said before Padilla could respond.

"You can give him an iced tea. I want a beer," Padilla said.

"Okay fine," Chance replied. "Two beers then. We heard about this place. It got some good reviews."

"Yes. I'm always looking for positive reviews," Chad replied.

"You the owner of this establishment?"

"Yes sir."

"Had it long?"

"Bought it in '95. So, yeah. You could say that."

"Been in Ensenada for a while before that, or did you just come down across the border to buy this place?"

Chad eyed them critically. "Why do you ask?"

"Well, I'll be honest with you," Chance said, pulling out his wallet and opening it to display a federal ID card and a shield. "We are federal agents. We are investigating the disappearance of a man named Thomas Cromwell, who went missing in 1985. And we believe he went missing in Mexico."

Chad Green had always anticipated the possibility of someone asking questions about the disappearance of Thomas Cromwell, so he wasn't taken entirely off guard. "Well, my name is Tom Cromwell, and I'm obviously not missing, so, you have the wrong Tom Cromwell. Besides, aren't you guys just a little bit out of your jurisdiction?"

"We are, but we can still ask questions, right?"

"I suppose so." Chad turned his back to the pair and started arranging glassware from a dishwasher rack.

"Aren't you even a little bit curious as to why federal agents are looking for a missing man by your name after so many years?" Chance asked. "Or... do you already know?"

"Okay, I'll bite."

"He's a suspected drug smuggler, and is wanted for questioning in the homicide of a federal agent."

"Well. I can honestly say that nobody has ever accused me of being either a drug dealer, or a murderer."

"He was from a well to do family, and was a Yale law school student. He made a trip from Connecticut in his Land Rover, with a substantial amount of mafia money, and his last verifiable location was San Diego."

If there was any doubt before, there was none anymore. They were talking about the same Thomas Cromwell. I can still be Chad Green if I need to be. But he doesn't have to be Chad Green. All that is important is that he actually isn't Thomas Cromwell. "Well, I'm not your man."

"Tell you what, Tom," Chance said. "It's not that I don't believe you, but I have an idea that could clear this up once and for all. And, to be clear, you don't have to do it, but would you be willing to offer up a DNA sample so we can compare it to the parents of the Thomas Cromwell that we happen to be looking for?"

There was a long hesitation. Then to both Chance's and Padilla's surprise, he agreed. "Sure," Chad responded. They were fairly certain that they would have had to get his DNA surreptitiously through a handled item, such as the bar glassware.

They turned to each other with a puzzled look. Chance nodded at Padilla, who exited the bar and returned with a small kit containing gloves, plastic baggies, and cotton swabs. "I'll just need to get a swab of your cheek please."

Chad complied, reasoning that it would get anyone trying to follow Thomas Cromwell's trail, off of it. At least in connection to himself. "I'm not trying to tell you guys how to do your job, but if I'm lying, and I am actually the fleeing fugitive you seek, what's to prevent me from disappearing, the minute you leave?"

"Well, you have a point there," Chance said. "To be honest with you, we didn't actually expect you would end up being the person we are looking for. But I have to tell you, the circumstances are pretty strong."

The men left. Maria had been silently listening from the back room behind the bar. "Tom, for years I had wondered where you got the money to buy this place. I've wondered why you never talk to family and nobody ever comes to visit you. I have wondered why we have never visited the United States. That wallet I found and asked you about. I wondered why you never made an effort to return it to its owner. Is there something that you want to tell me?"

Chad held his head low in his arms in despair. "Sit down, Maria."

The memories were trickling in, portions at a time. She remembered having been in London before, but never particularly cared for it. It was quaint, the people speak with quaint accents, but then again Svetlana herself has an even quainter accent when she speaks English. And she can't use an article in a sentence to save her life. "Article useless! Article serve no purpose. Russian do not use article in language!"

She was able to gradually move from the immigration detention center, to a home, courtesy of Dr. Katz' family's network, where she was allowed to bed down, and go about restoring pieces of her life. Her ultimate goal was to return to the United States. She had an incredible story to tell the United States Embassy in London – it was too incredible to believe. A story of a terrible accident, and misidentification, and an illicit journey. But, in the very words of GRU agent Sarkov just weeks earlier, 'fingerprints don't lie.' They wanted to contact and interview Bruce Highland, but she convinced them that it was both in her best interest, and his best interest, if they don't, besides, they did not need his corroboration to establish her identity.

It should have been a simple process, but it wasn't. It took some time and effort, and the ability to convince trained professionals as to her authenticity, but she finally was able to secure her first major milestone. A re-issued United States passport. That was a huge hurdle, and it should solve everything, right? Wrong.

She and Bruce were married later in life than typical spouses marry, for the first time. Consequently, she always maintained her own bank account. She learned California was a joint property state, and that Bruce was entitled to her assets in her death, but she also learned that no application had been made to declare her death. The Russian Government never did issue an official statement of death – at least in her case, not in a form that was acceptable to the US government, so consequently, she wasn't officially dead yet. It takes five years of absence under presumed demise for a court to issue a determination of official death. And it had only been three.

She banked with a major institution, one that had branches worldwide. Including London. The banker at the desk examined her passport, and pulled up some records on a computer terminal. She made a call to her supervisor. "I'm sorry ma'am, but you must have at least three forms of identification with you in order to be able to verify that you are the owner of the account in your name."

"Passport not good enough?" Svetlana asked.

"I'm afraid not. Usually in these circumstances we not only require three forms of identification, we also require that you answer a series of questions related to your past which are not publicly available."

Svetlana sighed. "Can you at least tell me if there is money in my account?"

The girl studied Svetlana carefully. Russians can be crafty con artists. But it's the men, and they use the Internet to con people. "No. I'm sorry. But if you are able to produce the documentation that is required, in your home country, I think you will be satisfied."

"Thank you."

Of course, that begged the question. Would Bruce Highland still have her things? Her papers? Her naturalization documents? Her birth certificate? She was sure she would have lost her driver's license in the crash. Why wouldn't you take it with you on a trip? But that can be replaced. And her bank cards? She would have needed them on the trip, and those were exactly what she was trying to restore when she went to her bank's London branch.

The answer was staring her in the face. She mentally kicked herself for not seeing the notes collected by the consulate staff in San Francisco. Maya Goldman realized that she had Bruce Highland's phone number all along with a reason to call it. He left it with a bartender at an American Legion post in Monterey and the word was spread around.

"Hello?" Bruce said as he answered an unknown number.

"Mr. Highland?" Maya said.

"Speaking."

"My name is Maya Goldman. I ran across your name and phone number in Monterey. I research secret, controversial government installations, and right now I'm focusing on a historical site called Area 91. I was told you are the man to talk to for information."

"I think that is a little bit of a stretch," Bruce said. "I'm not sure I can help you much."

"Can I meet up with you to talk about it?"

"Well, I... where are you?"

"I am in Sacramento. The downtown area."

"Okay, I'll tell you what. I am currently at a place called the Crop & Saddle. I'll be there for another hour or so."

"I'm familiar with it. I was just there the other day. I can be there in ten minutes."

Maya waited in her rental car, which was parked outside of the Crop & Saddle, for ten minutes, and then went inside. She stood at the bar and ordered a glass of house white wine. Bruce, who was standing next to her, recognized her voice, which had an odd accent. "Are you Maya?" he asked.

"Yes. You are Bruce Highland then?"

"I am. You look slightly familiar."

"I might be. I've been here once or twice."

"I see. So, why are you researching these, how did you phrase it, secret and controversial government installations?"

"I plan to write a book."

"Hmm," Bruce said. "Okay, well, before I get into it, can you tell me what you know about Area 91?"

"It was an American military research facility in the 1980's. There was some kind of accident there, and the researchers were killed."

"Well, I hope I haven't wasted any of your time, but that's pretty much everything I know about it." Which wasn't technically true, but that was more or less the extent that Bruce would have been willing to share.

"Can I ask why you are researching it?"

"It just happens to be related to a client investigation that I am involved with," Bruce replied.

"May I ask what is it that you are actually investigating?"

"It's a private matter. I don't discuss active investigations with non-involved parties. I'm not trying to blow you off, but my clients generally expect me to maintain confidentiality. I'm sure you can understand."

"Of course." Maya looked disappointed.

Her curiosity was starting to border on annoying. Bruce eyed her carefully. She was attractive. She had a nice figure. He placed her age to be in the mid-twenties, perhaps pushing thirty. In another time, in another world, he would have jumped at the opportunity to engage her further. Then again, available, attractive young women, or for that matter attractive women in general, have never been off the table before. It should be harmless enough to prod a bit. "Where are you from?"

"Tel Aviv, Israel."

"You traveled all the way here, just to get the scoop on Area 91?"

She smiled. "I have family here. Area 91 is a side venture."

"What do you do for work?" Bruce asked, as he reached for his automatic beer refill.

"I'm a massage therapist," Maya replied with an evil smirk.

"You have an interesting hobby, for a masseuse."

"I'm joking. I'm a data analyst for a major corporation. But I do give a mean massage," she said with a wink.

Was that an invite or what? Bruce could hardly believe his ears. Surely, he must be having a dream right now. "I might just take you up on that."

"That could be arranged."

Before Bruce could speak another word, his cell phone rang. It was Nielson. "Excuse me," Bruce said. "I need to take this call." He stepped outside of the building and walked out of earshot of the entrance. "What's up, Nielson?"

"Listen, Bruce, that inquiry I did came up with another hit, from an interesting source. The NSA has come up with some data and voice communications with the phrase Area 91, as well as some Internet searches. Not surprisingly, most are in California, and a couple were in Mexico. But... one hit was in Tel Aviv."

"Oh, I think I can explain that one," Bruce said.

"You can? I'd love to hear that explanation, because it was in a phone call from a known Mossad agent."

"What?"

"That's right. An old timer named Ari Rosenfeld. He's pretty high up the food chain."

"I'll be damned. We spy on... Israel?" Bruce said in disbelief.

There was a short silence. "Bruce, monitoring foreign countries, is something that we... do."

"I guess when you put it that way. Can you run a name for me? Maya Goldman?"

"Who's that?"

"My brand-new unsolicited lady friend. I think she is about to rub me the wrong way."

It took some searching and a FOIA request, but Bruce finally held a piece of paper that contained the names of the casualties that perished in the Area 91 incident. It confirmed what the former MP named Delmar Washington said. Eleven casualties, and not ten, and Chad Green was on the list of casualties. But, it was confirmed positively that he was still alive for at least several months afterwards. One name stood out in particular. Daniel Levin, from Tel Aviv. It didn't take a strong set of math skills to realize that Project Dark Fury must have been some sort of joint effort with the Israeli government, hence Mossad's interest.

Nielson's latest phone call revealed what Bruce had suspected after talking with him earlier on the phone at the Crop & Saddle. Maya Goldman was formerly a lieutenant in the IDF, who was discharged after two years then her history stopped – not an atypical background for a Mossad agent. And a good liar, also not atypical for a Mossad agent. Interested in Area 91? Truth. Writing a book? Lie. Data analyst for a major corporation? Lie. Gives a killer massage? Truth. Getting information out of Bruce was like squeezing water out of a rock. Getting Maya to complete the massage to a happy ending was like getting information from Bruce. Both left the hotel room in frustration.

One of the problems with a forty-year-old case is that personal information and history is hard to come by, at least using online resources. By knowing the area of expertise of the team members, one could piece together what the government might have been working on for Project Dark Fury. Daniel Levin was a microbiologist, a doctoral candidate that was known as the top in his field for his area of research, which was not specified. Another member with enough recognition to survive the annals of time was Andrew Spink, a leading expert in gene splicing. Gene splicing? Microbiology? Sounds suspiciously like a program for developing a new biological weapon.

Some things were bothering Bruce. A couple were in Mexico. Bruce was absolutely positive he had made no telephone conversations of any sort, nor made and electronic inquiries regarding Area 91. He was pretty sure that Melanie had not done so either, and even called her to confirm. She was adamant that she had not.

Unable to contain his curiosity, he called Nielson again. "Hey Nielson, got a minute?" Bruce asked.

"Only a brief minute. What do you have?"

"Remember in that one call you made to me? You mentioned that the NSA pinged a couple hits on Area 91 in Mexico. Can you tell me where?"

"Let me see." Nielson pulled up a screen on his monitor. "Ensenada. A couple Internet searches."

Ensenada. It was probably more likely coming from Melanie and she was drunk and forgot about it. Or maybe she just forgot about it. "Do you think you could put a name to those searches?"

"Hmm." Nielson typed a query. "No. The IP pings to an address, 35 Boulevard de Costero. That comes up with... a restaurant called La Estrella de Ensenada. The owner of the IP is listed as 'La Estrella de Ensenada, S. de RL.' So, probably the restaurant's WIFI."

Bruce pulled up a map. "Huh," he said audibly, with no audience as he had already hung up on the conversation with Nielson. Bruce was one hundred percent certain that it was not a restaurant that they had been to. And neither had mentioned Area 91 to any person while on the trip. But it was also possible that someone within earshot may have overheard it and decided to do a search on it to see what it was. Later. Well after the fact. Or, it could mean Chad Green was sitting right there in that very restaurant, looking it up, hiding in plain sight.

The smart thing to do was to just let it drop. Play stupid. Blow Maya off. It's clear she was here for one reason, and that was to milk Bruce for information. But it was obvious she must know some piece of the puzzle. There was no point in letting a resource go wasted, Bruce reasoned.

Like clockwork, she showed up at the Crop & Saddle at precisely three o'clock, bought a beer, and meandered over to Bruce's table, where he was engaged in some laptop research on another case. "Learn anything new?" Bruce asked.

She took a seat and rested her own laptop bag against the rustic brick wall. "Nope."

"Well, I got an interesting tidbit of information yesterday," Bruce said. "I got a hold of the casualty list. All eleven people that were reported as deceased in the accident."

Her eyebrows raised. "Oh? That's good."

"Did I mention that I seem to have a kink in my back? I think I pulled something at the gym this morning."

"Sorry to hear."

"So obviously, the casualty list isn't that good." Maya sat in silence. "You want to know a strange coincidence? There is a member on that team that was from Tel Aviv. A microbiologist named Daniel Levin."

"If you want these jeans to come off, you're going to have to give me more than that."

"How about we do this? Why don't you just cut the crap and tell me why you are really here? Oh, I know who you work for, and it isn't some private company."

She studied Bruce intently, and looked around. "Let's go someplace where we can talk."

"All right. Let's go sit in my car."

"I am here for the same reason you are," Maya said. "To find out what Daniel Levin was working on. To find out why he died. To find out what was so important between our two countries."

"Then why don't you go through the official channels to find out what happened?" Bruce asked.

"My boss has tried to do that for years."

"So, what do you guys know about this project?"

"Nothing. Only that it was a top-secret collaborative project to develop some new kind of weapon that would serve both of our purposes." Maya cleared her throat. "And that it was supposed to be a two-way street. But it wasn't."

"So why are you – or your organization rather, suddenly interested in it now?"

"Because we had been alerted that there was new activity and interest in the matter, and that we might be able to finally get some answers. And hopefully some return on our investment in it, which was the life of a revered university scholar and researcher."

"Then I'm pretty sure I'm not going to be able to help you any more than you are going to be able to help me."

"Why don't you meet me back at the hotel to talk about it more? These jeans are starting to feel uncomfortable."

"As much as I would love to jump on the gracious offer of your virtuosity, if that's what you're implying, just talking to you could potentially land me in federal prison on treason charges. And you probably shouldn't consider yourself to be as immune from spying charges as you think you might be. So, good luck with that, but don't involve me any further in your efforts."

As Bruce drove home pondering a serious missed opportunity, he mentally reminded himself that this woman did not travel 7,700 miles as the crow flies to give up so easily. A part of him wanted to turn her onto Roland Macleod, but at this point in the game, that probably wouldn't be a very good idea.

Chad Green was now spooked. He abruptly woke from a bad dream, bolted upright and was sweating profusely. "Are you okay, mi querido?" Maria said with a yawn.

"Yeah, I'm okay." He lay back in bed. First, it was the woman. She introduced herself as Ana. She explained that she was seeking older people, especially Americans, that might have been around back in the 1980s who knew, or knew of an American named Chad Green. Then, there were the two DEA agents that were looking for Thomas Cromwell a mere few days later. Was Area 91 rearing its ugly head after so many years of silence and inactivity? Did somebody make the connection between the two?

It occurred to him that he had not set foot on US soil since entering Mexico in 1984. Back then, all you needed to cross the border was some form of picture ID that was usually a driver's license. Now you can't. In a perfect world, he would obtain a passport in the name of Thomas Cromwell, but without backup documentation such as birth certificates and social security cards, that wasn't going to happen. His US passport expired thirty years ago. He did have the documentation necessary to renew it, but the last thing he wanted to do is reactivate Chad Green's existence, which he had wiped from the map, or so he assumed.

Then again maybe he was being paranoid. He forced the bad thoughts out of his head, and replaced them with images of brown skinned dancing natives coming into his bar wearing dresses so short it would be unnecessary to disrobe for a gynecologist visit, and pounding Pina Coladas like they were the latest fad, making Chad both wealthy and happy at the same time.

Bruce was troubled by the report of a second unknown individual looking for Chad Green in Ensenada. But he still wasn't sure that Macleod, or someone else would have been able to make the connection. After double checking Melanie's social media posts, he confirmed that she only shared her own status and did not even post any photos of herself and Bruce online. Which, led to another interesting theory. These days it's dirt simple to discreetly install GPS tracking devices which use the cell phone network to covertly transmit the location of a target vehicle. They can even be used on airplanes and boats, just not in real time once they leave the cell network service area.

To that end, like a hungry cartoon coyote whose ACME Prime subscription lands him a box dropped off in the middle of the desert, Bruce unpacked his latest toy. A professional RF detector. This five hundred dollar investment would reveal if someone did stick something on his car. He couldn't find anything in the usual hiding places, such as on the underside of a plastic bumper panel, but it didn't mean there still couldn't be one there. He wished he could have found one – at least the mystery would have been solved. But it wasn't a waste. He would probably use it again.

He called Melanie. "Hi Bruce," she said, balancing the cell phone on her shoulder as she stirred a pot of soup on the stove.

"I don't want to get your hopes up, but I got a lead that suggests that your brother may actually be in Ensenada."

"I don't know, Bruce, I'm getting kind of frustrated here. We seem to be spinning in circles and getting nowhere."

"In the search for your brother?"

"Yeah, that too."

"I need to be straight up with you about something."

"Please do. I don't need lies, deception and false promises."

"I've given you exactly... none of the above. But you do need to know that Svetlana is not legally dead, and I am still legally married."

"You told me she was killed in a plane crash three years ago."

"No death certificate was ever issued and no body was ever recovered. It was such a bad crash that most of the occupants were burned not just beyond recognition, but beyond identification. Plus, the Russians handle situations like this differently than we would over here."

"I see. I guess I should be more understanding. All right, this is what I'm going to do. I am going to hit the reset button. We are back to strictly business. How sure are you about this lead you have?"

"Not very, but it's worth taking a second look."

"So, are you good with this... status, between us?"

"Sure. That kiss never should have happened. I'm sorry."

Chapter 7 – Just missed

The young lieutenant glanced over at the latest edition of Playboy sitting on the captain's desk. August, 1967 featuring Playmate DeDe Lind. He picked it up, and started flipping through the pages with a smile. He heard horror stories about Vietnam. So far, his first few days in Long Binh seemed to be more like an endless party than it did a combat zone. But the heavy fighting was up north, and the chance of an MP officer meeting his demise at the hands of the relatively ill-equipped Viet Cong weren't particularly great, he learned at the makeshift bar.

No sooner than he made his way to the centerfold, trying his best to lead up to the excitement, than Captain Jenks arrived. He immediately sprung from his chair and came to attention. "Lieutenant Macleod, sir." As he rendered a salute.

Jenks waved him off. "Sit down. We're in 'Nam. We do things differently than we do in the real world. But I guess you don't know that, do you Lieutenant? This is your first duty assignment, right?"

"Yes sir."

"Of course."

"All right, let's get started. You will be assigned to lead third platoon. You know what that means?"

"Yes sir. I'll take charge of the platoon and make sure they are the most squared away in this company," Macleod said with a beaming smile.

"Wrong. You have a hardened, experienced platoon sergeant under you. You will let him run the show, and you will back him up when he needs it. Frankly, in reality, he doesn't need you, nor do I. Oh, and you can dispense with the 'sir' crap when we are alone or in the company of other officers."

"Understood," Macleod replied.

"Scenario. You know the UCMJ sections regarding drugs, or you goddamn well should since you're an MP, but a corporal in your platoon busts five soldiers smoking dope in a tent, and Staff Sergeant Deluna quietly lets the whole thing go and you find out about it. What do you do?"

"Hell, I'd have Deluna in cuffs along with the other five miscreants to face courts martial charges."

"Wrong. The hell you will. I need Deluna, you need Deluna, and we need every single goddamn soldier that we can get in this hellhole. If you haven't noticed, or heard, we're losing men left and right."

Macleod squinted at Jenks in a sideways stare. "Okay."

"You got a problem with that, Lieutenant, because you sure look like you do."

"I'm ready to go to work. Sir."

"I asked you a question, Lieutenant. I expect an answer."

"I do have a problem with that."

"All right. Fair enough. I expect honesty and I respect candidness and the unwavering ability to stand your ground."

"You mean this was a test?" Macleod asked in a confused tone of voice.

Jenks looked up. "Yes."

"Well, I guess I'll fit right in after all then."

"I said I respect candidness and steadfastness, not that I want it. I need lieutenants that will go with the flow. I'm up for rotation stateside in four months. Four months is a long time for you to deal with me and vice versa. I suggest you make your way back to Saigon and find MACV headquarters. There is a man there named Mr. Ding, who is looking for officers for a special project back stateside. They are pretty picky about who they choose. They didn't want me. You might give it a shot though."

The massive two-story complex at Tan Son Nhut Air Base was often referred to as 'The Pentagon East.' After some misdirection, Lieutenant Macleod found his way to the MACV command headquarters, informed the Duty Charge of Quarters that he was looking for a Mr. Ding, and took a seat in the lobby.

"Excuse me sir," the sharply dressed sergeant said. "I made a few calls around, and I'm coming up with nothing. Someone must be messing with you. Real sorry about that."

"That's all right sergeant. Thank you. Whelp, back to Long Binh I guess."

No sooner than Macleod stepped out of the building to await a shuttle, than a black Plymouth pulled up alongside of him. A window rolled down. "I understand you're looking for Mr. Ding."

"That's right."

"Get in."

Macleod was driven to a building in downtown Saigon, and led up four flights of stairs and told to wait inside of a small, air-conditioned office overlooking the busy street below. A gaunt man walked in wearing a light-colored suit. "You Lieutenant Roland Macleod?" he asked.

"That's me. You must be Mr. Ding?"

He cracked a slight smile on an otherwise expressionless face. "For your purpose yes. I'm a little bit perplexed though. Normally we come looking for you guys. Not the other way around. How did you hear about us?"

"Let's just say that when I reported to my captain for duty, we didn't hit it off very well so he suggested I go see you. He said you had some stateside assignment and that you were looking for officers."

"Before we go any further, I want to make something very clear. We are very, highly selective on who we choose for the program, and the chance of any given officer we interview being selected, is frankly minimal. You are not to discuss what we've talked about, who we are, where we are, or even acknowledge that this conversation has ever happened. Do we have an understanding on that?"

"Yes."

"Good, because your captain obviously did not, and that was a move that just may earn him another combat tour up north in Danang or Pleiku." The man leafed through a manila file folder. "Ordinarily, we wouldn't talk to you, but you're already here, so we might as well. I need you to fill out this form, read it, and sign it, so we can pull your service records."

"Can I ask a question?"

"Sure."

"What is this program of which you speak? What would I be doing?"

"If, after the next five hours, we decide to bring you on board, we will tell you then."

The Joint Task Special Projects Office was on the top level facing the lagoon. It was Lieutenant Macleod's official duty assignment, and Colonel Meacham was his official commanding officer. Where he physically worked may vary, and what he actually did was something that Meacham himself didn't even know. His duty assignments were issued by a group within a massive secure complex in Langley, Virginia.

The surf was crashing outside as Bruce and Melanie enjoyed a beer at the center of an upscale beachfront restaurant. The midday crowd was light. Tom Cromwell really turned this place around. Bruce did his due diligence. It was co-owned by an American man and a Mexican woman. Thomas Cromwell would have been in about the right age bracket. But Ana even remembered talking to him, and didn't feel he bore much resemblance to the last known photo of Chad Green.

"Your brother has some pretty good taste, if he hangs out in a place like this," Bruce said.

"He wasn't much into material things, from what I remember," Melanie replied. So, what's the plan?"

"I don't know. For right now, just be observant and see if there is anyone sitting around that looks like him. It's like looking for a needle in a haystack, I know. But you know, I did consider the possibility that it might even be the owner himself. If he's been living here since 1985, he would need a job, and being a restaurant owner is the type of thing an American with limited Spanish skills could pull off, if he has the help of a local."

"I just don't know if I would be able to recognize him."

"Yeah, that is the million-dollar question. When I was in high school, there was no Internet. Now, these days, I see a lot of my old classmates on social media. A couple look like they never aged a day, some looked just like they did back then but older, and many I wouldn't even have a clue if I ran into them on the street."

"I could say the same about some of my own." Melanie gazed off in the distance, fixated on a couple of surfers as they tried to catch a decent wave in the choppy surf. "You know, Chad always wanted to learn how to surf. And he took it up when he started working in Monterey."

Bruce chuckled. "He could be out there." A server dropped off a bowl of fish ceviche and some tortillas. "Hmm. Oh look, pickled fish."

"It's called ceviche. It's good."

A short while later, an older Mexican woman came over to their table. "How is everything?" she asked.

"Good," Bruce replied. "I read a lot of good reviews on this restaurant. I hear one of the owners is an American?"

"Yes. Thomas."

"I'd love to meet him. Is he around?"

"I'm afraid he's away on family business."

Bruce studied her face. "Well. That's understandable. You know, we're here on family business as well, believe it or not."

"I hope all is well then. Let us know if you need anything." She started to walk away.

"I suppose, while you're already here, we might as well ask you. We are here to find her brother. A man named Chad Green. Do you know anybody of that name by chance?"

"Older brother. Much older brother," Melanie interjected.

The woman paused and looked at Melanie for several seconds. "No, I'm afraid not."

"Sorry Melanie," Bruce announced. "Hopefully he'll turn up someplace."

The woman again paused, and then walked away.

Bruce smiled. "She knows something."

"Why wouldn't she tell us then? How do you deny someone you know of their long lost relative?"

"Because we very well could be here under false pretenses trying to pass you off as his long-lost sister in order to flush him out."

"Who would do that?" Melanie scoffed.

"I would," Bruce retorted, as he made a ceviche taco for himself.

Nielson sat in his corner office fixing his gaze on the dense tree line just past the massive Langley headquarters parking lot. It felt a little like jail. When you are a little kid, and you do something bad, you get sent to the principal's office. The principal is... the man. Top dog. Head honcho. Big cheese. The principal is the one that calls the shots, the principal is the one that is all-knowing.

But directors come and go. They are appointed, not thoroughly vetted by means of slow and exclusive progression through the ranks and levels of trust. Hence it is so rumored that there are, in the most top-secret agency in the world, with twenty-three thousand employees, sections that are reputed to be above the director. Whether they are or not, in any case, any given individual man serving a limited term of appointment can't know everything going on in it.

Buried deep within the bowels of Old Headquarters Building, through endless card lock security corridors is an unmarked office, which contains some of the longest serving and highest-level access individuals in the entire agency – the Overwatch Group. Even Nielson himself doesn't know where it is, and Nielson is actually quite high up the food chain. So high up that he personally interacts with the Director himself. Nielson is neither the bad little ninth grader nor has he been sent to the principal's office. The man sent to escort him to the secret dungeon is someone that he sees regularly buying a coffee and a Danish at the same deli kiosk he frequents himself.

The fluorescent light fixtures in the windowless office look like they date back to the 1960's. It looks straight out of an episode of Adam-12, except the characters have modern computer terminals with flat panel displays. Seated at a central desk was a massively tall man wearing an impeccable, dark pinstripe suit but with a cut that goes back four or five decades. He would not look out of place wearing a derby hat. He resembled a proverbial man-in-black with deep, inset eyes and gaunt features. "Hello Mr. Nielson, please have a seat." The man's desk placard read 'Mel Givson.'

"What can I do for you gentlemen?" Nielson asked.

"You have made some queries about Project Dark Fury, which happens to be one of our custodial responsibilities. And well, we would like to know why."

Ohhhhhh shit. "Because the site itself had been brought to my attention by one of my assets, who was looking into it for an unrelated reason. Is there a problem?"

"Well," Givson replied. "I certainly hope not. But now we're somewhat intrigued, because it appears as though, that there isn't a single person alive that actually knows what Dark Fury is about."

"I don't understand," Nielson replied. "You guys don't keep records on these things you're in charge of?"

"No, we generally don't, other than the period of overwatch protection of the project site, and why it is being protected. Which, in this case is both a matter of national security, and a grave threat to public safety if breached. The project files are old enough that they aren't electronic, and the Agency contact retired years ago. We wouldn't ordinarily bring a person like yourself, who by the way has an impeccable service record with the agency, down here but we thought you might be able to tell us something about it that we don't know."

"Well, I'm sorry, Mr. Givson, I'm afraid if any of us has learned anything, it's me."

"We're a little bit concerned, Mr. Nielson, that for whatever reason, the Mossad seems to be taking an interest in it, and we don't know why."

"Your guess is as good as mine."

"Fair enough. Oh, and Mr. Nielson, you would be wise to inform your asset to tread very lightly on this one. Very lightly."

"That goes without saying, and I assure you, he knows the rules as well."

"Very well. Good evening, Mr. Nielson."

Nielson looked confused. "Evening? It's ten o'clock in the morning."

Givson turned around and glanced at the twenty-four hour format digital clock. "When you spend twenty hours a day down here, you tend to lose track of time."

Undaunted, Maya drove through the mist along the boundary of the Presidio of Monterey, and scoped out what appeared to be a suitable entry point in a wooded area at the base of the hill on which the Area 91 site was located. There was an obvious trail in the brush, and a breach in the cyclone fence suggesting that others had routinely make the same trek.

She wondered why she was even making the journey up the dirt road in the light rain. Maybe the site would reveal some clues. Did you even look at the site? That would be the first question that Ari would ask upon her return.

She double checked the crude map, and the GPS coordinates with her cell phone, which both suggested that she was at the right location, but there was nothing except a small gravel clearing in the trees, and a concrete pedestal at the center. She paced the perimeter of the clearing, and proceeded to take several photographs with her cell phone. It was no sooner than she was ready to head back down the hill, that she heard the sound of two approaching vehicles. Realizing she was in a place where she was not supposed to be, she quickly scanned the trees, and pushed her way through the dense brush to hide. Both vehicles pulled into the site and stopped.

In a white marked pickup truck was a uniformed MP with a police dog. In the other black Tahoe were two plainclothes law enforcement officers. All exited their vehicles with guns drawn. "Ma'am! Federal Marshals! Come out with your hands up, or we will send in the dog! You will get bit!"

Sheepishly, Maya extricated herself from the brush. She was immediately tackled, and handcuffed by the marshals.

The lead marshal thoroughly frisked her, coming up empty save for a key fob and a cell phone. "Got any identification?"

"I left it in the car," Maya replied.

The marshals placed her in the rear of their car, and drove off post to the location where Maya had parked her car. One marshal got out and retrieved her purse, and went through it, and retrieved her passport. "Yeah, it's her."

"What seems to be the problem, officers?" Maya asked, in her best poor innocent me voice.

"Problem? For starters, illegally entering a federal military installation, and trespassing on a restricted classified facility. And suspicion of espionage."

"Am I under arrest?"

"Not yet. For now, you're just being detained. You will be transported to Atwater."

"For how long?"

"For as long as we want. The Patriot Act is in effect, lady."

Ari Rosenfeld took a seat in a small, empty conference room inside the US Embassy in Tel Aviv. Fifteen minutes later, a short, curly haired man in a black suit walked in, closed the door behind him, and took a seat. He smiled, and sat down. "How are you doing, Ari? It's been a while."

"How am I doing? How am I doing? Your agency has crossed the line!" Ari screamed at the top of his lungs, shaking his fist.

"Now calm down Ari, we've known each other for a long time. And... and... and, technically, it wasn't our agency, your counterpart who nabbed her."

"Your government. Same thing. And why are we even having this meeting at the embassy? Are you afraid we will illegally detain you and stick you in a jail cell too?"

"Well, I mean, the Mossad has been known to take an eye for an eye, just saying."

"So, what did she do wrong, for the sake of god?"

"C'mon, Ari, you guys can't just come over onto American soil under false pretenses, break into military bases and spy on American facilities. You know that."

"Spy? Spy! What the hell are you talking about! That was a joint project! How the hell can we spy on our own joint project?"

"Look, there are proper channels that you can go through if you have issues with a, what did you call it? Joint project? Is it a joint project? Nobody at my agency seems to be aware of that. Did you ever give your good friend Sal a call to look into things? Hmm, let me check my phone... No messages, no calls. Nope."

"Your predecessor did nothing for us. You guys have your heads up your asses. You're too big and have too many people for your own good. And you act like six-hundred-pound gorillas."

"Well, you guys act like six hundred one-pound piranhas, but that's neither here nor there," Sal replied.

"So, what do you want from me?"

"Well now that you ask, there has been this nagging issue that we have been having... and we've talked about it, surely, we did. Malik Jafir."

"Malik Jafir is a filthy Iranian terrorist pig! And he is our Iranian terrorist pig. No you can't have him."

"Okay, well, if that's how it's gotta be, I understand. You have your policies and we have ours. Surely you must want her back."

Ari shrieked a falsetto laugh. "You want her? You keep her. You feed her. You house her. You pay for her health care."

"I'll tell you what Ari. Let's do this. How about I throw in Yassir Faheem as well? You get your girl back, free of charge, and Faheem? Give us Jafir? Hmm?" Oh, hey, free of charge! Get it? Charges? No? Too soon?"

Ari threw up his hands in despair. "Okay fine, you can have Jafir. Faheem is worthless, we don't want him either. Just promise me, just promise me that you will look into Project Dark Fury. Tell us what it was our man Daniel Levin died for."

Sal hastily wrote down a note. "Project Dark Fury?"
"Yes."
"I'll do what I can. Oh uh, and by the way, congratulations on your grandson's Bar Mitzvah."
"Yeah. Whatever."

The streets looked familiar. Market Street. Cuts diagonally through the city and splits the skyscrapers. Geary Street. One of the steepest public roadways in the world, and it cuts right through the area named Little Russia. Golden State Park. This was the place. This was the place where Svetlana moved after fleeing Russia. She had family here; she just knew it. But she didn't remember them, except for some fleeting glimpses. There was a brother.

She was successful at reinstating her bank account access. There was enough in there to live on for a while but not for a long while. Especially not here. She needed an income. Or a man. But she was different now. She had no memory of passion. No memory of love. Not even enough to further check into Bruce Highland. Not enough to disrupt whatever life choices he had made.

For right now, she opted to share a single room in a tiny flat in the Richmond district with a woman who was also from Ukraine originally. It wasn't cheap, but it was at least in an area that she knew and could remember. Places she could remember. Faces not so much. Names much less.

You were a former cryptologic officer with the GRU. She knew she was good with computers. She began to remember that it was working on, and with computers which supported her previously when she lived in San Francisco.

She went out for a stroll, down to the Theater District. And then, there it was. It was a fleeting glimpse. 1191 Market Street. It was significant. She didn't know why. She didn't live there. It wasn't an apartment or condominium high rise.

Returning, she made her way up Webster Street to the corner of Bush Street, took a left and passed an inviting looking street level pub. She poked her head in, and decided to take a seat at the end of the bar. She had the feeling that she had been there before. It wasn't particularly crowded as it was the middle of the day and the lunch crowd had already departed.

The bartender was an aging hipster of a man, with a salt and pepper goatee wearing a flat cap. "What can I get for you?" He focused in on her with a slight hint of recognition.

"I don't want vodka." She said. "Beer."

"What kind of... I think I know what you want." He poured a lager and gave it to her. "Yeah, I think I remember you. You used to come here a lot."

"What was my name?" Svetlana asked.

"Oh, I didn't know you by name."

"When was this?"

"Maybe I'm thinking about someone else. Obviously, you would have remembered if you came here a lot."

"I had an accident three years ago. I was in a plane crash. I lost a lot of memory."

"Oh. Well, I'm sorry to hear. I'm glad you're okay. Or I guess you're okay. Maybe not as okay as you would like. But you're still alive."

"Yes. So, when was this?"

"Let me think... hmm. It has been a few years. Hmm, the Syrian refugee crisis was going on at the time. So, about eight years ago. This place has been open something like fifteen years. I started working here ten years ago."

"Did I come here with anyone?"

"You knew people from here at the time. They most all moved on. I don't know that you showed up with anyone on a regular basis."

"Do you know the names of anyone I knew?"

"I mean, not by last name. People would run up tabs so I knew some first names. We weren't actually taking credit cards at the time yet. Old man Herman finally gave in to modern technology about five years ago."

"I see."

"So... this plane crash, it wiped out your memory. I guess you're lucky to have family to take care of you."

"I don't have family to take care of me. I recovered in a rehabilitation center in Russia. They let me go when they considered me able to live on my own."

"Man, that's tough. Are you doing okay?"

"I do okay. I live with another woman from Ukraine."

"Well, if you ever need help with anything, my name is Matt. You can find me here."

"My name... Svetlana."

Matt chuckled. "Had to think about that one for a bit did you."

"For three years, I did not even know my own name."

"Oh, sorry. I guess that was an insensitive thing for me to say."

"Can I ask you something Matt?"

"Sure."

"I live here before. People were in my life. I don't know if it is fair to intrude on their lives."

"I don't understand, why would you be an intrusion?"

"I was told I was married. He would have assumed I was dead. Lost in the plane crash. He may have someone else in his life by now."

"Yeah, oh boy. That is a sticky one. I see where you are coming from there. I don't know, I don't have a good answer for that one." Matt broke off to serve another customer and returned. "You know, thinking on that a little bit, I'd probably leave that situation alone."

"I figure same thing. You have girlfriend or wife?"

"I had a life partner. She um... I lost her to leukemia two years ago."

"Sorry to hear."

"Yeah well, people come and go. I try not to get hung up over that too much anymore."

"Same for me."

Svetlana ordered two more beers, then walked back to her apartment flat, left with more questions than answers.

Dragovich. Sergio Dragovich. The man, the GRU agent that visited her in St. Petersburg, his name was Sarkov, Svetlana thought to herself. Sarkov told her that she was married to a man named Bruce Highland. But she remembered Sergio Dragovich. A Russian helicopter pilot. She remembered the funeral. That was her husband. She was now more confused than ever.

It was the same sidewalk café in Tel Aviv that Maya Goldman met up with Ari Rosenfeld nearly three weeks prior. It was the same thing. A pot of tea, a bagel, a newspaper. He lowered the paper and raised his eyebrows, as if slightly surprised to see her.

"Do you have a few minutes?" Maya asked.

"Sure. Have a seat. What is on your mind?"

"I'm sorry. My assignment was a failure. Not only did I fail to find out the information that you requested, I caused an international incident."

Ari put the paper down. "I wouldn't exactly agree with you Maya, in our business, failure is more common than success. Certainly, I will not lie to you, this... international incident, as you phrase it, put me in an awkward position. But at the same time, it put some things in motion that would not have been put in motion otherwise. Would I have liked to see things play out differently? Yes. Am I sorry I sent you? No."

"Really?"

"I would not lie to you."

"The reason I came here, is I wanted to talk to you one last time. My intention was to resign my position in Mossad."

"Well then, I'm glad you came here, because you can't resign your position with Mossad. You are with us for life unless we decide otherwise. And the number of unfit agents we've had under my watch, I can count on one hand with four of my fingers missing."

"So, your report to my superiors will be favorable?"

"I don't report to your superiors."

"Okay, thank you."

"Don't thank me. In thirty years, you will probably be sitting at this very table, sending the agent you mentored on an impossible assignment that you knew had little chance for success."

Chapter 8 – Being watched

It stood out to Bruce for no other reason than it, although it wasn't entirely impractical, was way overpriced and pretentious for what it was; a sport utility vehicle. A white Range Rover Discovery. You pay about two to three times what you pay for your basic Japanese big three model of the same type and class.

He didn't think much of it at first when he spotted it parked in the far end of the parking lot of La Estrella de Ensenada, but when they reached the motel, and decided to grab some dinner at a restaurant a short distance away, he saw another one parked across the street in front of another motel – or it could have even been the same one. It piqued Bruce's interest enough that he took a stroll across the highway, and noted the plates. They were California plates.

There was nothing in itself suspicious of either a late model Range Rover, or the fact it had California plates. Probably a quarter of the vehicles parked in the tourist and residential district of Ensenada had California plates. Something else caught Bruce's eye, which warranted a closer inspection. And that something was a small blue on white sticker emblazoned with 'City of Monterey Residential Parking Permit' with a string of numbers.

"Shit!" Bruce said. "We've been had."

"By who?" Melanie asked.

"What is the likelihood of any given vehicle hanging around bearing a Monterey parking sticker? And I think, but I can't be positive, I saw the same Range Rover parked out in front of the restaurant earlier today."

"You think it's Macleod?"

"Let's go back to the motel. I need to make a couple calls."

They went back to Bruce's room. He booted up a laptop computer, and entered the license plate identification of the

Range Rover. It was registered to an LLC corporation. "I'm either being paranoid or he's one smart bastard. Someone is hiding the registration behind an LLC."

"If it is him, how would he know where we are? Could he have followed us?"

"I suppose it's possible, but it would be pretty hard to do without being noticed. And, I tend to notice things like that more than the next guy." Bruce peered through the drawn curtains. "Damn. Either I'm reading too much into this or he's onto us. The Range Rover is gone."

"What does he want?" Melanie asked.

"I have a strong suspicion that the car accident that killed those two surviving researchers in 1984 was no accident. Your brother Chad got away and Macleod is using us to track him down and finish the job."

"Oh my god. You think?"

"The Agency is actively protecting the Area 91 site, and I don't think it's any coincidence that he just randomly happened to show up at the site when you were there. I would not be at all surprised if he is in fact, the custodian in charge of protecting it. I've been told the man spent his entire career in the Pentagon save for that one command assignment at former Fort Ord."

"I don't know, Bruce, it seems kind of far out there."

"Trust me, I've seen the Agency go further than that to hush a witness."

"So, what do we do now?"

"I don't know. Let's go eat. I hope I'm wrong."

"Sounds good to me. Oh, I forgot when we left before but, can I stick my purse in your trunk again? I don't trust leaving it in the room."

"Sure. I don't blame you for not wanting to lug that massive... wait a minute. How often do you go through your purse?"

"Well, every time I need my keys or my wallet."

"No, I mean completely, accounting for everything that is in there."

Melanie chuckled and blushed slightly. "Bruce, there are things buried in there I haven't seen for months."

"Let's go over to your place. I realize that going through a girl's purse is a more intimate action than the lovemaking process, but I just want to rule out the possibility that someone didn't put a tracking device in there. These things are small enough these days you could bury one in that behemoth of a bag you carry, and you would never know."

Ten minutes later, with the contents sprawled all over Melanie's bed, she held up a small square blue plastic device, devoid of markings other than molded FCC compliance notice and string of serial and model numbers. "Okay, this is definitely not mine."

Bruce examined it. "Bingo. That's how he was able to follow us. I use these things myself sometimes. Same model in fact. How do you think it might have got in there?"

"There is a million ways it could have gotten in there. But a funny thing happened the very next day after meeting Macleod at the site. A random guy bumped into me at the store as I was shopping, and I thought he was trying to steal my purse. I'm almost positive his hand was in it. He apologized and left. I checked inside and nothing seemed to be missing, so I didn't think any more of it."

On the way to the restaurant, they passed some container trucks parked on the side of the road. There was a Hispanic man smoking a cigarette outside of one of the trucks. "Adónde vas, Senor?" Bruce said to the man.

"Honduras," The man replied with a smile.

"Perfecto," Bruce said. He doubled back behind the container, and dropped the tracker in a recess in the frame. "Let's go eat."

Melanie dipped forkfuls of lobster in melted butter in between sips of wine, which turned into gulps. "Do you think we should to back and warn that lady at the restaurant that Chad may be in danger?"

"Oh, I think he knows that. If he's here, or had been here all this time, he knew that a long time ago," Bruce replied.

"You know, it occurs to me that we both engaged in an activity that was more intimate than the lovemaking process itself, in your words."

"Yeah, the thought had crossed my mind, actually. I wasn't going to bring it up." Bruce ordered more drinks nonstop.

Melanie's pale skin revealed itself as the layers came off. A long throbbing kiss turned into a voracious entanglement of waves of carnal ecstasy, culminating in a volcanic eruption of passionate crescendo, feeding the hunger of desire, fueling desperate connections.

Bruce woke to the sound of a maid banging on the door. He was sprawled face down in his bed. He looked around. He was alone, in his own room. He felt depleted. After sitting on the floor of the shower for thirty minutes with a soft, cool stream of water raining down on him, he felt well enough to go to the lobby for a cup of coffee. Melanie was there, nibbling on a croissant and reading a magazine. I had the time of my life, and as always, it had to be a goddamn dream.

"You sleep okay?" she asked.

"Yeah," Bruce responded. "You?"

"Yeah."

There was a long, awkward silence. "I had an interesting dream last night," Bruce said.

"Oh?"

"I dreamed I kissed you."

"I guess it's good it was just a dream then, because I would have slapped you."

"It was a dream, right? I mean, nothing else happened between us?"

"I don't even know how to answer that, Bruce. Actually, to tell you the truth, I kind of feel hurt and insulted. I would hope that if we actually had an intense night of passion, you would remember it."

"Well of course I would have remembered it."

"For the record, if you must know, we did kiss, and you conked out cold and went to sleep. I stayed with you for a couple hours to make sure you were going to be alright, then I went next door and went to bed. You should drink less."

"Where uh, did you stay, on the couch?"

"If your heart gave out or you quit breathing, how would I have been able to tell from the couch?"

Chad Green endured a grueling ride in a soft top Jeep in high winds, with sand flying everywhere, to a remote ranch in the Mexican desert roughly halfway between Tijuana and Mexicali. He rapped on the door of a rusting metal barn, and a minute later a man held it opened and he entered.

They called him 'Horsey'. Back in 'Nam he flew CH-46 airplanes for Air America. These days, he ran small planes across the border to deliver heroin and cocaine. And occasionally, the paying passenger. The paying passenger in this case was an American, who had the unique problem of, while documented and able to move about freely within the United States, could not cross the border legitimately through a point of entry.

Horsey wasn't a bad man, or an evil man. He just thrived on adrenaline. He understood intrinsically that importing illicit drugs was a bad thing, but he viewed it as a victimless crime, sort of like prostitution. Don't want to end up dead in a ditch? Don't do drugs. Your choice.

Inside the creaking barn, with sand flying about through the many voids in the corrugated paneling, was an aging Cessna 210, loaded with some precious cargo. With the apparent hurricane going on outside, Chad couldn't figure out why this pilot chose a day like this to make a border crossing into the United States. But the man must have his reasons.

The reason was called TARS – an acronym for the Tethered Aerostat Radar System. It is a series of unmanned airborne blimps held in place by a wire cables at an altitude of ten thousand feet, bearing downward looking radar at locations spanning the Mexican border. The idea behind TARS is that you can fly your plane low to circumvent ground-based radar stations, but TARS will see through that bullshit in a hurry. It does however have a vulnerability – high winds. During high wind conditions they have to pull the aerostat blimps down so they don't get shredded to pieces. Horsey was waiting for the right moment, where conditions were just good enough to be able to manhandle the aircraft outside the barn and take off, but not quite good enough for Homeland Security to raise the TARS aerostats.

"Give me a hand with this door," Horsey said as he rattled loose a rusted latch. The two men dragged the heavy door across the dirt. Satisfied that the door was going to stay put, he motioned for Chad to climb into the passenger seat. "Here, put this on." He said as he handed him an aviation headset.

"Don't you need to pull the plane out of this building?" Chad asked as Horsey performed a quick mental startup checklist.

"No real need to," Horsey said, well aware that he was about to stir up an internal dust storm from the spinning prop. After a few pumps to the primer, he cranked over the engine, and it fired to life. The plane slowly taxied out the door on its own, and Horsey did an on-the-go runup as he approached the graded dirt strip. The engine wasn't technically warm enough yet, but then again it only needed to last until just over the border, to a location less than ten miles away, to a dry river bed where Horsey had a waiting Jeep parked. If all went well, they could be airborne, fly over the border, land, and drive away before the Border Patrol could even react.

The 210's Continental engine slowly came to full power, and after a bouncy run over the rough dirt surface, it became airborne, crabbing in the strong wind after takeoff.

"What's the plan?" Chad asked.

"Once we land, we're going to load up the Jeep with our payload, and we're going to head directly towards a small airport. From there, you're on your own, and I'm heading five hundred miles north in another plane."

"I don't understand. If we're headed to another airport, why not just fly there?"

"Too risky. The longer we stay in the air, the more risk that we get picked up on radar and tracked. Plus, even if I managed to get in and out of Agua Dulce before anyone catches wind, eventually the Feds will make the connection and that route is dead. I kind of want to keep it alive as long as I can."

"What about the plane?"

"This one? Oh, it's a throwaway. The DEA will seize it, and eventually I might buy it back for cheap at an auction. Most of the throwaways come from DEA auctions. They're cheap – it's too expensive to make them legally airworthy but they still fly. That's all I care about."

Chad Green pondered his next move at a local bar and grill. Agua Dulce was confounding – the town center was a couple of strip malls in the middle of nowhere with a faux old west motif. What he needed was wheels. Or some sort of transportation and none was to be found here. A quick search on his smart phone revealed that the nearest bus station was in San Fernando; which, although technically within walking distance, would be one hell of a long walk. And speaking of long walks, one would have thought Horsey could have gone a couple miles further and dropped him off in 'town', but, when one is carrying enough bricks of heroin in the back of his Jeep to finance an upper middle-class retirement, one goes straight to the destination, and does not stop, or detour.

He didn't get the phone call from Maria until he had already landed. Through the years, he kept up on the whereabouts of the family. Mom and Pop passed a few years ago. Hazel was still in Ohio. Melanie was in Redwood City. But was it really Melanie looking for him with another gentleman as Maria reported? He mentally cursed himself but then again, he figured it was likely a trap. How the hell would she know where he was? She was a little girl back then. Feisty, with fiery red hair in braided locks. The girl described would have generally fit the description of what she might look like today. Chad wished Maria had presence of mind to take a photo. But either way – Chad realized that, to his horror, his cover had been blown.

His destination was Redwood City. His goal was to connect up with Melanie, somehow. Or Hazel, but Hazel was a couple thousand miles away, versus four hundred. If she was actually in Ensenada looking for him, she would probably already be back home. If not, it's probably best he lay tracks far from Ensenada. Either way, she's probably about the only one he can turn to at this point.

Thirty years of owning a bar taught Chad a set of bar social skills that would be hard to match by even the most diehard alcoholic. A grizzled old cross-country trucker with a white beard and a cowboy hat named Skelton was a fortunate solution to the problem of reaching Northern California on a less than exorbitant travel budget. He was tired, but it was a little bit hard to sleep with Skelton grinding up and down the gears in the hilly Southern California desert with its share of intersections. Once over the Grapevine north of LA, down into the Central Valley basin, the drive was boring, but steady. Even Skelton himself appreciated the reduced workload.

He wondered if he was looking at things all wrong. Maybe he should just quit running and face the music. His original plan was to wait it out until the heat died down over Project Dark Fury and Area 91. It never really sunk in that it had been nearly forty years. Five years of destitute paranoia turned into ten years, which turned into twenty, and well now here he is. He reminded himself that the reason he stuck it out so long was because he had a story to share. If it was even a story that should be shared.

The 1952 expedition of an uncharted and unnamed island in a remote location of the South Pacific was prompted by Professor Charles Ellerbee's accidental discovery of an 1859 voyage manifest buried in the archives of the British Royal Academy of Natural Science a few years prior. It told of a small, lush, unpopulated island a thousand miles from the nearest landfall, encountered by chance from a tramp steamer out of Auckland bound for Santiago, blown off course during a storm. A landing party's exploration was cut short by a pack of vicious predatory animals, who reputedly devoured a boatswain's mate, stripping his flesh within seconds. The landing party retreated in haste back to the ship. Descriptions of the animals given by the landing party were somewhat inconsistent, other than generally bearing a reptilian appearance, but otherwise maybe some type of cat, but no one could agree on an exact identification.

Ellerbee was keen to realize that often times sailor's descriptions of sea life can be grossly distorted, resulting in stories such as massive sea serpents swimming in the Sargasso Sea. Nonetheless, the Royal Academy's team of scientists came prepared and armed. The team had in fact encountered an island so described in the location noted in the manifest. It was so remote that confusion between it and another island would have been impossible unless the navigator was several hundred miles off, which, he couldn't have been, since the steamer arrived at Santiago precisely as charted.

What they did find was in fact an unknown, uncharted and uninhabited island, but they did not encounter any sort of vicious predatory animals. Or for that matter, any mammals at all save for some ground burrowing moles. But there was evidence that there was plentiful mammal activity judging by bones and historic animal trails. Wild boar. Small primates. Fallow deer. Island wildcats. But aside from bone remnants, the island was otherwise devoid of them. The team was baffled. They didn't starve to death, there was lush vegetation available to support a complete food chain with no evidence of sudden or catastrophic depletion. It was as if they were hunted to extinction, except that every single mammalian species had been wiped out save for ground moles.

There was evidence of human visitation. Notably, two landing sites, one with the decaying remnants of an ancient Polynesian seagoing canoe, and the other with the remains of a more recent wooden skiff dating back to the 1700's, and what appeared to have possibly been the start of a campsite, littered with some small pottery fragments. It was unclear how either vessel got there. Seagoing canoes have been known to travel great distances. The skiff was thought to possibly been from a ship that might have foundered off the coast.

The Ellerbee report was destined for publication in scientific journals as a groundbreaking exploration, and would have certainly gained worldwide attention, if it hadn't been for the untimely death of Charles Ellerbee, who in a drunken stupor, mistakenly poured himself a double shot of formaldehyde during a late-night lab session at the Institute. As a result, the report never was submitted, and eventually ended up in the hands of a young American professor named Irving Fuller, who was on sabbatical from Harvard twenty years later, as a prize for having won a pub bet in London with one of Ellerbee's understudies.

The thing about Irving Fuller, is that he wasn't the type to be a professor of natural resources. He should have been a corporate CEO, or a wealthy entrepreneur. But he wanted fame more than money, and he was searching for his ticket to rise from the ashes of academic ubiquity to a world-famous scholar. It took a lot of politics, conning, sweet talking, and ambitious promises to leave a Harvard mark on the world, not that it needed another, but after pressing full court he was finally able to get a Harvard led follow up expedition funded and organized.

Fuller's report from the expedition would indicate that what they discovered on that island, was something that Ellerbee's party missed. Something so incredible, that it would shock the scientific world, and catapult Fuller into a demigod status, not just among his peers, but even to the public eye. Snippets of his discovery eventually got out. And then the men from the government showed up one day in his office. Irving Fuller's world, as he knew it, changed from that point on.

The rain had finally let up, so the man seated in the white Range Rover got out, threw on an overcoat and a flat cap, and lit a cigar. A short while later a black Crown Victoria pulled into the gravel clearing of the Area 91 site. A large, tall man in a black trench coat got out, walked over to the Range Rover, and leaned against it.

Roland Macleod snuffed the cigar on the ground and placed it back inside an aluminum tube before pocketing it. "Mel, what is so all fired important that compels you to come all the way out here from Langley?"

"How are things going?" Mel Givens asked, as he fanned away the residual cigar smoke.

"Fine," Macleod answered.

"All well with the site? Any developments I should know about?"

Macleod paused. Givens wasn't asking the question to make small talk. "Well, there has been a revival of local interest in it. And of course, the Mossad incident, but you knew about that. Everything is under control, if that's what you're asking."

"I have no doubt it is," Givens replied. "But what about you personally? How are you doing?"

"Quite well, why do you ask?"

"You have served the Agency well beyond our requirements and expectations. Let's face it, Roland. You are not a young man. You're about to turn eighty."

"Next week yes."

"Although the Agency appreciates your continued service, we do realistically have to consider a succession plan. You aren't going to live forever, and we can't be left scrambling to find a suitable replacement should you suddenly depart us."

Macleod fished the cigar out of his pocket and lit it. Damn Givens. "I don't blame you for your concern. And I'm not surprised you came out here to bring that up. Been expecting it for some time honestly. But I think we can kick the can down the road for another year at least."

"Just the same, we have an individual that I would like to send to you, that you can prepare and educate to take over your custodial duties. The transition does not have to be immediate."

Macleod's Scottish drogue became more pronounced as he spoke. "I'm not ready for the pasture, Mel."

"I'm sorry, Roland but I've made the decision. This is not an option."

"Yes... sir. Is there anything more?"

"You should count your blessings. I've been going over your file. Because of your assignment with us, you were one of the youngest officers in the history of the Army to make colonel. Hell, the only reason you didn't get a flag rank prior to your retirement was because you would have stood out too much. The protection of national security is a bigger issue than your own ego and personal desire."

"Can you say the same about yourself?" Macleod blew a ring of smoke.

"Absolutely. One hundred percent. My days are numbered as well. But the difference between me and you is, I work in a dark, damp cave from the moment I set foot on the Agency campus until I leave, and there are times when I won't see the light of day for a month. You on the other hand, spend your days in a beautiful coastal city, doing whatever the hell you want, only exerting yourself when you have to tell a base commander that he can't build anything on that property, or check out the occasional intruder."

Macleod resisted the urge to blow smoke in Givens' face. "It's a little bit more involved than that. There are some aspects to this position that even you don't know about. Sir."

"Regardless of any difference that you have with me, can I trust you to handle this assignment in a professional, and diligent manner?"

"Of course." *But my definition of professional and diligent may be different than yours.*

The visibly run down, nine story glass encased tower in Khodinka, just north of Moscow, is nicknamed 'The Fishbowl.' It serves as the GRU headquarters, and is connected to support facilities and residential housing for current and former GRU employees. Nikolai Sarkov was busy at his desk, scanning over the daily intelligence briefings. His section chief took a seat beside his desk.

"Yes Andrei?" Sarkov asked. "You look troubled? Do we have a problem?"

Andrei flopped a stapled report down on Sarkov's desk. "Well, I'm not sure, Nikolai. I'm a little bit puzzled. I have been informed by our embassy in San Francisco that

Svetlana Petroya appears to be alive and well, in the United States. That seems to contradict what you say in your report to me."

Sarkov looked up. "Does it? I simply said in my report that the woman I was sent to investigate at the rehabilitation center in St. Petersburg was not Svetlana Petroya."

"Then who was the woman named Elena Yakut?"

"Presumably Elena Yakut. But I was not sent to determine who she was. Just who she wasn't."

"It's troubling that Svetlana Petroya was determined by the aviation authority to have perished in an airline crash, yet, there she is."

"I reviewed the report. They were unable to determine that she perished in the crash of Aeroflot flight 7230. No identifiable remains were ever recovered. We don't even know that the Svetlana Petroya that was supposed to be on that flight was the same person, our former agent. For that matter, we do not know that the Svetlana Petroya reported in the United States is, either."

"Petroya is an uncommon Russian surname."

"So, what do you want me to do?"

"Nothing, Nikolai. Nothing. Everything is... fine."

Sarkov watched carefully as Andrei returned to his glass windowed office. He closed the door, and immediately made a telephone call. Sarkov could only guess who that telephone call was to, and what it was about, but he had a bad feeling about it.

The street level pub on Bush Street was an inviting distraction to Svetlana. She deliberately chose a time of day when the establishment would be least busy. Matt smiled as she sat down at the bar. "Usual?" he asked.

"Usual," Svetlana said.

"How are things coming?" Matt asked.

"Things coming well," Svetlana said in her characteristic broken English. "I take job in corporation close by for computer IT support."

"That's good," Matt said. He looked to his right and left. "I like the quiet downtime, but man, this isn't good for tips."

"I think maybe that will change," she replied, motioning to a younger man with shoulder length dark hair and a pencil thin mustache.

He took a seat at the bar next to Svetlana and ordered a beer. "Cheers," he said in a thick Russian accent.

"Cheers," Svetlana responded, also bearing a Russian accent.

"You Russian?" The man asked.

"Originally from Ukraine."

He became animated. "Oh Ukraine. That is good. Mikhail. Na Zdorovie," he said, toasting this time in Russian.

"Svetlana. Na Zdorovie." Svetlana sensed something was not right. The man looked nervous, and compulsively stared at her glass.

Several minutes later, he got up to use the restroom. Matt came over. "Be real careful of that guy. I have seen that look before. Watch your drink. I think he might be trying to put a roofie in it."

"Roofie?"

"Date rape drug."

"Can you do me favor?"

"Sure."

"Do you have dirty glass, preferably handled by another woman?"

Matt looked confused. "Yeah, actually I do have some dirties down here."

"Can you replace with my glass?"

"Yeah, I guess, why?"

"No time to explain. Leave empty but on the bar. Tell him I left. I be back in a while." Svetlana used the opportunity to do some shopping and returned a short while later. A few more customers gathered but the young man was gone.

"I'll be damned," Matt said. "You'll never guess what happened after you left. Oh, wait a minute. Maybe you can guess, now that I think about it. The sonofabitch grabbed the glass by the inside and ran out the door with it. How did you know? I'm assuming that's why you had me switch glasses."

"It is old trick used by Russian government to get identification from fingerprints. And these days, by DNA as well."

"Is there something you want to talk to me about?"

"There are a lot of things I would like to talk to you about. But maybe not that one."

"I don't mean to pry, but are you running from something?"

"I rather not talk about it right now."

Chapter 9 – So sorry

Sal ran his fingers through his dark curly hair wondering if he was doing the right thing. The last meeting was at the US embassy. This meeting was in a coffee shop not far from Mossad headquarters. Ari seemed to have calmed down the last time he spoke with him over the phone. This time, it was Ari that entered, followed by Maya Goldman.

"Oh yeah," Sal said as the two took a seat at a table. "Maya, right?"

"That's correct," Maya said.

"I trust you had a pleasant flight back from the United States? I believe we put you up in first class, did we not?"

"What are you asking Mr. …?"

"Just call me Sal. All of my friends call me Sal."

"If you're asking if the French wine and Filet Mignon at thirty-seven thousand feet made up for the first-class treatment in your Atwater prison, it did not," Maya huffed.

"Anyway," Ari interjected. "Why are we even here? If you had anything of substance to give me, we certainly wouldn't be talking about it here. We should be discussing it at our headquarters, or at least a place more private."

"Oh, headquarters, right, well, see I have this thing about being manhandled down hallways with a bag over my head so I don't see anything I'm not supposed to on the way to a room that resembles Stalin's interrogation quarters. I just wanted to tell you face to face that we seem to have a slightly embarrassing situation on our hands."

"Oh? What's that?" Ari asked.

"Those responsible for handling Dark Fury, have absolutely no idea what it is about. Nobody seems to."

"I find that a bit hard to believe. I'm sure the Agency stonewalls its own members when they sniff around in areas they have no business in. We do that ourselves."

"Well, yes, but, generally, if someone high up in the Agency makes a statement to the effect of 'I do not know what this is about' to another person high up in the Agency, which I am by the way, it genuinely means, 'I do not know what this is about.'"

Ari stared at him incredulously. "You don't keep records? Bullshit!"

"Ari, hang on. Okay the project itself was being run out of the Pentagon. Both program managers from the Agency and the Pentagon have been since deceased. And the records... well, we had this incident which occurred on September 11, 2001, where, we had this jet airliner crash into the Pentagon. A lot of records were lost that day. Dark Fury was one of them."

"What about the project site itself?"

"The project site? Area 91? The entire structure has been backfilled solid with concrete. Retrieving anything useful from that would be impossible. So basically, what I'm saying to you, is that I am at the end of the line of anything that exists that I can give to you."

"Well, I guess it is what it is," Ari said. "You ready to go, Maya?"

"One more thing, Mr. Sal," Maya said. "There seems to be an issue with my travel visa. Do you think you could at least sort that out?"

Sal sighed. "The State Department is real funny about things like, oh, breaking and entering federal properties and suspected espionage activities, so..." Sal eyed Maya up and down with a predatory, carnivorous stare. "Tell you what. Why don't you give me a call later, and I'll see if there is something that can be done." Sal fished out a card from his wallet and slipped it to Maya.

Ari glared at him. "Maya, wait outside a minute for me please." As soon as Maya left, Ari focused back on Sal. "Our employees are strictly off limits. Do I make myself clear on that?"

Sal grinned. "I think you give me way too much credit."

"You're right. I give you way too much credit; that much I agree with."

Ari walked lock step with Maya back to the headquarters building. "I feel that it is a little hard to believe that the Americans backfilled the structure with solid concrete, given the steps they are taking to protect it."

Sal was beside himself in anticipation. Of course, he made a promise that he couldn't deliver, but all he said he would do is make a few calls. He didn't actually promise results. And Maya seemed to buy that. Or at least accept it. He nervously paced the hotel room, awaiting her arrival. Wine, check. Purple pill, swallowed.

It was eight o'clock. Sal responded to a sharp rap at the door. It was Maya of course, wearing a very alluring, silky dress and high heels. She shut the door, and started to pull it off, stopping halfway, revealing the sheer black laced panties underneath, and then pulled it back down. "Just one rule," Maya said, as she pulled out a black silk scarf. "You need to wear this." She wrapped the scarf tightly around his head, completely obscuring his vision. "It doesn't come off until I say it is okay to."

"Wow, okay," Sal said.

"Then go ahead and strip completely." She then opened the door, and unbeknownst to Sal, let another person in the room then closed it without making a sound.

Sal complied, and moments later, he felt a warm wet sensation on his genitals, and started moaning loudly. After five minutes, he climaxed uncontrollably. Immediately afterwards, he heard the door open. "Okay you can go ahead and take the blindfold off."

"What, exactly the hell?" Sal uttered in disbelief as he stared at Maya while she stood in the doorway with a video camera in hand. She closed the door behind her and left. He then stared straight down at a smiling, ninety-year-old crack whore, completely toothless, making gurgling sounds. "Holy mother of Jesus. What the hell just happened?"

Melanie peered through a slight opening in the blinds in response to the ring of her doorbell, undid two deadbolt locks and a slotted security guard, peered to the right and left and let Bruce Highland inside. "Thanks for coming."

"Okay, so tell me what's going on," Bruce said.

"Somebody's following me," She replied.

"Your ex?"

"No, I don't think so. A much older man but I can't really see his face well because he wears a hoodie. I saw him at the coffee shop. I saw him at the bar. I saw him in the parking lot outside my work. This is really creepy, and it's upsetting me."

"Did you call the cops?"

"I did but they told me there wasn't much they could do. If I could give them a name, they could talk to him but that's about it."

"Right."

"Macleod possibly?"

"No, wrong build. I don't know what to do. I guess I could get a gun."

Bruce rubbed his chin. "It's not that I don't advocate ladies carrying around personal protection, but to do so legally and stay out of jail is a process that needed to have been started months ago. Sooo, I guess I'm camping out with you for at least a couple days. If you would like."

"I don't want to impose on you too much. Okay maybe I do. But you don't have to."

"I've got a go bag in the car. I'll be right back." Bruce returned a couple minutes later with a travel bag and a laptop computer. "I do a lot of my work on the go anyway, so it's not a big deal."

Bruce set up a work area on the coffee table in front of the fold out couch. In no time, he was almost in a trance, updating case reports from his field notes, and conducting information searches. Melanie slinked up next to him and peered at his computer. "So, this is what detective work looks like huh."

"Like I said, ninety nine percent is pretty boring." He glanced over at the time on the screen. "You wanna... go out and grab some dinner someplace?"

"Actually, I thought I might make dinner tonight. Do you like lamb chops?" she said with a smile.

"Well, does a cat like catnip? Yeahhh."

"Good."

The place settings were perfect. Melanie dimmed the lights and poured two glasses of a high-end Pinot Noir, and lit a candle. Bruce felt like he was in another world. The lamb chops were roasted to perfection in a reduction wine sauce. The garlic mashed potatoes were done up as if by a pro chef. "Wow, this really looks and smells good," Bruce said. And then he looked up at Melanie and smiled. "The food too."

"What's the plan for tomorrow?" Melanie asked.

"Go to work as usual. Go to your coffee place. Stop off at your bar. I'll follow behind. If you see the guy, pretend not to notice him and call me."

The dishes were all done, and Bruce was wrapped up in his work as the nine o'clock hour approached. Melanie came out of the bedroom in her nightgown. "I'm going to bed. Tomorrow is my gym day. Do you want to come?"

"Sure. How do I fold this thing out?"

"Oh that? That thing doesn't work."

"Oh. Okay well. I'll manage."

"I have a queen-sized bed."

It's an awkward discussion to have. It always is. But the reality of the situation is that, upon hearing the statement that 'I am unable to conceive a child' is best not met by a response of 'oh that's great,' even if in fact, it really is great.

It was convenient but not surprising that both belonged to the same national health club chain. Bruce was mesmerized as he sat in the passenger seat of her Mercedes sedan on the way to an early morning workout session. The Mercedes sort of fit her. It was not a particularly top of the line model, nor was it particularly new. But the subject had been brought up before. She bought it at an estate auction for pennies on the dollar so why not?

"Do you like James Bond?" Melanie asked.

"That's a random question," Bruce responded. "You mean the character? The actors?"

"The character."

"Anyone with a modicum of knowledge of international intelligence cringes at the thought of a character like James Bond. In real life he qualifies as nearly the worst choice one could make to employ as an intelligence operative."

"I think he's a snake. A womanizing scumbag. He seduces women and throws them to the side."

"Fair point, there have been times when women seduced him and thrown him to the side."

"Name one movie where that happened."

"Let me get back to you on that. And... and I never claimed to be James Bond. I'm quite the opposite, if that's where you're going with this."

"So, do I consider you my boyfriend? And do you consider me your girlfriend?"

"I kind of feel as though that line had been crossed prior to last night."

"See Bruce, you distance yourself. At first, I thought it was because you couldn't let go of your former wife. But I think it's just the way you are."

"Can you live with that? I can't play the part of an emasculated clingy romance movie character to save my life."

"I know that."

"How are you going to introduce me?" Bruce asked.

"To who? I don't interact with anyone there sufficiently to warrant an unsolicited introduction. But to answer your question, I'm just going to introduce you as my friend and leave it like that, to my friends, and let them read into the dynamics as they may."

"I'm perfectly fine with that," Bruce said.

"I figured you would be."

"So, back to the task at hand, which is, actually, why I came down here in the first place... you know that typically, stalkers are almost always someone that the victim knows. Can you think of anyone that you know, or are around on a regular basis that pays any undue attention to you?"

"Well, there is this one dude at the gym that tries to chat me up all the time, and he creeps me out a little bit. But he doesn't exactly single me out either. Other than him, honestly, no. But it's not him. He's black. The guy that has been following me is white."

"So, you want another go at him?" Ari said as he sat at his favorite street corner café table. "How's that going to work? You're compromised."

"I don't mean directly, face to face. Follow him. Tail him at a distance. See what he does. See where he goes." Maya compulsively fiddled with a hair clip.

"We have local assets that can do that, a lot more economically, and at a lot less risk."

"Just give me one week. One week. I'll stay out of trouble. I think I have some ideas."

"You're forgetting one minor detail. Your travel visa has been revoked. And right now, you're one of the last people that will qualify for an alias passport."

"Oh, that's been taken care of."

Ari raised his eyebrows in amusement. "Oh? How did you manage that?"

Maya pulled a thumb drive out of her purse and handed it to him. "With this. I need to get back to headquarters for a meeting."

Ari sat in anticipation as he booted up his laptop, twelve stories above the crowded streets below in his high-rise condominium. He inserted the thumb drive and opened a video file. His jaw immediately dropped open, and ten minutes later, he erupted in to a fit of hysterical laughter.

"Ari, what is so funny?" an elderly woman's voice yelled from the kitchen area.

"Oh, nothing Myrna. It's just that one of our agents just won a week's paid vacation to California."

It was a chilly night, certainly for Tel Aviv. Drugs and prostitution run rampant in Neveh Sha'anan, the old central bus district regarded as the worst of the dregs of the city. Heroin is the primary drug of choice, but anything can be had and the dozens of tweakers and junkies can be spotted on any given block. Sal Moon was frankly in the wrong place. Just his mere presence in the area, without a compelling intelligence reason could earn him a reprimand. He isn't a field agent. He's a high-level liaison officer.

Growing up in Central Philly, he despised the Kensington District and couldn't even fathom the thought of even going within a five-block radius of the place. Philadelphia's Kensington District is one of largest, most populous enclave of homeless drug addicts not just in the United States, but the civilized world.

Addicts shoot up right in the middle of the street, freely, and without policing in Neveh Sha'anan. There is a brothel not just on every street corner but in nearly every other building in between. Sal used to thumb his nose at those people. He now feels just slightly sorry for them.

Sal browsed through a small convenience store, doing his best to exercise his limited comprehension of Hebrew. His grandmother tried to teach him. It never sunk in. He never actually thought it would be useful. The Agency sent him to language school, and he did just well enough to convince his superiors that he could manage an assignment in Tel Aviv. Almost all of the people he would be associating with spoke English anyway.

"What are you doing here?" an old man wearing a kippah atop his bald head asked him.

"I'm just looking over some magazines," Sal replied.

"No, I mean in this area. Do you live on this block?"

"No, I don't. I… am here to see if there is anything I can do to help with the problems."

The old man shook his head. "When you pee into an ocean, don't expect it to rise."

"Shalom," Sal said as he exited the small store.

"Aleichem shalom," The man responded.

Sal walked methodically down the street, with the lapels of his overcoat turned up as if to maintain some level of anonymity and discreetness. One thing became apparent to him. There was what could best be described an inverse age range ratio. The greatest number of addicts were in the early to late twenties, there was somewhat of a gap in middle-ages, a spike in the forties to fifties, and a sharp decline of anyone older. It was an artifact of when people would typically enter that form of lifestyle. Old crack addicts don't start out as young crack addicts. The middle-age demographic is less represented since more are successful income earners. But they all generally die within months to a few years of entering that lifestyle.

He came upon an alleyway, where at the end there was a burning fire barrel. He stepped over individuals tweaking and sleeping on the ground, and found a small group of very old people. He kneeled down and looked at them. They were nearly catatonic. That one woman looked like a living corpse. She could have been Asian. She could have been Jewish. She could have been Russian. You wouldn't know.

"Can you stand up?" he asked in English. She didn't understand. He motioned for her to stand up. Slowly, she arose.

"Do you need some money?" he asked. She again did not understand. He held some US dollars in his hands. Her eyes lit up. "Come with me." Again, she did not understand. He motioned.

Even the seedy hotel manager looked at him cross-eyed as he lay down some cash on the counter for an hour of usage of a dirty, foul-smelling room with plastic tarp laid over the mattress to protect it from being soaked with excess sweat and bodily fluids. Which it didn't, because the mattress was soaked with sweat, blood, urine, and other bodily fluids.

Sal had a fascination with crime even as a child. Face it, the clean-cut kid had a dark, secret desire that had been locked up and stored away in his psyche his entire life. Necrophilia – the truly victimless crime. It was that one time when his best friend Tim's aunt passed away. Sal was drawn to Tim's aunt. He desired her. He fantasized about her. When he stared at her lifeless body in the open casket, he secretly wished he could have some quality private time alone with her. He knew those feelings were bad. He hated himself for it.

"Damn you, Maya!" he screamed. It was like screwing a corpse. She practically was. And it's not like he hasn't had intimate relationships with otherwise healthy women closer to his own age, but it was an incredible, erotic situation he had ever experienced in his life.

He felt a rush of adrenaline as he wobbled down the street after leading her back to her place in the alley way. He wasn't much of a drinker, but he purchased a bottle of cheap liqueur at a corner store, and drank it openly in the street. He wasn't a smoker, but he purchased a pack of cigarettes and smoked two in rapid succession, causing him to collapse on a small metal bench.

Sal spent all of Sunday and Monday evening in a Synagogue distant from his place of residence and the embassy, in a silent search of atonement for his sins. Tuesday, he was a peace with himself. Thursday, the cravings started to come back. Friday night, he was back in Neveh Sha'anan with a wad of cash, and a lust for adventure.

The gym had been uneventful, but some things stood out. This was Redwood City. They had the latest machines on the floor. And almost none suited Bruce's preference. They had the most advanced elliptical cardio trainers. And half were out of service. The showers were tiled with fusion granite with individual doored stalls, and towel service. But a gym is a gym. Melanie's pre-described player wasn't present, so Bruce couldn't make much of an assessment on him. The rest of the people were….

There was no sense of community. People generally didn't talk much to each other. And they were generally the older crowd.

Bruce camped out in a coffee house, where he set up a mobile workstation, while Melanie enjoyed a latte at the other end of room. No sightings. She continued on to the lab for work. And at the end of the day, she went with a group of coworkers to the sports pub. The ex and his boys, thankfully, were not present.

The first day was a total and complete bust. Bruce was wondering if Melanie was just being paranoid, or if it was an excuse to have him come over lacking a better one. He quashed that thought quickly from his head. The second night was delivery pizza. A massive Italian combo. And beer.

Bruce felt a little bit guilty. He worked with FBI agent Kim Park on several cases before Svetlana's disappearance in the plane crash. There were sparks between them. She was an attractive Korean girl – very slender, and perfectly shaped. Her eyes were captivating. And she was a ball of fire when she needed to be. But they always kept themselves in check; sometimes by choice, and other times by unfortunate (or fortunate, depending on one's perspective) circumstances.

And then there was that one case after Svetlana left. They did end up consummating their relationship. But in the end, it didn't work out. Bruce felt guilty. Park felt guilty, and in the shadow of Svetlana, who she had met and actually, ironically, liked.

In the end, Kim Park wanted to be a wife. Bruce didn't want another wife. He wanted a girlfriend. He was starting to have second thoughts about Melanie. Was this all a big mistake? The attraction wasn't just physical. There was something more with Melanie. But there was something more with Park too. And something more with Svetlana, although, just not physically after the ring went on. He was beginning to wonder if he wasn't feeling a sense of buyer's remorse.

"I need to head back to Sacramento," Bruce announced. "Just stay in public places, and during the daytime, and be conscious of your surroundings. I'll give you a call later to check up on things." He gave her a quick peck to the lips and walked out with his travel bag and laptop, threw them in the Altima, and drove off.

But he didn't leave. He doubled back and parked discreetly down the street but within view of her apartment. Ten minutes later, a figure appeared, wearing a hoodie, out of a small park nearby. He crossed the street and walked past Melanie's apartment, appearing to pay undue attention to it. Then he turned around, and walked up to the stairway, as if he was deciding whether or not to ascend it. Bruce fired up the ignition and was ready to tear out of the space towards the apartment should he make a move. He called Melanie immediately. "Try not to be obvious, but look out your window and tell me if that's the guy standing on the sidewalk."

"That's him!" she replied.

Just as Bruce was about to put the car into drive, the man balked, and slowly walked back across the road and back into the park. We are going to end this once and for all. He shut the engine off, reached in his jacket to snap the shoulder holster open, and started to exit the vehicle when he saw a white Range Rover stop in front of the park. And it was none other than Roland Macleod himself that got out of the vehicle.

What the hell, is it one of Macleod's henchmen? Bruce did a speed walk to the park, and converged on both Macleod and the stalker seated at a table at the same time, both to their surprise. Instinctively, Bruce reached his hand inside his jacket for his Sig no more than ten feet away from Macleod. As he did so, Macleod did the same. After a brief hesitation, both men drew their pistols simultaneously and leveled them at each other.

"Highland!" Macleod said in a commanding voice. "Put the gun down."

"What the hell are you doing here Macleod? Trying to off someone, like my client?"

"God no, Highland. I'm here because of him." He nodded toward the hooded figure.

"Hey man" The hooded figure responded holding his hands up. "Whatever is going on, I want no part of it. So, I'll just be on my way."

"No, you stay there!" Bruce demanded, not sure who to train the gun on. "Macleod, you sonofabitch. You used me, and Melanie, to try track down Chad Green for you, didn't you?"

"You're absolutely right, Highland."

"Who is this guy, and what is his involvement?" Bruce asked.

"Why don't you ask him yourself?" Macleod responded.

"All right," Bruce replied. "Who are you, and what are you doing here?"

"You guys win. You got me. You might as well get it over with and take me out right now," the man said in a resigned voice. "Yeah, I'm Chad Green. What am I doing here? I'm trying, with no success, to talk to my sister."

Bruce looked puzzled. "Well guess what Macleod, you're not going to get away with it. I'll take you out in a heartbeat if you try."

Macleod shook his head. "Please, let's put our guns away. Yes, I did use you to find him, but not so I could kill him."

"Then why the hell did you declare him dead in the compound when you knew he was alive? I don't get it?"

"I was trying to protect him, dammit."

There were a lot of confused stares. Chad broke the silence. "Actually, I think he's telling the truth, mister. Whoever you are. You know, I remember that day, that afternoon, clear as a bell, as if it happened yesterday. I saw on the news that Dr. Fuller and Sarah Lock had been killed in a car crash. I kind of suspected something was wrong, as if they were targeted, but then I got a phone call, from a man with a Scottish accent, telling me that if I did not want to end up like Fuller and Lock, that I needed to leave immediately, and start a new life. That's the same exact voice I'm hearing from him as he speaks."

Bruce slowly lowered the pistol, and Macleod did the same, replacing it in his shoulder holster, briefly displaying a shield and an ID badge. "Who are you, Macleod?"

"I am a federal agent. I'm assigned to the CIA's Protective Service Division, the Agency's cops, as an officer on special assignment. That assignment is the overwatch protection of a top-secret government project, and its facilities. I have had that same assignment for the last forty years. They assigned me to be the Provost Marshal of Fort

Ord so I could have some say about what went on in regards to Area 91 and its personnel."

"So, what is it that you want with Chad Green?" Bruce asked.

"You have no idea what it is like to protect a site like this for four decades, having no inkling of what went on behind those fortified doors, not knowing if there was an extreme hazard to public safety, or not. Mr. Green here is possibly the only living person that holds those secrets."

"Before we get too far into it," Bruce said. "Chad Green, my name is Bruce Highland. I am a private investigator. Your sister Melanie hired me to find you."

"Okay," Chad replied.

Bruce pulled out his cell phone. "So, Chad, tell me something significant that happened when you were still together with your sister."

"Hmm. Well, on her eighth birthday, I just graduated with my doctoral and was back in Canton and I gave her this stuffed horse. Her older sister hid it and pretended that it was stolen, and she started bawling her eyes out."

Bruce dialed Melanie. "Hey, me again. Did your brother give you a stuffed horse on your eighth birthday?" There was a brief pause. "Well then you will never guess in a million years what is going on outside of your apartment in the park."

Melanie's only demand? Give me a couple hours alone so I can talk to my brother. Then we can all have a big happy discussion. To that end, Bruce and Macleod rode together to a sports pub to have a couple of beers.

"So you knew about the killings of Irving Fuller and Sarah Lock then?" Bruce asked.

"Actually no, but I suspected they were in danger, at least Fuller anyway, and I did call him and tried to warn him. But I was too late. When I heard the news of the crash, I immediately put two and two together, and assumed Chad Green was next. So, I found his contact information, called him to warn him, and then officially wrote him up as a casualty in the accident so the hounds at the Agency would not come looking for him."

"Why would they want these people dead?"

"My guess? Once the project was for all intents and purposes dead in its tracks, the survivors represented a potential security risk to its secrecy."

"What about this report that says the site was entirely backfilled with concrete?"

"That was what Fuller recommended and as far as I know, he intended to do so, but never made it that far. The person I reported to back in Langley told me to concrete the entrance shut and bury it. So, I guess they didn't want to destroy whatever was inside. I would assume they would want to exhume the site at a later date and have another go at whatever they were trying to do, but that never ended up happening. But in any case, Fuller was adamant that there was an extreme public risk if that site was ever opened."

"Why do you care after all this time?"

"They want to replace me, Highland. They think I'm too old. And they are probably right. Never mind that I go back to Langley twice a year for health and fitness checks, and recurrent firearms qualification, which I have managed to pass flawlessly to date. Highland, are you a man of religious conviction?"

"Well, I believe there is a god. I don't go to church, nor do I believe Christianity is the sole pathway to God and spirituality."

"So, in other words, you don't take things on blind faith alone?"

"That would be accurate."

"I'm going to have to train someone to do my job. Which, admittedly, is not very hard, but how can I impress on them the importance of what they are doing, if I can't tell them why they are doing it? And for that matter, how can I convince a person that they are protecting a real threat when I don't even know if I believe it myself?"

"I see your point. But it is a little hard to believe you had no inkling of what was going on."

"My job was to protect it, not to be part of it. I suspect that if I did actually know what they were working on, I may well not have stayed above ground much longer either."

"Do you still think there is a danger to Chad Green?"

"After this much time? I doubt it. I can tell you that our overwatch protocol for this facility does not include tracking down former associates. In fact, both the Agency and the Pentagon's program managers have been deceased for some time. So, I don't think anybody actually 'owns' Dark Fury."

Chapter 10 – Revelations

The atmosphere in the apartment had an ethereal quality to it. There were four people. Melanie, Chad, Bruce, and Macleod. "Should I open a bottle of wine?" Melanie asked.

"Well, I guess it's his turn to ask the questions." Bruce motioned towards Macleod.

"Sure. Why not. It has been years in coming," Macleod said. "So, Mr. Green, can you tell us what you guys were working on?"

Chad downed a glass of wine in a single gulp. "Got time?"

"Oh yes," Macleod shot back.

"I'm not even sure where to start," Chad replied.

"How about from the beginning."

"Okay. In 1859, a steamship travelling from New Zealand to Chile went off course in a storm, and they happened upon an uncharted island, very remote, in the South Pacific. It recounted an event where members of the ship boarded the island, one of the crew was eaten by wild animals, and the boarding party fled. The journal was lost but rediscovered almost a hundred years later by a professor in England, who organized an expedition in 1952. When they reached the island, they noticed that, although mammals once flourished in the forested hills, none remained. Well, fast forward, in 1972 it was Dr. Fuller himself that came in to possession of the documentation of that expedition, which was never released for whatever reason. And... he actually organized a third exploration of the island." Chad stared at his empty glass.

"Another?" Melanie asked.

"Yes please. Anyway, on this third voyage, they did a thorough search of the island, and found the remains of these unique animals, that had never been seen before –

and, they weren't actually remains. They weren't actually dead. They were dormant."

"Whoa," Bruce said.

"Oh yeah. Dormant. They weren't rotting. They weren't decomposing. But nothing had changed there in years. See, it had been theorized that there was some sort of predatory species that literally ate itself to death with a limited island food supply. Except that they didn't actually die. They went dormant."

"Then what happened?" Macleod asked with keen interest.

"Dr. Fuller brought these dormant animals back to the United States for further study. Eventually, the government found out about Fuller's find, took a look at the reports, and decided that there was a potential military application of these newfound creatures. A powerful, unstoppable predator with no natural enemies. Revive them, breed them, train them to recognize NVA soldiers, and release a few in Northern Vietnam, and the war would have been over in short order. So, basically what happened is that the government took everything over, sequestered the project scientists, added a few more, and began studying this new species in secret. It would take about five years, in other words the late seventies, before they could be revived from a dormant status, but after that, it soon became apparent that they would need a place more contained and secure than the Harvard University campus. In the early '80's, the project moved to Area 91. That's when they brought me aboard."

"What did you do?" Macleod asked.

"I was an animal behavioral scientist. My job was to see if these things could be trained, and their behavior predicted."

"Could they?"

"No. They behaved like no other animal species we know of. They had a keen sense of their own self-preservation, but beyond that, they were unpredictable and untrainable. But... they were very intelligent."

"What did these things look like?"

"They were reptilian in appearance, but not like lizards or alligators. They had the equivalent of opposable thumbs. They normally traveled on all fours. But they were extremely fast, and extremely strong. But the thing about them that set them apart was their resiliency. They were very difficult to kill. You cut its foot off it regenerates. You cut its head off it regenerates. You starve them they go dormant. You cut their air off they go dormant. They had a very simple organ structure. And a unique cellular structure that nobody had ever seen before. But that wasn't my area of expertise."

"So, they couldn't be killed?"

"We had to incinerate the problem ones."

Everyone in the room was completely mesmerized. "So, what happened, in um... the accident?" Macleod asked.

Chad let out a deep sigh, and motioned for another glass of wine. "You have over a dozen top level scientists, each coming to the realization and agreement that these animals were dangerous. In fact, they were so incredibly dangerous – a nearly indestructible predator with no natural enemies, and a propensity to shred all living animals to pieces for sustenance, that if released and unchecked, they could potentially wipe out the entire human population, save for holdouts in fortified shelters. It would make a nuclear holocaust seem tame in comparison." A tear welled up. "Sorry."

"It's okay Chad," Melanie said.

"Okay so, we all were in unanimous agreement. This project should be stopped and the animals destroyed. Dr. Fuller was told no, and to continue on no uncertain terms. But we knew the risk was too great, so we decided to destroy them anyway."

"Were they destroyed?" Bruce asked.

"I'm getting to that. No. See, I told those guys. I told them. Do not, under any circumstances, discuss any such plans within earshot of them. The animals understood what we were talking about. They didn't believe it. So, on the day they were to be destroyed, they managed escape their steel cages, and they just ripped through the containment structure, shredding staff like a banana in a blender, or a cow in a lake of piranhas. Dr. Fuller, Sarah and I were able to get outside and seal the containment hatch before they got to us."

"Chad..." Macleod asked. "It's been forty years almost. So, you are saying the containment structure was sealed up, and none got out. Surely, after that amount of time, they must be dead by now?"

"I wish I could give you a straight answer on that, Mr. Macleod. Conventional logic would agree with you. But when those dormant animals were found in 1972, nobody knew how long they had been in a dormant but still viable state. Remember, the previous expedition was twenty years earlier, and apparently, they were not active then, so, it's possible that they could have lived through at least twenty years of dormancy."

"Where did these things come from?" Bruce asked.

"That is a great question. They were so unique there was not a genus to assign them to. We jokingly called them 'Ripalots.' Like an Ocelot that likes to rip things to shreds. Who knows? Probably some weird mutation. One thing is for certain, if they ended up on any other island besides the one where they were found, life on earth as we know it would be very different."

Macleod cleared his throat. "Chad. My guess is you probably don't know the politics outside your former team, but do you have any idea of why Mossad, the Israeli intelligence agency, would have an interest in this?"

"Probably because of Daniel Levin. He was one of the brightest molecular biologists in the world at the time. He flat out told me his country, Israel, also held a stake in this."

Bruce perked up slightly, having had a faint recognition of that name. Then he remembered the conversation with Maya Goldman. He decided to keep it to himself for the time being.

"Mr. Macleod, can I ask a question of you?" Chad inquired.

"Of course," Macleod replied.

"Do you think it is safe for me to come back? To come out of hiding?"

"I suspect so. But I can't say with absolute certainty either."

"My assumed identity was the result of a very lucky break. I don't want to start over again with a fresh identity. I'm too old for that."

"Well, I think that choice has already been made for you anyway, at this point."

"Oh, one more thing," Bruce said, directing his attention to Chad. "You were involved in this thing from the beginning, right?"

"No. Actually I was brought in towards the tail end. I spent two weeks getting briefed by Dr. Fuller and a few of the other team members. And the next two weeks working inside the compound," Chad replied.

"Oh. Did you work closely with these animals?"

"Not really. I got to see them from a distance a few times. There was some sort of internal politics going on. The handlers were really protective of them."

Alexandri 'Alex' Petroya walked up the steps of his Anza Street townhouse, fresh from his morning run to the beach. He passed the mail carrier, who simply handed him a stack of bills and junk mail. "Thank you," Alex said as he opened the door.

"No problem. Saves me the trouble of trying to fit all that crap through your mail slot."

After a quick shower and a shave, Alex settled down at the kitchen table to sort through the mail, discarding the junk flyers, putting the bills in a small growing stack, and singling out a subscription Russian language tabloid, featuring a particularly unflattering caricature of the Russian Premier on the cover. A dark-haired woman with fine features entered the kitchen in a nightgown. "Hey Volga, look at this," Alex said with a smirk as he held the magazine up.

"How disrespectful," she said. "Did you make coffee yet?"

"No. I was going to get some at the office. You aren't working today?"

"No. The building is shut down for electrical repairs."

"Lucky you."

"Unlucky me. It means I will have twice the work to do tomorrow. Did you drink all of the orange juice?" Volga asked as she rummaged through the refrigerator.

"Yes. Three days ago." Alex flipped through the magazine, and smiled at the article claiming the Russian air force had forged an alliance with space aliens, complete with a crudely Photoshopped image of a general shaking hands with a smiling creature resembling ET. Then the doorbell rang.

Volga peered through the peephole. "What? No... this can't be."

"Who is it?" Alex asked. He got up from the table and walked over to the front door. Volga opened it as he approached.

The two of them stared at the woman, who blankly stared back. "Alex? Volga?" Svetlana asked, halfway wondering if she had in fact come to the right house.

"Who are you?" Alex asked.

"You do not recognize me?"

"You look just like my sister, Svetlana, but she is...."

"Alive. I lived through the crash, but my memory had been so badly damaged that I did not even know my real name until about two months ago."

"Well, come in." Alex gave her a big hug. "Please have a seat."

Volga eyed her with suspicion. "Alex, can I talk to you for a minute in the kitchen?" The two went back in the kitchen area and Volga spoke in a whisper. "This might be some kind of scam."

"I think I should know my own sister."

They returned to the living room. Alex looked Svetlana up and down. "I hate to ask you to do this, but can you please lift your shirt up to just above the bottom of your bra?" Svetlana looked slightly embarrassed but complied. The two telltale moles just below her right breast confirmed that indeed it was Svetlana. "Yes, the moles. You used to be so self-conscious of them that often you would wear an athletic top at the swimming pool."

"Forgive me, but my memory comes back very slowly and in pieces. After the crash, they took me to a rehabilitation center in St. Petersburg, but they misidentified me. It is long story but eventually I was identified correctly. So, when we talk about past events, I may not be able to relate."

"Where are you staying? What are you doing?" Alex asked.

"In the Richmond district, not that far from here with another Ukrainian woman. I just get job as an IT technician at company close to apartment."

Alex chuckled. "Your English is getting slightly better. Okay, does... Bruce know you are back?"

"No. I know of him. The GRU sent a man to identify me when they heard I had possibly been identified as myself, Svetlana Petroya. He told me about my life here, and about Bruce Highland. He also told me to leave Russia because people within the GRU wanted me dead. I will tell you the truth, I have some fleeting memories. But that is it."

"Are you going to tell him?"

"I don't know. He may have another woman in his life. From what little I remember, I think he always had other women in his life."

"I never felt that he was right for you. But again, I never felt anyone was right for you. I wish I could tell you what his life situation is but we have not spoken in maybe two years."

"How did he react?"

"It almost destroyed him. He was deeply sad and depressed for a long time. I think he should know you are alive."

"Please let me make decision."

"Okay. So. How about you come over for dinner?" Alex looked back at Volga. "Maybe tomorrow?"

"Tonight is good," Volga said. "I might as well do shopping today."

"Oh," Svetlana said. "I know you want to, but please do not tell rest of family in Russia. As I say, there are people in GRU that dislike me."

"I understand. But not many are left anyway. Mother passed last year."

Macleod found Bruce seated at his table at the Crop & Saddle, hacking away at a laptop. "People like you and I don't change. Always seated in the corner facing the entrance, with one eye on the doorway and the other eye on everything else," Macleod said.

Bruce motioned for him to sit down. "What brings you here?"

"Chad Green told a pretty incredible story, don't you think?"

"That he did for sure."

"What's your take on it?" Macleod asked.

"What do you mean?"

"Do you think he's spinning a yarn?"

"Hard to say," Bruce said. "The man has lived most of his adult life in a paranoid existence, hiding his own identity. And he's not a young man. He could certainly be delusional. Of course, the risk here is that he isn't. Taken at face value, Area 91 could be one hell of a Pandora's Box."

"So, you can see our conundrum, can you not?"

Bruce raised his eyebrows. "Our conundrum? As I see it, my job is done."

Macleod sighed. "Of course it is. What would you suppose is inside that concrete three-story vault?"

"If you were to infer from Chad Green's story, the remnants of a research facility, some old bones, and some dormant mutant creatures, frozen in time."

"Let's say that there is just that, Highland. If you were in my shoes, what would you do?"

"That's a tough call. If you wanted to remove the risk to humanity, then you would incinerate the dormant mutant creatures. But of course, if you do, you've destroyed valuable scientific evidence of an undiscovered animal species. That's a hell of a call to have to make."

"That would appear to have been the call that Irving Fuller's research team unanimously made."

"You yourself thought that Chad Green's story might possibly be the embellished ramblings of a delusional madman. So, I don't know what to tell you there, Hoss."

"You don't feel the slightest inkling of social responsibility in the matter? Unburdened with the knowledge that you are one of four people in the entire world that harbors a terrible secret?"

"The satisfaction of burdened knowledge does not pay my utility bills. What is it that you want from me, Macleod, affirmation? If so, consider yourself affirmed and move on."

"I want to take a look inside of that structure. And I could use some help."

"Help is a dime a dozen."

"You already know the background, plus, you are an investigator. I am not. I would like to find out if there is any credibility to Chad Green's claims before making any major and potentially career ending decisions."

"Fine. My normal billing rate is eight hundred a day plus expenses."

"Done."

Bruce raised his eyebrows. "I said that was my normal billing rate. The Agency normally pays me double that, for services to the Agency."

"Well... okay. I can make that happen."

"I said that was what the Agency normally..."

"Stop! Take it or leave it!"

Bruce let out a heavy sigh. "Well let's see, what do I have going on... an insurance investigation into the sinking of a twelve million dollar container ship hauling thirty million dollars of cargo, a cheating spouse investigation of a celebrity with a ten million dollar prenup agreement at stake, both of which have percentage bonuses for claim avoidance, and a lost cat. Doing the numbers, you fall roughly between number two and number three, with a priority level closer to that of the cat. But you know what? Fine. We'll go with double rates."

He squinted his eyes in adjustment as he flicked on the light switch of the bathroom. His head was pounding. A beer at the Sacramento pub turned into four, followed by a very long drive back to Monterey, with a stop at a liquor store for a bottle of Wild Turkey. Macleod fumbled for some aspirin, downed them, and looked at the mirror of his short beard and mustache, proud that at eighty years old, it still hadn't gone gray. He flicked the light back off and climbed back into bed. Just as he dozed off, the doorbell rang.

Go away. Macleod pulled the pillow over his head in a desperate attempt to block the ringing that still continued in his head. Then the doorbell rang again. And again. And again.

Oh bloody hell. Macleod threw on a bath robe, donned some slippers, squinted through the peephole, and saw the figure of a young woman. When he opened the door, he saw that it was a young woman, with two large suitcases at her feet. She was blonde, with long braided hair, dressed in business slacks and a jacket. "Can I help you?" Macleod said, trying his best to shield his eyes from the morning sunlight.

"I'm Mary Adams-Wentworth."

Macleod's eyes darted between her low-cut blouse, her curvaceous hips, and the two large suitcases. "Whatever it is you have to sell I'm not interested. Now if you'll excuse me, I need to catch up on my beauty sleep." He shut the door and started to walk away. The doorbell rang again. He returned and opened the door, this time with an angry demeanor, and was presented with a shield and a federal identification badge. "What is the meaning of this?" Macleod demanded in a stern voice.

"I'm your replacement, Mr. Macleod. Mel Givens sent me. You're supposed to train me."

Macleod was aghast. "I see. Well, find yourself some suitable accommodations and come back later at a decent hour."

"This residence is an Agency owned asset, Mr. Macleod."

Macleod was beside himself. "Ohhhhhh, no, no, no, no, and a final.... No! Absolutely not! Young lady, if you think you are camping out here, you are sadly mistaken."

"Oh, well, you're right, I don't plan on camping out here."

"Good. Then it looks like we have an understanding. I will see you..."

"I plan on moving in here," She announced.

"Okay, again, let me make myself perfectly crystal clear. You are not, under any circumstances, moving in here."

Macleod could not shake the callous sense of the invasion of his personal space. He flipped through the local newspaper at the kitchen table, and sipped a glass of orange juice. His concentration was broken by the sound of someone rummaging through the refrigerator. "I trust the second-floor guest bedroom, with its attached bathroom, will accommodate you suitably, Miss Wentworth?"

"It's Adams-Wentworth, and it's Ms. Adams-Wentworth thank you very much. But you can call me Mary. The bedroom will work. My god, don't you have any real food in this refrigerator? And what's up with the Sunny D?"

"I'm afraid I didn't get around to picking oranges from the citrus tree to provide you with fresh squeezed orange juice. How rude of me. Oh... wait... alas, I don't even have a citrus tree."

"You kind of remind me of that guy that starred in those really old James Bond movies."

"Hmm. Yes, well, I get that a lot. I guess that is a compliment."

"I thought he was a womanizing cretin."

"Hmm. Yes, well, I... actually don't get that a lot, to be honest."

"So where do we start?"

"I guess we'll drive out to the site. That's as good of a starting place as any."

"So which car do I get?"

"Huh?"

"Yeah, I mean, there is a Range Rover and a Jaguar parked in the garage. I have to drive something."

"My god, woman, that Jaguar is my personal vehicle, it is a classic E type, it's valuable. It's not to be driven every day. Besides, it has a manual transmission. Your generation doesn't even know how to drive one."

"Oh, trust me, I know how to work a stick. Especially an old, classic one."

Macleod blushed slightly "My, that's good to know. Let's get going, shall we?"

Mary stepped out of the Range Rover and surveyed the clearing. "This is it?"
"That's right. See up in those trees? There is a camera there. We can watch the site from the house."
"Okay, but I don't see anything except a rocky hillside."
"It's buried in there."
"So, what are my duties?"
"To ensure it stays buried in there."
"Okay."
"From time to time, either a base commander, or a public works officer, or a private land developer will propose to develop something on this hill. In order for them to do that, they have to get permission from you. Your job is to tell them no."
"That sounds easy enough."
"I never said it was a tough job. And in the event that someone shows up unannounced, and takes undue interest in the site, you investigate them. If they try to disturb the site, you call base security, and if necessary, federal marshals."
"What do I do when I'm not doing either?"
"You might consider improving your tennis game or taking up a productive hobby."
"So, what's the deal with this place? Why is it being protected? What is so important?"
"I have a few things for you to read over when we get back to the house. Other than that, nobody really knows."
"It sounds like you've pretty much did all the training you needed to do," Mary retorted.
"Well, well... I mean, no, not by any means. I have to... see how you're going to react under different situations. It could take weeks. Months maybe."

"All right. Well, I guess I'm good here. Are there any contacts here I need to meet while we're on base?"

"In due time lass, in due time. Oh, and I hope this goes without saying, but the location of the house is strictly confidential. For the purpose of having a mailing address, your official residence is in Salinas. It's not far away. I'll take you there at a later time."

Hazel Green was like an older version of Melanie, taller and a bit plumper. She could hardly believe the news when Melanie called, and immediately boarded a plane to California. Melanie invited Bruce over for dinner with Hazel and Chad. She seized the opportunity to introduce her 'friend' and hired private investigator Bruce. Bruce seized the opportunity to dig through Chad's story more thoroughly. What he was looking for was some sort of documentation trail – not necessarily of the project itself, which Chad probably never had access to, but to the events leading to the project. But it all lead back to Irving Fuller. And Irving Fuller had been long since deceased. The best Chad could offer up was to possibly pay a visit to Harvard University.

"Have you decided what you are going to do?" Bruce asked Chad.

"I kind of like it down in Ensenada," Chad replied. "I have a girl down there. I have a successful restaurant. Maybe I'll get my paperwork up to date so I can travel back and forth. As Chad Green. Funny thing is, I've been living as Thomas Mallory for so long, I'm not even used to using my own name."

"What's the story behind Thomas Mallory?"

"Story? A few months after I fled California and ended up bumming around in Ensenada, money started drying up. There weren't many options for work for a non-Spanish speaking American, so I decided I would just disappear in the hills and end it all. In doing so, I stumbled across four dead bodies, two vehicles, drugs, and a ton of cash. It was obviously a drug deal that went bad and they managed to kill each other. One of the dead guys was Thomas Mallory, and he looked a little bit like me, so I drove away with his wallet, his Land Rover, and duffel bag with enough cash that I could live quite some time on it."

"Weren't you worried that someone would come looking for him?"

"Sure, but nobody ever did – until, coincidentally, a couple of days before you showed up. There were a couple plain clothes DEA agents looking into cold case investigation involving him. It didn't go anywhere. They ran my DNA and of course it didn't match, but the whole thing spooked me, which prompted me to find Melanie. I didn't really want to involve her but felt there was nowhere else to turn."

"What are your thoughts on the possibility of opening up the site at Area 91 and taking a look?"

"That place is pure evil. Absolutely do not do that. Trust me on this."

On the surface, the idea of poking around Harvard to get some information on Irving Fuller seemed to be a fruitless dead-end pursuit, but the one thing about academia, is that people in his field tend to remain in academia, sometimes their whole life. It was worth putting out a few calls and some online requests to seek out former students and associates of Irving Fuller. Somebody had to know something. And in the best-case scenario, there was a box of his 'stuff' sitting in a faculty storage room or a lecture hall basement. Of course, that would be like finding a needle in a haystack. But Bruce was perfectly happy to rack up double-rate billings at the Agency's cost, courtesy of Macleod.

After speaking to more than a dozen former students, one name kept circling back to Bruce. Henry Blue Horse. Henry Blue Horse was a tenured professor of natural history. And he indicated that he might possibly be able to help. But there was a condition – he was completely unwilling to discuss anything about Irving Fuller over the telephone, or electronically.

Henry Blue Horse was born Heinrich Blaupferd in Argentina, the grandson of a wanted Nazi SS officer who fled Germany in the last days of the war. He came to the United States on an academic visa, in an effort to leave the stigma and history behind. He ended up at Harvard and never left.

Everything looked old on campus. Even the new red brick buildings looked old, and the old red brick buildings looked even older to Bruce. He found his way to Henry's office with the help of some directions by students walking the streets. He was a frail old man, who squinted through a pair of spectacles to grade the morning pop quiz on the evolution of insect species in Madagascar. He critically eyed Bruce as he entered the office, and beckoned him to have a seat.

"Thank you for seeing me, professor," Bruce said. "Irving Fuller was working on a government research project which reportedly started here at this university. Can you tell me anything about that?"

"I was one of his graduate students at the time. I was aware that he had just returned from an oceanic scientific expedition, and had brought back some groundbreaking findings, and was studying them. That much I know. Exactly what it was I don't know, because he and the rest of his team were tight lipped about it," Henry replied.

"Tight lipped? Was the government involved at the time?"

"I don't know. I don't think so but you have to understand, often times when game-changing scientific findings are made, they are kept in secret until the team involved is ready to publish their findings. I mean, university research does have a business element to it, and they don't want to risk diluting the credits."

"Do you know if it involved animals?"

"Maybe, I couldn't say for certain. But one really strange thing happened. About a month into it, Fuller and his team basically... left, literally overnight. Then government agents interrogated myself and the rest of his students on our knowledge of the project, and were told not to discuss it further under threat of prosecution."

"Can you think of anyone else that you might know that might have something to add?"

Henry's eyes lit up. "Why yes. In fact... wait... no I'm sorry. He died ten years ago."

The bar and its patrons reminded Bruce of an old television series featuring... a bar and its patrons. Tell me something I don't know. The trip had been a complete bust. At least the beer was good.

Chapter 11 – Unexpected ally

This is the high rent district. Bruce's older model Altima stood out among the shiny new BMWs, Mercedes, Porches and Infinitys. And the occasional Teslas just to prove the homeowners' dedication to the green movement. Macleod certainly isn't living a frugal lifestyle on the government's dime.

"Would you like a brandy or a single malt?" Macleod offered as the two sat in his spacious living room with bricked walls and stained hardwood trim.

"Considering it's eight thirty in the morning, I'll take a pass on that," Bruce replied. "I am however a little bit surprised you've offered up the location of your lair."

"I think security went out the window, at least in regards to your involvement anyway. So, what did you learn?"

"Nothing that could really corroborate Chad Green's story outside of what we already could have put together. But even in talking to him, he never did come across as delusional. Maybe a bit paranoid yes. And, granted, although he throws a government conspiracy on the table, which, by the way, there actually is, he hasn't gone into the realm of ghosts or space aliens. But he was very adamant that the bunker should not be breached."

"Well that isn't much help," Macleod said, as he fished out a large cigar from a wooden box.

"I'm just thinking out loud, but what if say, we dug into the hill a bit to expose a wall, then drilled a small hole through the concrete? Say, like an inch, and ran a camera probe through it, just to take a look inside? In fact, you could maybe even put a gas sniffer in there and pull out some material samples and send them to the lab for toxic chemical analysis?"

Macleod expressed a slight facial gesture of approval. "That's not a bad idea, actually."

"And in the worst case, if there are toxic chemicals, or killer space aliens ready to pounce, we could always seal it back up fairly easily."

"That would be something to consider, however that would be a serious breach of protocol."

"Good point. Certainly, a serious breach of protocol could indeed be a career ending move." Bruce abruptly looked up. "Oh wait. Sorry. Too soon?"

Macleod chuckled, "Touché. Well, let me think about it for a bit."

The silence was broken by the shuffling of footsteps descending the staircase. A female figure wearing nothing but a bra and panties walked into the kitchen past the two men as if she was wearing blinders, opened and shut a cupboard door, and then walked back into the living room, freezing as she finally noticed the two men. "Oh... um. Hi. I thought you left for the morning," she said, addressing Macleod.

"Well... hi," Bruce said sheepishly.

"Oh bloody hell," Macleod said. "Meet my replacement. Miss Mary Adams-Wentworth. Oh, excuse me. Ms Adams-Wentworth. I am supposed to train her."

"Well, so far you're doing one hell of a job, from where I'm seated," Bruce retorted with a smirk.

"Who is he?" Mary asked.

"Bruce Highland," Bruce introduced himself. "I'm the hired help."

Mary looked confused momentarily. Then she brightened up and smiled. "Oh, okay. Great. Can you be a darling and help me move a dresser?"

This time it was Bruce that was confused. "Sure – I'll be right up." Mary ascended the stairs to the guest bedroom. "She thinks I'm the butler?" Bruce asked in a hushed voice.

Macleod pondered the situation. "Apparently yes. Well, then let's just go with that for now. Go make yourself useful," Macleod said with a grin. "I'll be back in a short while. I'm just going to make a quick run to the store."

Bruce knocked on the partially opened door, then entered after there was a muffled response. "Oh, I'm sorry. I'll just give you a few minutes to put some clothes on."

"All my casual wear is in the dryer right now." Mary was seated on the bed, trying to massage her lower back.

"You okay?" Bruce asked, noting the partially moved dresser angled out on the floor.

"I pulled my back trying to move that thing."

Bruce proceeded to move the dresser into its presumed destination in the corner as Mary pointed. "Is that good?" he asked. Mary nodded. "Can I get you some aspirin or something?"

"No, but could you be a real dear and rub this knot out of my back?"

"I can do that I guess. Just um, lie face down."

Bruce proceeded to rub her back with his thumbs. "How is that?"

"Oh, that feels really good. You're a professional at this, aren't you?"

"I know what I'm doing," Bruce said, trying his best not to fixate on her ass.

"I knew it. Can you go lower?"

The massage was now encroaching on her panties. "Better?"

"Oh yes. A lot better. You said you're a professional, right?"

"Sure," Bruce said nonchalantly. Just not a professional masseur.

"Oh good." Mary stripped off her panties. "Can you go lower?"

Oh my. "How's that?"

"Ohhhhh, yeah. Lower."

Bruce started to rub her upper legs. "Better?"

"No, no, up slightly."

"That's a mighty... private area," Bruce said.

"Just... do it!" Mary said as she gritted her teeth.

"If you insist."

Bruce was busy surfing the web on his tablet computer in the living room as Macleod entered the house. "Would you like a glass of orange juice?" Macleod asked, toting a paper grocery bag to the kitchen.

"I'll pass, but I'll take that shot of whiskey if you've got it."

Macleod squinted out the patio window through the slats. "What the hell is she doing back there?"

"I think she's trying to smoke one of your cigars."

"That's odd. What's her problem, did you manage to rub her the wrong way?"

Bruce contemplated the question. "I'm going to go with no."

Bruce tossed and turned. He was in a twilight state. Not completely asleep, and not completely awake. Too many things were going through his head at once. He kept cycling through the possibilities of what lay behind the walls of Area 91. Chad Green's story did indeed seem far-fetched. If you were to believe him, opening the site could potentially expose the continent, if not the world, to a massive life extinction event. But even that scenario was purely based on conjecture. Experts have been known to be wrong before. A more likely case was that he was generally right but had embellished and overstated the threat. It's also very possible that there was some sort of chemical accident or a fire perhaps, but the confounding problem was that someone in the know, at the time, deemed the site to be an extreme hazard, regardless of the actual reason.

For this reason, Bruce was apprehensive of his own suggested solution. Which, wasn't actually a solution, it's more like dipping one's toe in the water to see if it's cold. One might be able to eliminate some chemical or radiological hazard – at least at the location of the exploration, but one couldn't rule out the possibility of a boogeyman waiting to pounce from a hidden room. In his last detailed conversation, Chad outlined that the team had hypothesized that these 'Ripalot' animals as they termed them, ate themselves to the point of starvation and went in a dormant state. So, it follows that, if Chad was to be believed, then these animals, if they were still even viable after nearly forty years, would at least be in a harmless dormant state.

Following up on that begs some serious ethical considerations. You go in, you find these dormant creatures. You know they have the potential to be revived and become potentially extremely dangerous, so what do you do? Do you kick the can down the road, and let a future generation figure it out and deal with it? Do you document what you know and hope that someone won't try to misuse these creatures for nefarious purposes? Do you incinerate and destroy the creatures to eliminate the potential for any future threat? Or do you preserve them in place, in the name of science?

Irving Fuller wanted to fill the entire vault with concrete. Bruce didn't know exactly how big it was but it had to be big enough to require enough concrete to build a small dam. And that doesn't exactly 'solve' the problem, as concrete can be busted up, but it would certainly slow it down and probably destroy valuable documentation that may still be present in the vault.

Bruce sat bolt upright, now fully awake. In any case… in any case, the Agency isn't protecting this thing out of a sense of altruism or public service. No, some sort of weapon, some sort of military application was being developed, and they are protecting its secret. No, it's things like this that become ultra-destructive and potentially civilization ending when misused. Like nuclear energy. It has peaceful uses that make our lives better. It has lifesaving medical uses. And between the United States, Russia and China, we all have enough nuclear weapons to turn the entire earth into a massive, lifeless, toxic wasteland.

It had been going since late the previous night, and that was the smoker in Bruce's back yard. It was Bruce's first try at smoking beef brisket, a cut that requires a solid seventeen hours of smoking time if it is to be done properly. Bruce surveyed the living room. He hadn't gone through the entire twelve pack of beer. There were still a couple left. His head was pounding and he still had to take about ten pounds of meat off the smoker and do something with it and store it. Its destination would have been next door at Steve and Matilda's but that backyard party was canceled due to a family emergency and all the other neighbors made other plans.

Bruce looked down at his cell phone and saw a text. It was from Melanie. From a few hours ago. Are we still on for this afternoon? Bruce saw that he replied. Yes, come on over. Then he looked in the back yard. Melanie was lounging in a lawn chair engrossed in her phone.

"Sleep well?" she asked, not taking her eyes off the phone. She didn't sound happy.

"Yeah. Sorry I dozed off."

"Dozed off huh. More like passed out drunk. I could have had a better conversation with my Bonsai tree."

The instructor barked orders to the class as if he were a Marine drill instructor, and in fact bore a strong resemblance to a notable actor portraying a DI during wartime Vietnam – meaning, he didn't look quite right dressed in cycling spandex.

The lights came on, as the music waned from high energy techno dance mix to a slow R&B wind down set. Mary couldn't help but notice the girl on the stationary spin bicycle beside her with the bleach blonde hair. "Now I recognize you," she said. "I've seen you jogging in the neighborhood."

"Right," The girl said. "I recognize you too."

"Do you live in the neighborhood?"

"No. I live in San Francisco. But I come down here regularly to visit my boyfriend."

"Mary, by the way. Good to meet you."

"Maya. We should have coffee sometime."

The Agency warned her. Macleod warned her. If you want to have a relationship, get a dog. But Mary reasoned that coffee with a random occasional neighborhood and gym mate was harmless and it would help her blend in better anyway. "Sure."

"In fact, I'm going to get a mocha drink at the place across the street after the gym."

"Sounds fun. I might try it one of these days."

"You're welcome to join if you would like," Maya said.

Mary made a slight grimace as she pondered the offer. She felt like a deer caught in the headlights. Oh well, let's just get this over. "Okay. Sounds good."

The two women sat across from each other holding steaming espresso drinks. "So, what's your story?" Maya asked. And she wasn't actually clear what her story was. Or for that matter who the man was. And for that matter, why Bruce was there.

"Oh um, I just moved in. I'm... I'm renting a room."

"Nice place."

"Tell me about it. It even comes with a male housekeeper."

Is she talking about Bruce? Maya wondered. "Sounds nice. Is he attractive?"

"Oh yeah. And, gosh... he has the most magical hands. Why he was able to... um, anyway. Yeah."

"What do you do for a living?"

This was a really bad idea. "Oh, I'm a... a government worker. Procurement. I do paperwork. Really boring. How about yourself?"

"I'm an investigative writer. About, like, conspiracies and stuff. You know, like secret bases in Nevada."

"How interesting."

"You know, I had heard of a place around here, actually."

After a fresh shower, Mary settled down in the living room enjoying a small pot of tea. The early morning espresso drink threw her off. Macleod was busy reading the Wall Street Journal. A red light flashed by the large screen television, followed by a short, faint audible alert. "What was that?" Mary asked.

Macleod smiled. "That my dear, is how we monitor the site without physically going out there and sitting on it. The proximity alarm has been tripped." Without even touching the television or a remote, it automatically displayed a bird's eye view of the site. Macleod held up his smart phone. "And if I'm out someplace and I have a wireless or a data connection, I can even see what's going on through this."

Mary stared at the screen intently. There was a small SUV and a minivan parked in the clearing. A man wearing dress slacks and a pressed shirt climbed out of the SUV, walked to the edge of the clearing as if to verify that they were alone, and walked back to the minivan. A woman wearing nurse scrubs climbed out of the driver's seat of the minivan, opened the side door, and they both went inside. "Holy moly. I'll bet I know what's going on there."

Macleod laughed. "A lot of times animals will trip it. These two happen to be a little bit ahead of schedule today.

The man is a civilian administrator at the base clinic, and the woman is a nursing assistant."

"Are they like... having an affair?"

"Well, what do you think. Why else do you go to the most remote location on the post to play hide the salami?"

"Are you going to call security on them?"

"Why? It's a waste of their time, plus the less people that figure out the site is under video surveillance, the better."

"So, on another note. Just a hypothetical question, but, if I'm randomly out some place, and someone starts talking to me about Area 91, how should I handle it?"

"Well, it does have some local legend attached to it, so it's not an impossibility that someone may randomly bring it up in conversation. And at some point you will be a named, published point of contact for it on the post directory, so, it's not entirely infeasible for some tinfoil hat whack job to try to track you down in order to speak with you. Those people have tried to talk to me over the years. They just can't manage to find me. Another reason to have your official address in the next town over. If for some reason they do manage to track you down, you're just a property manager and that's it."

"Okay. What if I suspected that they were actually trying to breach security?"

"Use your judgement, I guess. Ninety nine percent of the time these people are harmless and just curious. Anyway, let's take a run to Salinas. I'll show you the official address. I need to pick up my mail anyway."

"Where is Bruce today?"

"Oh him? He doesn't come every day."

The outdoor shed was years in the making. It could have been as simple as calling Insta-Shed and have them build a twelve by ten foot outbuilding in the back yard, but Bruce simply wasn't going to have a wood floor on dirt for a foundation. He viewed the outbuilding as sort of his own above ground man cave more than simply a storage area, but the need for such had waned somewhat. It morphed into open air, covered concrete patio so he could grill or run the smoker at will, rain or shine.

Tommy was a retired contractor that lived two houses down, and did handyman work just to keep busy. He put the finishing touches on the wood structure, and stood back and admired it. "Well, what do you think, Bruce?"

"I like it. When is it going to be ready for use?" Bruce replied.

"You can use it now if you want. Concrete is cured enough."

"Hey Tommy, random question. Let's say I need to drill, oh, a one-inch hole, though... Mmm... say two feet of concrete. Horizontally. How big of a deal is that?"

"Piece of cake. You can do a two-inch hole up to four feet with a handheld diamond tipped wet core drill. Well, okay you need a stand to go that deep, but it's a one-man job. Why, you got another project for me?"

"Well, it's not local. It's in Monterey."

"Oh. You can rent the equipment and do it yourself if you want. It's not a huge deal."

"There is no power out there I don't think."

"You just need a small portable generator then. You can rent that too."

It was actually Bruce's turn to go to Redwood City to keep Melanie in company, but as luck would have it, she had to go to downtown Sacramento, in person, to help clear up a certification issue with the analytical laboratory she works for, acting in place of the laboratory director. It turned out to be a simple misfiling, and the matter was cleared up in minutes. She was pleasantly surprised to see a sober and alert Bruce Highland when she knocked on the door.

"What do you think?" he asked, as he led Melanie out in the back yard, and pointed to the new covered patio.

"It has a patio, and a roof over it. So I guess you can fire up the charcoal grill in the rain? Is that why you built it?" she asked.

"Exactly."

"Sorry for the short notice. I thought I was going to have a long day and then have to go back."

"I didn't really plan anything. I was actually going to head over to the Crop & Saddle to meet up with a client."

"Oh, no problem. You can do that. We can hang out another time I guess."

"Why don't you come? This particular client gets five minutes of my attention tops. I promise."

True to promise, the client, a clean-shaven younger man, nerdy in appearance wearing a sharply pressed but otherwise rather cheap suit and a tacky thin tie suggestive that his occupation may be a cycling evangelist. He was in and out in four minutes and thirty seconds, leaving Bruce with a small manila packet.

"How did you manage to cut that so short? Usually, you wine and dine clients at bars," Melanie said.

"He's a devout Mormon and despises bars. That's why I like to meet him here. It keeps the meetings short and brief."

"What does he have you working on?"

"It's called cleaning house. His local church wants to excommunicate members that they believe are engaged in philandering and other sinful pursuits."

"Seriously?" Melanie narrowed her eyes.

"Hey I'm just the investigator, not the judge or the jury. Besides, if my work leads to them getting kicked out of the church, I'm probably doing those members a favor anyway."

"I suppose if you look at it that way. I don't think I've ever eaten here. Is the food any good?"

"It's... okay. Burger is decent. Fish and chips aren't bad. We can go someplace else to eat if you would like."

"That's okay. I'm not really all that hungry anyway."

Bruce couldn't help but feel a gaze from the far end of the bar. He couldn't place the man at first, but then he realized who it was. Someone he hadn't seen in over two years. It was Alex Petroya. "Hey uh, I'll be back in a minute. I need to go talk with someone real quick."

"No problem."

Bruce walked over and stood next to the man. "Alex, what brings you down here?" Bruce asked.

"I just wanted to check up and see how you are doing." Alex glanced over at Melanie, who was seated at a table. "You appear to be doing fine."

"Why are you guys so interested in my well-being all of the sudden? You guys have never been thrilled with me from the start."

"I have never held hard feelings towards you," Alex said, as he took a shot of house vodka. "I will admit, our mother has not been a fan of yours, but she has passed a while back."

"Okay. So, what did you come to see me about?"

"I see that you are happily settled, so it's of no importance. I guess I will be on my way."

"Whoa, wait, Alex, what the hell do you mean by that?"

"Goodbye, Bruce." Alex walked stiffly out of the bar, climbed into his black Mercedes SUV, and drove off.

"Is everything okay?" Melanie asked.

"Yeah, fine." Bruce looked visibly disturbed.

"If I tell you something, will you promise not to take it the wrong way?"

Bruce was slightly taken aback. "If you have to put it that way, I'm not sure I can."

"Okay I'll just tell you then. I kind of feel a little bit weird here."

"The bar? Like I said, we can go someplace else."

"No, I don't mean here specifically, I mean Sacramento. Your place. I feel like I don't belong. I feel like I'm in the shadow of another woman."

"If you had to script my life, I'm the action hero. The guy that isn't supposed to end up with the girl, living in a house with a white picket fence in a suburban neighborhood, coaching baseball while mom drives the van to the soccer games."

"You have a magnetic draw to women, Bruce. You are fun to be with. They like you physically. They probably love you. But emotionally, you are closed off."

"You're absolutely right. But don't interpret that to mean that I don't care."

"What about that Korean girl you told me about? What was her name? Kim Park? How come things never worked out with her?"

"She was getting too close."

"See that's just it. You don't want anybody to be close. It's like, there is a burst of physical affection, and then, you think about it, and say wait a minute, I'm getting in too deep, and you shut down."

"Well, like I said...."

"I need to get going Bruce. I have to get an early start tomorrow."

"All right. Let's head back to the house." Bruce kissed her, and saw her off. She made a fair point. Love and hate are two very strong words. Hate is easy to use. Love is hard to use. Hate is easy to come by. Hate is easy to acknowledge. Love is hard to come by, and harder to acknowledge.

Use your judgement, I guess. Those were the sage words of arguably the oldest living staffer in the history of the Agency. He seemed to be remarkably lackadaisical compared to most of the hard liners back at Langley. Mary's new found friend had been a dedicated stationary cyclist and workout partner, a morning coffee companion, and now, they would encroach on a new boundary, drinks at the wine bar. Mel Givens made it agonizingly clear that there would be no room for relationships in this assignment. But Mel was clearly talking about Men. Certainly, there is nothing wrong with girls getting together to discuss girl business, right?

So, tell me about your boyfriend. The glasses clinked, and the two girls toasted a cheer. A glass later, and Maya started to turn a slight shade of red. Oh, my boyfriend. It occurred to Maya that the only thing close to a boyfriend that she ever had was that one upperclassman that she dated when she was at the university. "He's older. Professional. Le'Chaim!" Maya said, raising her glass.

"Cheers," Mary said, with a slightly puzzled look.

"Oh, sorry. Yiddish grandmother." Maya's accent started to become slightly more pronounced. "So do you have a boyfriend?"

"No," Mary replied. Then she downed her glass and smiled. She started to speak, and then checked herself. Agency rules on this assignment.

"Sounds lonely," Maya said, more out of a conditioned response than actually being able to relate. "But, truth be told, my journalistic pursuits break my loneliness, boyfriend or no boyfriend. "And while I'm here, I would like to look into Area 91. I've been reading up on the rumors and hearsay."

"Well, that's what they are, rumors and hearsay," Mary replied.

"Oh?" Maya said, pretending to be surprised. "Do you know anything about it?"

"I might know a little," Mary said, as she started to sip her third glass of wine. She was starting to feel the buzz. "I mean, I work in procurement, so... it's one of the things we... I... deal with." Mary was getting the distinct feeling that Maya was staring at her bust line.

"So, they say the place was some kind of research facility. Do you know what they were researching?"

Use your judgement. String her along. "Well, it's... a secret."

"Secrets. Ah yes, secrets. I understand. Well let's leave that a secret. But hey, have you ever played share the secret game?"

"Where if I share a secret, you share a secret?"

"Yes, that one."

"Okay, I'm game. You start," Mary said.

"Well, I tried it with a woman once."

"Oh my god, what was it like?"

"Oh, it was incredible. So sensual. I almost couldn't go back. Okay, your turn," Maya replied.

"Well, I know this is going to sound totally crazy, but I've always wanted to try it with a woman." Mary couldn't believe the words that just came out of her own mouth. She chalked it up to the wine talking.

The conversation became awkwardly silent. Maya smiled. "What they don't know won't hurt them," she said.

The hell did she mean by that? Mary wondered. "Definitely. I need to get up early tomorrow." She threw some cash on the counter to settle the bill.

Her lips were moist and succulent, unlike any that Mary had encountered before. They gradually moved lower, invisibly, in the darkness of the night. "Tell me another secret," Maya said, as she brushed her tongue below the navel.

Finally, Maya's tongue had reached the forbidden zone. Mary cried out in ecstasy. "More, please!"

"Tell me about Area 91"

"No don't stop there!"

"Then tell me about Area 91!"

Mary shuddered and woke, sitting bolt upright in bed, covered with sweat. The wine buzz was wearing off. There was no Maya, No lips. No tongue. She slowly pieced together the progression of the evening. They met at the bar. They got drunk. They talked a little bit about Area 91. Then they started having a very personal, drunken conversation, which was about to turn physical when Mary freaked, paid off the tab and jumped into a ride share back to the house. Other than that, she was certain of nothing, other than the fact that the morning's gym session was going to be a tad awkward. Try as she did, she could not manage to get back to sleep. She was unsure if she woke out of a state of fear, or a state of climax.

Chapter 12 – Not what we thought

Macleod had arranged for a backhoe to be brought to the Area 91 site in the very early morning to dig out a section of the rocky soil on the embankment until concrete was exposed. The operator and backhoe were in and out before anyone noticed its presence. Bruce decided that the logistics of machine rental, generator, water feed, and a whole slew of hand tools and implements was a little bit more of a deal than he was willing to take on, so he enlisted the paid help of his neighbor Tommy, who already had everything packaged in a utility truck with the exception of the boring machine itself.

Bruce estimated that the concrete walls would be about two feet thick. They were slightly over two and a half feet thick, but Tommy came equipped to go three feet so the boring went off without a hitch. Thank you, Tommy. Here's your fifteen hundred bucks for a really long drive and about two hours of work. And remember, it was just some random coastal buried concrete structure down south. In fact, better yet, forget about it.

Bruce fished some plastic sample tubing connected to an industrial air quality monitor through the hole, and as far into the interior as he could reach and activated the sensor. Carbon dioxide levels were normal, and there were no detectable levels of hydrogen sulfide or carbon monoxide. There were some trace volatile organics, but only slightly above outside ambient air.

Macleod stood impatiently as he awaited the results. "What's it looking like?"

"Looks pretty good, actually," Bruce replied. He sniffed the opening. "Smells kind of musty, but that's kind of what you would expect." Bruce put away the air quality monitor. "Now for the fun part."

"What's that?" Macleod asked, eyeing the long-coiled wire attached to a small handheld video monitor.

"It's called an industrial endoscope, or snake camera. We can go up to fifty feet in there and see what is inside. At least, as much as the small lens at the end can catch."

"Is there going to be enough light in there?"

"It has lights built into it. I brought some half inch PVC pipe sections we can use to push the end inside the room. Okay, well, I've got enough for twenty feet. Hopefully it should give us an idea. Help me tie this thing onto the end of the pipe."

Both men stared at the small color screen as the probe slowly advanced past the opening in the concrete, gradually drooping to the floor as it flexed. "Huh," Macleod said as he gazed at the screen.

"What do you make of it?" Bruce asked.

"I kind of expected to see carnage. Bones. Dried blood. But it looks more or less like a normal room might look, after being sealed up for forty years. Caked dirt on the floor. Patches of peeling paint on the walls but not too bad. A lot of dust everywhere. Can you manage to prop that thing up somehow so we can see the tops of those tables?"

"Not with what I brought with me. This stuff is too flexible. But remember, this is just one room. Some kind of lobby. Whatever happened may not have gotten this far, and if it had, three people might not have gotten away."

Macleod scratched his head. "True. I wish we could fly a drone around in there or something."

"Air quality readings are looking pretty good for a sealed underground vault. I'm thinking we can safely go in there."

"I don't know, Highland. That's a tall order."

"We've come this far."

Ari Rosenfeld held a plastic pen in his teeth as he searched the Internet on his laptop in his private study. Without breaking his gaze, he reached over for a blister pack of throat lozenges. Feeling it, he could tell he was out. He broke his concentration and looked at the depleted bubble pack. "Myrna? Did you already leave?" he asked in a loud voice. There was no response. "Oy vey." He focused back on the task at hand. And that was researching his old charge, the man responsible for causing Maya to spend an extra week in the United States to find out any information she could find regarding his demise. He stumbled upon his university's obituary.

Daniel Moshe Levin, noted University of Tel Aviv doctoral graduate and leading researcher in microbiology, 1960-1985. Ari stared at the brief obituary turned up in a search. They have the wrong year of death.

Maybe it is the wrong Daniel Levin? Ari did further searches on the same name, and age bracket and only turned up another obituary, dated 1985, this time from a newspaper. Daniel Moshe Levin, a leading microbiologist at the University of Tel Aviv, has passed at the Chaim Sheba Medical Center on November 13, 1985 from terminal brain cancer. He is survived by...

"No! This cannot be!" Ari exclaimed aloud to a non-existent audience. It must be the wrong Daniel Levin, Ari reasoned. Perhaps, that was the official explanation for Daniel Levin's death? They still have the date wrong. It's almost a year too late. But the more Ari thought about it, he never actually knew what the official, recorded cause of Levin's death was to begin with. That wasn't his department.

Ari's first stop was the hospital. Of course, the response he got when he tried to verify the death over the phone was 'we cannot release that information to a private party but you can go through...' so he instead chose to go into the records department and wave his Mossad card. There was a record of his diagnosis, treatment, and eventual death that spanned a two-year period. Okay, well, so, a man named

Daniel Levin of about the same age died here in Tel Aviv in 1985 of brain cancer. It was signed and dated.

Ari's next stop was the University of Tel Aviv. They confirmed, there was one, and one only, Daniel Moshe Levin, doctoral fellow then graduate, leading microbiology researcher, up until his death in November of 1985. Ari stood dumbfounded. Well, if it wasn't Daniel Levin that I met and recruited at the University of Tel Aviv, then who the hell was it?

Bruce had a hard time sleeping and couldn't shake the feeling the rest of the day. There was something basically wrong with Chad Green's story. The big problem is that he is the sole survivor of the incident, yet, he was the newest member of the team, having only been on board with the program for a total of four weeks. Bruce couldn't quite put his thumb on it, but something seemed amiss, regardless of the plausibility of mutant killer animals.

Bruce went back to the news searches of June 6, 1984. Dr. Irving Fuller, and Sarah Lock, killed in a vehicle accident on Highway 1 in Monterey. Reported on the local news and in the local newspaper. Bruce dialed Macleod on his cell phone.

Macleod responded. "Hello?"

"This is Bruce Highland. Listen, think back to June 6, 1984. Specifically, the traffic fatalities involving Irving Fuller and Sara Lock. How did you learn of them?"

"From the evening news, why?"

"Did you ever get the report from the CHP or the local cops?"

"No, I don't believe I did."

"You said you're a federal agent, right?"

"That's right."

"Can you have them pull the report?"

"My god man, that was nearly forty years ago. I doubt they still have it."

"It was reported as a fatal road rage incident. A crime. A murder. They have it. They just don't want to dig in their hard copy records to find it. I'd do it myself but you will have better luck getting some of their time than I will."

"All right. I'll do that. I don't see how it's going to make a difference one way the other, but I'll humor you."

"It's almost certainly going to be on file with CHP. If not, then either Monterey city cops or Monterey County sheriff."

"What am I looking for, pray tell?"

"That it exists."

Four hours later, Bruce was twenty ounces into a five-glass bender of German Pilsner at the Crop & Saddle when Macleod called back. "Highland speaking."

"They didn't have it," Macleod said. "And I tried all three agencies."

"Well, what did they have for that day?"

"CHP and County Sheriff have a record of three traffic fatalities in the City of Monterey on June 6, 1984. One was a double fatality on Highway 1, suspected road rage, and the other a single vehicle accident into a phone pole on Beach Street."

"Get the names?"

"Double fatality on Highway 1 was William Lerner, 43 and Julie Lerner, 39, residents of Monterey. Single vehicle accident was Jose Mendez, 87, resident of Salinas."

"The news reports for that day identified three fatalities in two accidents, Irving Fuller, 43, and Sarah Lock, 39, residents of Monterey, and Jose Mendez, 87, resident of Salinas."

"My god Highland, what the hell happened?"

"Oh, see... I had this nagging, sneaking feeling something wasn't right. Someone, possibly at the scene of the accident, reported the false names to the media and it aired that way."

"For god's sake, why?"

"I have a feeling that our esteemed professor didn't die in a traffic accident that day."

"Again, why?"

"I don't know, Macleod. But I'll tell you one thing – I really want to get inside that vault."

"All right. Let me work on that."

"Oh... by the way, my source at the Agency apparently had a chat with your boss. Or more accurately, the other way around. He reported that the Agency contact for Dark Fury had retired several years ago. Do you know, or can you find out who that contact was?"

"Let me think. The DOD manager at the Pentagon was a Colonel Reston. I dealt with him. I met the Agency contact once. The name was..., let me think a minute. Risso. A lady. A real looker at that. Karen Risso was the name. She was an officer. A high-level program manager."

The week was nearly up. In fact, if you factored travel time back to Tel Aviv, she would technically have overextended her trip. Maya started to pack her things. She felt a twinge of guilt, as if she should somehow reach out to Mary and let her know that she had to return to her home country. She was starting to feel a bond. Bonds are dangerous in this business, nobody had to tell her twice. Her burner phone rang from an unknown number, probably another burner phone. "Hello?" she replied.

"This is Ari. Have you started back yet?"

"I booked the flight and I'm packing, but no, not yet."

"Cancel it for now. Something very strange is going on."

"What is that?"

"It seems that Daniel Levin did not die in an accident at Area 91 in 1984. He died of cancer here, in Tel Aviv, a year later. Or, at least that's what the records reflect."

"If that's true, it would seem like our work is done."

"Our mission is not to bring closure to a suspicious death. Our mission is to protect whatever interest Israel has in this project we shared with the Americans."

"Right."

"I want you to stay there. I am going to travel over there to meet up with you. We are going to get to the bottom of this, one way or the other."

"All right. Give me a call when you get here. I will pick you up from the airport. Which one will be your destination?"

"I don't know. Probably Los Angeles. No matter, I will find my way to Monterey."

Maya felt slightly insulted, as if she was judged so incapable of doing her job that Ari had to fly all the way out to do it for her. But, in Ari's defense, she wasn't getting anywhere. Yet. That said, there was also an upside to the extended stay.

Maya dialed another number. "Hey Mary, just checking in with you. How are you doing, girl?"

First things first, Bruce reasoned. Find the death record for Professor Irving Fuller. There wasn't one issued in 1984. Of course, there wasn't. Who would have issued it? The news media? No. The county coroner. For that matter, Bruce was not able to locate a death record for Fuller subsequent to 1984, so he still could be alive. On the other hand, Bruce can't conveniently track the whereabouts of the professor either. He never re-entered academia, and there are a hell of a lot of Irving Fullers in the phone book. He could be hiding in plain sight under his own name, and nobody would even notice unless they were actively looking for him. There are only two people that could know where he is – and that is the tax man, and the social security lady. And if you don't collect benefits, or earn a reportable income, you don't need to talk to either.

What about Sarah Lock? There are lots of Sarah Locks in the phone book too. There was no record of a GS worker named Sara Lock. Bruce made a call to Nielson, who did a clearance check on all of the known members Bruce was aware of. Irving Fuller and Chad Green were issued Top-Secret clearances. Daniel Levin was issued a Limited Access Authorization Secret Clearance equivalent, which is the highest level clearance that may be issued to a foreign national. There was no record of any clearance issued to anyone named Sarah Lock. Even admins for top-secret programs must be cleared. Hell, the coffee barista in the CIA headquarters food court has a top-secret clearance. It doesn't mean he has access to any form of classified information whatsoever, it just means that he can be reasonably trusted to keep his mouth shut if he overhears something he shouldn't have.

There were two more players who needed to be researched. Colonel Reston. Reston led top-secret Special Forces missions in Vietnam and Honduras, and then was assigned to the Pentagon. He retired in 1995 and passed away in 2014. Can't talk to him anymore. Karen Risso was a mid-level officer in the Agency, resigning her employment in January 1985. Presumably over the Dark Fury debacle. Current and former staffers, particularly high-level, aren't easily tracked. And there are enough Karen Rissos in the phone book that singling out the right one will be tough. Nielson could confirm her name and position but he did not have access to her personnel records. Bruce could estimate her age roughly by conjecture, but that alone without knowing a place of birth wouldn't be particularly useful in finding her. And she wouldn't exactly be a spring chicken by now, so there is no telling if she was still around.

Bruce had one nagging issue, which was completely unrelated to the effort in which he was currently engaged. He did a search through his paid LEO/bonded investigator access portal for State Department records. Low and behold, a replacement passport was issued in London to none other than Svetlana Petroya.

Bruce was shocked beyond belief. He didn't know whether to be happy, sad, angry, or maybe he had run into some misinformation. But he was very specific on the information he entered and received. If it hadn't been for the odd encounter with her brother Alex, he would have chalked it up to probably identity theft. It still could be. He fumbled for his cell phone, dialed a number, and it went straight to voice mail. "Hey Alex, this is Bruce. We need to talk."

For lack of a better resource, and because he was already someone involved anyway and liked challenges, Bruce brought in his neighbor Tommy and two of his buddies, who arrived with a small skid steer excavator towed behind a pickup, and a jackhammer. After three hours of work, they removed the concrete covering the heavy cast iron door that served as the entrance to the structure. After breaking the corroded padlock away and applying a gallon of penetrant to the hinges and doorway edges, they were finally able to slowly pry it open sufficiently to enable Bruce and Macleod to walk inside. It's a confined space. Tommy was insistent that they remain clear of the structure until a ventilation blower could circulate good air inside for twenty minutes.

"Does this thing still have power?" Bruce asked rhetorically. He opened a large breaker box and threw the main breaker. A couple of fluorescent lights overhead popped and fizzled, and emitted a flickering yellowish light. "Looks like we're in business."

It was like a time capsule. There were some yellowed magazines and newspapers dated 1983 and 1984 on the lobby area tables, some desks with telephones, and some old vintage IBM PCs. There was a thick layer of dust over everything, and old cobwebs everywhere. Moving on to the second level up a concrete stairwell, there was a laboratory. There were lab counters and worktables on which rested centrifuges, tests tubes, microscopes, and a couple more PC's. There were file cabinets. Supply cabinets. Desks.

Up on to the third floor, there were some stainless autopsy tables, large empty cages, and more supply cabinets. "You know what's wrong here?" Bruce said to Macleod.

"Yes, the lack of carnage and bones," Macleod replied.

"More than that. There were animals in here. How did they get fed?" Bruce opened empty storage lockers and refrigerators, also empty save for tie packs of plastic water bottles, most of which had disintegrated to the point of losing their contents. "And look at these cages. They look like they are made of sheet metal curtain rods." Bruce poked around the area some more, and rifled through the drawers of a metal desk. There was a folder inside filled with receipts. One in particular caught Bruce's eye. It was a return receipt in the amount of five hundred dollars, from a company called Shimano's House of Effects in Pasadena. Bruce pocketed the receipt.

Bruce proceeded back down to the lab area. There were rows of black binders neatly arranged on the shelves. He pulled some out. They were all maintenance manuals for industrial HVAC systems, pumps, forklifts, and beverage bottling lines, probably scabbed from a factory. The equipment itself appeared to be old and outdated for the era, mismatched, and largely non-functional. Half of them were placed in areas nowhere near an electrical outlet. The lab sinks and faucets were not plumbed into anything. "Well I'll be damned Macleod; do you know what we're looking at?"

"What's that, Highland?"

"You want to know what this place is? It's a goddamn movie set!"

Macleod could only respond with a stare of disbelief. He poked and prodded at the equipment as well, and opened the file cabinets, only to find bankers boxes of old apartment rental records, and binders full of old commercial construction project records, probably recovered from dumpsters. "All this time. I've been protecting what appears to be one, big, huge, massive lie! I don't get it, Highland. I don't fucking get it!"

"I don't either, my friend. I don't either. But I'm beginning to think I might have an idea."

"I can't believe I actually, seriously listened to what that man... Chad Green, said that one night!" Macleod announced angrily.

"I wouldn't be too quick to vilify him, at least not quite yet." Bruce walked outside the shelter with Macleod. There were now five people standing outside. Tommy and his crew, plus a girl that both Bruce and Macleod recognized as Maya Goldman, who was accompanied by an older man.

"You!" Macleod announced to Maya. "Didn't they teach you not to interfere with classified government facilities the first time?" He looked over at the older man. "And just who the hell are you?"

Ari motioned downwards with his hands, as if to diffuse Macleod's harsh tone. "My name is Ari Rosenfeld. I am a senior operative with Israeli intelligence. The reason we are here, is because we were told we lost a brilliant mind of our own, a man by the name of Daniel Levin, to a fatal accident here at this facility. And I want answers. And I want to know what we, and I mean 'we', as it was a joint project, have a stake in."

"Do you?" Macleod replied. "All right. Well, it's all in there. Go ahead. Take a look inside. Take your time." Macleod fished out a cigar, cut the tip off and lit it with a butane torch.

"Cigar huh?" Bruce said. "I'm not sure what there is to celebrate. Other than maybe that the threat was never real to begin with."

"I haven't smoked a cigar out of celebration since landing Captain Ella Crabtree in a Saigon hotel bed when I was a lieutenant," Macleod laughed. "Come to think of it, she smoked one too."

"All, righty, thanks for the graphic there," Bruce replied.

Macleod thought for a minute and turned red. "I didn't mean exactly that way, but yeah."

A half hour later Ari and Maya returned from inside the bunker. "This was all some big joke? Is that what you are telling me?"

"I'll have you know that I myself am just finding this out, today in fact," Replied Macleod. "But I'm pretty sure I can safely say that your man Daniel Levin almost certainly did not perish here in a terrible accident."

"I've come to that conclusion myself," Ari said. "I just don't understand what the hell is going on."

"Nor do I," Macleod said. "But I doubt it concerns your interest at this point in time."

"Apparently not. Come on, Maya. Let's return home." Ari and Maya drove off in a rental car.

"What now?" Bruce asked. "Case closed?"

"No," Macleod said. "Not yet. We can see what has happened, but not why. Maybe I'm missing something."

"I don't think you're missing anything, other than being party to one of the biggest snow jobs in recent history. But... if we can find Fuller, we might possibly get our answers."

"All right. Consider yourself still on the clock."

"Are you guys done with us?" Tommy asked.

"Cut the power and get that door closed," Macleod said. "I'll throw a lock on it later."

"How are you going to handle this with the Agency?"

"I don't know yet. I suppose that may be somewhat dependent on what our friend Dr. Fuller is able to share with us."

"I have something to tell you," Bruce said, as he took a seat on Melanie's couch.

"Go ahead," she said. Usually, when it's the man that needs to have either 'the talk' or 'has something to tell,' it's pretty big. Men hate talking and shudder at hearing the words 'I have something to tell you.'

"Svetlana is back."

"What? I thought she was dead?"

"So did I. Long story. Her death was never confirmed. She was in Russia for the past three years in a rehabilitation center with no memory. Well, the memory thing appears to be changing and she is now back in California."

"You just found that out?"

"That guy in the pub the other day I had to talk to. He was Svetlana's brother. He hinted that she was alive, but didn't outright tell me then. He told me later after I pressed him."

"Then I guess you need to make a choice."

"Well, see, that's the thing, Melanie, I'm not sure I actually have a choice that I am able to make. I still am technically married and she still is technically alive."

"You told me yourself that you felt things with me that you did not feel with her. Was that a lie?"

"No, it wasn't. Still isn't. In a perfect world, I'd have my cake and be able to eat it as well. But that wouldn't be fair to you."

"See Bruce, that goes back to what we talked about before. You are only comfortable with people you can't be close with. It sounds like a hell of a way to live your life, but that's just my take."

"I don't have a good answer to that. You do realize I broke my own rule about client relationships with you?"

"Well, you realize that I in turn broke my own rule about hired professional service relationships, right?"

"Understood."

"So, is this the part where you tell me that you'll get back to me after you figure out whatever you are going to do?"

"I wouldn't patronize you like that," Bruce said.

"Thank you."

"I need to get going." Bruce held her in his arms at the doorway.

"The door is open if you ever need to talk."

"Later," Bruce said, as he pecked a quick kiss on her lips.

It had been a long time. He still went by Alexandri back then, when they first met, and he didn't have that townhouse on Anza Street. And he had just met Volga, but they weren't serious back then. That was eight years ago. It was Bruce's first case where he worked closely with the Agency and was even employed as a staffer for a short period of time. He needed a computer hacker. They said to look in Little Moscow for a computer hacker. He met a friend of a friend of Alexandri's, who had a sister that was a top-level computer hacker. And sparks flew.

Bruce knocked on the door. "Hi Alex," he announced.

"Come on in," Alex said. "Svetlana is in the living room."

Svetlana stood up and embraced him as he approached. Then she sat back down on the couch. Bruce sat down next to her. "I wish I could tell you that I remember you better than I do."

"I understand," Bruce said. "I missed you. It was very hard at first. I did not handle it well."

"I did not handle things well either. It is very frustrating not even knowing who you are, or even what your real name is for almost three years."

"I can't imagine."

"I'm sure you have moved on by now," Svetlana said, with an expressionless face.

"I tried to. It didn't work out."

"Park. Yes?"

"You remember her?"

"The name just came to me. Right now."

"Do I have... things?"

"Yes."

"At your place?"

"Well, our place, but yes. I never expected you to come back, but I saved them just the same. Well, except for the car. Sorry."

"Um, Bruce?" Alex said.

"Yes Alex?"

"Do you have anything to add before we get off the subject of moving on?"

"There isn't much to add. I met a girl named Melanie. That's the one you saw me with at the Crop & Saddle. She was a client who hired me to find her brother. That case has been closed."

"She didn't look at you like just a person you work for."

"That part of the case has been closed too. Look, I want to make something clear. I made a promise to Svetlana and I have every intention of keeping it."

"Which part?" Svetlana asked. "The love, honor and respect, or the take care of in sickness and health? Because the first one I think you struggle with."

"I'm not perfect. But I would never leave you high and dry."

"You know you could have just left it alone, Bruce," Alex said. "What is your expectation from this meeting?"

"Me Alex? I could say the same of you. You approached me first, remember? You didn't come right out and say it, but you suggested that Svetlana was alive and back. What do you expect me to do? Ignore her? Turn my back on her?" Bruce felt frustrated. "What do you want to do, Svetlana?"

"I have job here. I have purpose. I don't know, Bruce. Obviously, we must have felt passion at some point in time. I don't remember it though. I am sorry."

"Don't be. You forgot about that part well over three years ago," Bruce replied with a snide look.

"Bruce!" Volga interjected. "That was uncalled for."

"You're right. Sorry."

"I...I don't know. Let me think about it," Svetlana replied.

"Take your time."

According to Chad Green, sometime between 1972 and 1982 Irving Fuller sought and received a grant to conduct an oceanic expedition of an uncharted island in the South Pacific, and subsequently organized the voyage and recruited some scientists to go along. A trans-oceanic venture of this nature is going to be very expensive, even with the lowest budget charter vessel available. It's going to be enough that in addition to department approvals and recommendations, the university itself is going to have to approve the project by a board, and it will be well documented. And it was. He secured a grant for a little over $1.2 million. However, aside from Fuller's expedition report, there is no other outside documentation to suggest that the trip ever occurred. Ostensibly, the 120-ton trawler New Zealand flagged MV Pegasus sailed from Christchurch on August 3, 1980 on a 3,100 nautical mile voyage to the island on a trip that lasted twelve days to the island, three days at anchor for exploration, and a return lasting eleven days. A record search conducted by Wellington Fisheries, Limited, owner of the MV Pegasus, revealed that indeed, on January 29th, 1980, a written charter quotation was sent via fax to Dr. Irving Fuller of Cambridge, Massachusetts for a private oceanic exploration totaling 6,200 nautical miles round trip. And no further communication was received regarding the quotation. In fact, the MV Pegasus was docked for repairs the entire month of August. There was no evidence that Dr. Fuller ever even set foot on New Zealand soil, much less with a research team in tow.

In contrast, the cited expeditions to the island conducted in 1859 and 1952 were, in fact historically cited as a matter of record. Bruce was beginning to see a pattern here. He pulled out his calculator, started adding up costs, based on a graciously emailed copy of the original quotation, threw in the costs of a research team, logistics, and other odds and ends and concluded that $1.2 million was an unrealistically low budget, but it probably represented the maximum that Fuller would have been able to secure, and who cares if the budget is light because Fuller isn't going on an actual expedition anyway. The university never even got the chance to scrutinize Fuller's full report because it was confiscated and censored by the CIA under federal warrant before it reached their hands. Try that today.

Bruce theorized that scamming the university wasn't Fuller's end game. It was chump change compared to what he could extract from a secretly funded military program with a huge budget and no outside accountability. But scamming the most powerful military and the largest intelligence agency in the free world is a whole new level above defrauding an educational institution. Fuller couldn't have done it alone. Fuller had to have some inside help.

It had to be someone that was part of the program. It had to be someone that was not just involved with the program, but involved at a high level. Someone that could either make decisions on large scale program expenditures, or have a strong influence in them. The only two candidates that were known to Bruce was the Pentagon manager, Colonel Reston, and the Agency manager, Karen Risso. One oversees the job. The other came up with the job, and funded the job. Risso wins hands down on this one. And she conveniently left the Agency after the program was put in hibernation.

Bruce had an idea. Irving Fuller is a wealthy man who could be living any place in the country. Or any place in the world, for that matter. Could the same be said about Karen Risso, who forfeited a generous federal pension? It was a long shot, but find one, you find the other. The problem is, how do you find one of them? You look for both of them together.

There was one huge loose end. And that was the people. The team. There were a total of thirteen people, four of whom were known by name. Fuller, Lock, Green and Levin. Fuller, Green and Levin are legitimate people. Lock is suspect, either by name, or possibly even by presence. Bruce called up Macleod on the phone.

"Yes Highland," he answered.

"Listen, think back to the days when the Dark Fury team was operating on the site. We know there were thirteen people. Have you ever seen them all?"

"No. I'd see people come and go. But not really much until the end. We opened it up in... eighty-two, there was a lot of activity for about a month. Trucks coming and going. Then there wasn't much activity until about a month before the incident."

"How many have you ever seen together?"

"Together? Maybe... two or three. But I wasn't keeping constant watch on it either. I did actually have to pretend to have a day job."

"Right. Thanks."

Undeterred, Bruce decided to reach out again to Chad Green, who picked up his cell phone after several rings. "Hey Chad, old buddy. This is Bruce Highland. How are things?"

"Good," Chad replied. "I'm back in Ensenada."

"Listen, uh... back when you were working at the site – Area 91, how many people were working with you?"

"Oh gee... let me think about that. I think... let's see... there was Dr. Fuller, Daniel Levin, two lab guys – not sure exactly what they did, and an animal handler. So, normally, six. So, on any given day in those two weeks, from four to seven."

"Was there a department secretary named Sarah Lock?"

"Yes, in fact there was. But I've only saw her once or twice."

"Wait... you said four to six. So, think back on that day. The very day the incident happened. How many people were working in that vault when the incident happened?"

"Let's see... six."

"I thought a total of thirteen people worked there?"

"Yeah, by roster but they were not all there at the same time. I only met seven including Dr. Fuller."

"Tell me about Daniel Levin."

"He was super intelligent. But he was real sick too. And he quickly decided that the program was flawed and he didn't want to have any part of it, so they ended up sending him back about five days before the incident. He wasn't there for very long."

"You told me that the animal handlers... I guess handler... was super protective of the animals. What about your lab guys?"

"Same thing. They didn't like me around. I hung out in the lobby a lot. Fuller told me that we were in a holding pattern awaiting the rest of the team."

"You told me a lot about these animals. About their behaviors. About how they couldn't be controlled. How were you able to determine that?"

"Pretty much only by what they told me. They wouldn't let me get very close to the animals."

"Did you have to write any reports?"

"I was working on one."

"Did you have contact with anyone outside of the immediate team?"

"Not really. It was Dr. Fuller himself that approached and recruited me. Oh...well, there was one thing. On the day of the incident, when all hell broke loose, the handler and a lab guy were covered in blood. They looked like they had been run through a grinder. They closed the door to the lab and were holding it shut, so Fuller and I could get out. But they asked me to make a call on the phone in the vault lobby to inform the higher ups of what was going on."

"So, it was just you and Fuller?"

"Yeah, Fuller told me to go home, and he would pick up the secretary, and we would regroup later to figure out what to do. Then I heard on the news about Dr. Fuller and the girl. Shortly after that, I got that call, by that Scottish guy."

"Hmm. All right. Thanks," Bruce ended the call.

Chapter 13 – Now we know

The massive ballroom was crowded with tuxedos and evening dresses as if it were a Hollywood gala, attended by the top television and movie stars in a highly publicized event to be covered in depth by every tabloid from Hong Kong to Rome. Except the stars were not Hollywood actors, they were professors, graduate students, fellows, and private foundation executives. This was the Natural History Symposium hosted in DC. Every university with a shred of accreditation was represented – and naturally, Harvard in force. The mood was somber – Ronald Reagan had just taken office having won the presidency over Jimmy Carter. Academia was unsure how this would affect educational funding and research.

A lanky, wavy-haired man in a black tux in his early thirties wearing thick, dark framed glasses loaded an appetizer tray with quiche tarts and cocktail shrimp. He couldn't help but notice the tall, broad shouldered blonde woman in the flowing turquoise dress approach him. "Irving Fuller, is that you?" she asked.

He did a double take. "Karen? My god, that is you, right?"

"Yes. Karen Risso. Remember? Oak Hill High?"

"Wow. That was a while back. What possibly brings you out here to DC?"

"I work here, Irving. I forget, did you go by Irving, or Irv? Everyone called you Irving."

"Irving works. Yeah, I um… I'm a professor of natural history at Harvard. Finished up my doctoral work a couple years ago. I'm here to support my department. What are you doing?"

"I have a… job with the government. I manage… programs."

"Oh. Nice. I'm surprised you noticed me. I kind of always viewed you as, how can I put it, out of my league."

"Yeah well, I guess I was kind of like that back then. But that was a long time ago. You had such a reputation for being a scammer. People would say you could con a rock out of its water."

"Well, that doesn't translate to being able to con the Virgin Mary of her chastity. I never did hit it off much with the girls."

"I'll admit you were kind of nerdy back then. But you've grown out of that, Irving."

"What kind of projects do you manage for the government? Or is it one of those things that if you told me you would have to kill me?"

Karen blushed. "Mm..." Karen looked around and lowered her voice. "Defense type projects."

"You mean like military?" Fuller asked as he bit into a chilled shrimp. "This thing needs sauce."

"Something like that."

"What would you be doing here then?"

"Oh, we go around to all of the big university events, looking for ideas, looking for projects. Obviously, we like engineering symposiums better, but you never know."

"Really. Say, would you like to have dinner tomorrow night?"

"I see your self-confidence has improved greatly," Karen said with a smile. "Ordinarily when guys, even good-looking guys ask me out, I normally decline."

"Well, I guess it is informative to know that I don't fall in that category."

"I didn't mean it that way. Don't you have to go back to Boston or New York or wherever the hell Yale is tomorrow?"

"Harvard. And it's in Cambridge. That's just outside of Boston. But to answer your question, no. This is a Friday, you know."

"Oh, it is, isn't it. I have such a busy schedule that I tend to lose track of which day it is."

"It gets that way for me too, during the school season."

"Anyway... you going to be here at this hotel tomorrow?"

"I can be."

"Good. I'll pick you up at six thirty then."

"I... did drive here. So I do have a car."

"Oh. Well, you can meet me at the restaurant if you want."

"I guess where I was going with that is I could pick you up at your place."

"I understand that. Be in front of the lobby, six-thirty sharp."

Bigger is always better. Until it isn't. The first thing that bothered Bruce when he came to the realization that Area 91 and the whole Dark Fury thing was a sham, was, how do you manage the charade act with a cast of thirteen players?

You don't. As far as Chad Green was concerned, he was absolutely convinced, and genuinely, that Dark Fury was real. Some had to be in on the game, and some were obviously not in on the game. Macleod got played. Bruce had previously held some residual doubts as to Macleod's authenticity, but they had since been allayed. What about Daniel Levin? Chad alluded that he was disillusioned with the project and it was his cause for leaving. Maybe he was on to it quickly. What about the others? Who knows? In any case, a team of five under you is easier to manage and control than a team of twelve. Bruce surmised that the remainder of the thirteen-person team existed in roster name only, and likely weren't even real people. Like Sarah Lock. Bruce suspected she was a paper person as well. But there is no good way of knowing for sure.

And of course, there is the possibility that Bruce was reading the whole thing entirely wrong. Kind of like when you expect to see a cat, and instead you are staring at a dog. You have expected the cat so long that you wonder if in fact, the dog in front of you is really a cat.

No, it's a dog. Bruce was pretty sure he generally had most of the pieces to the puzzle, but just not exactly how they all fit together. If you're building a jigsaw puzzle of a dog, and fit the pieces together incorrectly, the end result may well look like a cat.

Bob Shimano had crazy looking thick jet-black hair, and a full unkempt beard and mustache. He walked out into the lobby of his movie set effects workshop and greeted Bruce. "All right, let me take a look at that receipt. Man, that was a long time ago. I was like ten years old at the time."

"Can you tell me what it was for?" Bruce asked.

"Yeah, I remember my dad working on them. You know, we've rented these things out maybe three or four times since I've taken over the business. The Ripalots. That was actually the name given to the creatures by the guy that originally ordered them from us. We just kept the name after we bought them back from him."

"Ripalots. Yes. Vicious fictional animals."

"Yep. C'mon. I'll show you." Shimano led Bruce back to a massive warehouse, with all kinds of mechanized life like fake animals. "Obviously, you can see what we specialize in. That T-Rex over there. It was in 'The Land that Time Wouldn't Forget. A bad redo of a popular movie.'"

"Oh. Yeah. Terrible movie. Great monster though."

"Here we go. The Ripalots. Last featured in 'The Flesh-Eating Bog Monsters.' We've replaced the old controls with digital ones."

"The thing looks like an overgrown mutant Otter," Bruce chuckled.

"This one has a little bit of charge left in the battery." Shimano flipped a switch. "Watch your hands. Don't get too close to the mouth." Shimano slowly drew a long wooden stick to the robot's hairy face. Its eyes moved, it sounded with a faint snarl, and lashed out, breaking the stick in half with its teeth.

"Whoa!" Bruce said. "That thing scares the hell out of me, and I even know it's a fake."

"These Furbies on steroids are fairly popular." Shimano reached behind the robot's head, and flicked off the hidden switch. "Now I don't know the back story here, but it's not uncommon for us to buy back the props for pennies on the dollar after they are used in a movie set."

"What about stuff like fake blood and fake injuries and that kind of stuff?"

"Yeah, we do that too. And the nice thing about our stuff is it cleans up pretty easy." Shimano led him back to the end of the warehouse into a special shop. "There you go. Severed arms, shredded torsos, open brain matter head coverings, we can make you look pretty bad in a hurry."

"Oh my god," Bruce said, looking at a human looking dummy that resembled a female version of Frankenstein's monster. "Is that what I think it is?"

"Yes, we made it for the movie 'The Evil Gynecologist.' We sewed a fake vagina on the face where the mouth would be."

Bruce received a text message from Macleod, asking him to stop by Monterey on the way back from Los Angeles. He pulled into Macleod's luxurious house only to find three other black painted government vehicles parked outside.

The door was open. There were three men in black frantically pacing the living room, babbling at top speed on their cell phones. "So, what is going on, Macleod?" Bruce asked.

"I decided that sooner was probably better to bring my boss up to speed. And basically, your job is over." Macleod handed him a rather thick envelope stuffed with crisp one hundred dollar bills.

"You guys don't want me to find your perp, Dr. Fuller?"

"For what? To bring charges against him? To sue him? This has turned out to be a huge embarrassment. The Agency wants to bury it and forget it ever happened."

"Well, it looks like you're out of a job now," Bruce said.

"I was already out of a job, remember?" Macleod pointed as Mary entered the room, dressed in her workout spandex.

"What's going on here?" Mary asked, with a bewildered stare.

"Oh, um, Miss Adams-Wentworth. What a pleasure to have you back at the house. My dear, I believe you are shortly about to be reassigned to another program," Macleod announced.

Mary glared at Macleod, fuming over the 'Miss' reference. She looked about the room at the pacing men, and then over at Bruce. She let out a breath and calmed down. "Oh. Well, in that case, Bruce, can you uh, rub my back while you're here?"

"I'd love to, sweetie, but I really do need to head back home."

Bruce was still on a mission. A personal mission. It had taken a few weeks, but Bruce had discovered that Karen Risso's great uncle owned a property in the hills above the town of Bastia, Corsica. On a hunch, he started looking into the Corsica connection, and was in fact able to confirm that indeed, Karen Risso had purchased the property through a search of local records. What a perfect place to disappear. He tirelessly wheeled the tiny Renault rental car through the winding roads until he reached the address. He buzzed the intercom at the gate, and got no response. He could see a couple vehicles parked inside, so it stood to reason that someone should be home. More than likely, they didn't want to talk to anyone.

"Puis-je vous aider?" A voice behind him spoke. It was a neighbor across the street, who did not have a gated driveway.

"Monsieur Fuller et Mademoiselle Risso?" Bruce asked, struggling with his French.

The man shrugged and gave an 'I don't have the slightest clue' look.

Bruce was about to leave when a buzzer sounded and the gate swung open. A tall, thin wrinkled man wearing a floral pattern shirt and white trousers walked out. "Well, you got this far," he announced. "I suppose I might as well talk to you."

"Dr. Fuller?" Bruce asked.

He nodded. "Follow me." Fuller led Bruce back to shaded table on a patio area on a split level above a stone garage. "Have a seat."

"Do you know why I'm here?" Bruce asked.

"I have a pretty good idea. But why don't you tell me anyway."

"My name is Bruce Highland, and I'm a private investigator. I was actually hired to find a member of your team, Chad Green – which, by the way, I did. I want to know what happened at Area 91. And... I have been inside. I know about the fake animals. And I heard Chad Green's story."

"I figured it was a matter of time. I'm assuming I'm not in that much trouble, or you wouldn't have shown up by yourself."

"That's correct. The Agency doesn't care at this point. So basically, you're free and clear."

"Yeah well, that was important to me thirty years ago. I don't recon I have that many days left. Karen passed two years ago."

"So, tell me about it then."

"It all started shortly after I met Karen at a function in DC. I had come across some reports of two expeditions to an uncharted island in the South Pacific, and had wanted to organize a follow-up expedition for some time, but I quickly discovered that was easier said than done. I also knew from talking to Karen, that the government had seriously considered using trained attack animals against the North Vietnamese Army and the Viet Cong during the war, and we came up with this plan. First, get a credible expedition funded and approved, and find and bring back a stock of killer animals that we could train and develop into a military weapon."

"But that expedition never happened though."

"No, it didn't. An actual expedition would have cost about twice what I could have gotten funded, so I convinced the directors, got the funding, and... that's when Karen started selling the whole thing to the CIA. About the time I needed to show actual proof of expedition and research to the university, the government seized the operation and made it a classified program, taking the heat off."

"I figured that much myself. But why the elaborate deception in Area 91? And why bring in Daniel Levin and Chad Green?"

"Easy, I had to bring just enough recognized experts from the real world to be credible. The other three were washed out Hollywood actors. We had to fool Daniel Levin and Chad Green in to thinking the whole thing was real, so we spent two weeks rehearsing, and two weeks exposing Levin and Green to the site. Green was fooled, and Levin was not. Also, we needed to fool any visiting Agency personnel."

"Why the staged accident at the end?"

"You have to understand, I secured a huge, I mean a really big grant to fund this program. And things were finally catching up. Karen tried her best to keep the Agency at bay, but they wanted results, they wanted reports, they wanted a finished product. Which, of course I couldn't possibly deliver. So, the accident was the exit strategy. And to boot, I received a rather large fund to secure the site and make it safe."

"Which, you didn't spend much of on the closeout, did you?"

"No," Fuller grinned. "Karen got it placed in the Overwatch program, putting it in limbo for the foreseeable future."

"Roland Macleod was clueless about it?"

"I made sure he was never able to set foot in the place."

"Why was it necessary to stage your death? And an execution attempt on Chad Green?"

"Well, obviously, if I was alive and well, I would have to answer a lot of questions that I frankly didn't want to answer. They would have seen through the bullshit at some point. And Chad Green doing the Caspar? That was a bonus. He already did his job." Fuller rubbed his chin. "Besides, nobody tried to kill Chad Green. Macleod obviously read that into the situation and I guess he scared him off."

"Yeah. Well, it makes sense now."

"So why are you really here, Mr. Highland? If the Agency doesn't care, and your client is happy, what's it to you?"

"What's it to me? I dunno, Mr. Fuller. A miscarriage of justice? A massive defrauding of the taxpayer?"

"Justice? Fraud? Is that how you see it? Well... technically yes, but consider this. We left... literally about a billion dollars' worth of military hardware behind in Taliban hands when we pulled out of Afghanistan. Known terrorists. People that have sworn to kill us. Your government, and mine, was going to spend millions on building a destructive military weapon that could only be misused or go out of control. Wouldn't you rather it be spent on something that is harmless, than some actual program that could ultimately destroy the ecosystem and life as we know it?"

"That's a good way of rationalizing it. I commend you on that. Any way you break it down, I'm not walking away from here happy. I guess I just wanted to know, for my personal clarification, if I had you pegged right."

"So, you are self-centered as well."

"In that respect, yes."

Epilogue

The dinner table was dominated by an opened pizza box, littered with the remnants of a large Papa Guisti extra special Italian combination deep crust. As it had been, countless times in the past. Svetlana stared at the array of framed family photographs. "This... was me."

"Yes it was," Bruce said.

"What was our life like?"

"You're looking at it. Pizza. You ran a computer repair shop plus ran the books for the investigation business."

"I remember small pieces. I start to remember the house a little bit."

"Good."

"We ride bicycle a lot."

"That's right. It's still in the garage. All of your riding gear. All of your clothes, all of your things, I put them in the guest bedroom."

"Am I welcome back here?"

"This house is still yours too. That never changed." There was a knock on the door. Bruce got up and answered it. An Indian girl with flowing, jet-black hair and a slim figure walked in. "Remember Priya?"

Svetlana gasped. Priya ran over and hugged her. "Oh my god!" Priya said. "When I heard the news, I raced over as fast as I could. I can't believe you're back!"

"Forgive me, but my memory is very bad. It starts to come back, but slowly. You were my friend?" Svetlana replied.

"Yes. Well, I understand. I'm here for you. Listen, I can't stay long. I just wanted to stop by and say hi to you." Priya excused herself.

"I can't go back to Russia," Svetlana said. "I actually had to escape from there. There are people in GRU that still want me dead."

"We had had that conversation before you went on that trip. You were convinced it was safe. I was not very convinced," Bruce said.

"How is this going to work out?"

"You mean by you being back?"

"Yes."

"Let's take it one day at a time."

Mary Adams-Wentworth sat in an ornate metal chair in the street corner café in downtown Tel Aviv, next to Maya Goldman. "Thank you for meeting with me, Mr. Rosenfeld. I just wanted to introduce myself to you. I am the new liaison officer."

"Please, call me Ari. What happened to Sal?"

"He was um... discharged from the Agency. Our agency gets a little bit funny with senior agents that end up in foreign jails facing prostitution and drug charges."

Ari studied her carefully. "You look a little bit young to be a liaison officer."

"It's a long story. I heard there was an opening here and took advantage of it."

Maya grinned. "Yes, that's right."

Ari raised his eyebrows. "I see. I trust you're settling in nicely here in Israel, finding your way around?"

"Perfectly," Mary said. "I have some great help."

Maya grinned again. "Yes, that's right."

"Well," Mary said. "I guess we will... get going. Again, pleased to meet you."

"Very well," Ari replied. "Maya, can I have a private word with you before you go?"

Mary got up and left. Maya remained behind. "Yes?"

Ari leaned forward. "Is there something I need to know about? Or, more accurately, is there something I need to not know about?"

"You told me yourself that our agency encourages close working relationships with our counterparts."

"Tread carefully Maya, tread carefully."

"This is a really nice house," Jenny Murayama said. "How many years have we known each other at the gym, meeting for coffee in the morning afterwards at the café next door? Now I finally see where you live." She was a sixty-year-old second generation Japanese American with the body of a thirty-year-old.

"It's a long story," Macleod replied. "But I was able to buy this house from my former employer for pennies on the dollar. Fairly new electrical. Plumbing is in good order."

"Are you retired now?"

"I like to think that I'm not that old."

"So can you finally tell me what you really do?"

"Same as I've always told you. Government service worker, looking after properties."

"I had you pegged for some sort of super-secret spy or something."

"Well, if I was, then I wouldn't have been a very good one then, would I?"

"I guess not," Jenny smirked. She pulled out her phone. "I wonder if my masseuse can get me in this afternoon."

"Sore back?"

"Sore back, sore legs, sore butt... you name it."

"Well, I might be able to fix that."

"Really. All right. When?"

"How about right now?"

"Here?"

"Mm, why don't we head upstairs."

An hour and a half later, two unclothed bodies lay next to each other on a bed under a thick comforter. "That was a pretty thorough massage there, Roland. Plumbing appears to be in good order."

"All right guys, let's do a take here. We gotta make it quick before the base cops get here."

"Camera is rolling. Go ahead," the cameraman said.

"Hello, my name is Trey, and you... are watching the UFO Seekers, the channel that puts the 'you' in UFO. Today's segment is on an elusive secret government base called Area 91. And what we are going to tell you is going to blow your mind. We have some solid, concrete proof that this facility was used to house alien beings for top secret genetic research purposes."

"And my name is Carl, your co-host. We are a pair of investigative reporters and scientists that travel around the country exposing the most devious, derisive and repulsive secret government projects in existence. Back to you Trey."

"As we pan the camera out, here you are seeing it for the first time. The top-secret entrance to Area 91, exposed for the first time in nearly forty years. We have learned that in this very facility, human women have given birth to half-human, half-alien babies."

"Is there even a term for that, Trey? That goes even beyond bestiality. I would say, 'entiality' or relations between humans and space entities."

"Right you are Carl, oh, and you're seeing it on camera, the government camo men are on to us! They have come to shut us down! They have come to silence us! Keep the cameras rolling as long as you can! Oh, and please hit that subscribe button!"

The base security truck pulled up to the trio and the window rolled down. "What are you guys doing here?"

"Oh, uh, just shooting a short video. That's all."

"All right. Don't leave a mess, okay?"

"No problem." The security truck drove off. Trey looked relieved. "Well, there you saw it folks, a dangerous encounter with the camo dudes! All right, cut."

"Um, that's... not going to work as a dangerous encounter," Carl said.

"Not a problem. We have some stock footage of camo dudes I've been saving. We'll cut that in." Trey scanned the site, looking for other angles to record. "Oh, how's our CGI coming?"

"Almost done. We dressed Mason in a lizard suit and filmed him banging his girlfriend over the weekend. We're working on the delivery room scene now; except I don't think the Iguana is going to work out very well. We're going to have to find something else," Carl replied.

"How about a newborn dog? Those things can look pretty space alien if you don't know what you're looking at."

Carl reflected on the moment. "Don't you guys ever feel bad about, you know, faking stuff?"

The three young men looked at each other, exchanging confused glances. Then a loud round of laughter erupted. "This is going to take us straight to the mainstream channels, gentlemen! Cha-ching!" Trey exclaimed.

The veteran director stroked his beard and shook his head as he reviewed the footage. He clearly was not pleased. "Kyle, this is not a clean approach. You have to shake the camera a little bit to show we're on the edge here. Let's try this again. From inside the car."

The muscular, chiseled bald man wearing a tight-fitting black polo shirt in the passenger seat spoke in a hushed murmur to the cameraman. "All right. We're live in Ensenada, Mexico. Our team has managed to track down a former surviving employee of Area 91. He's legit. He's been verified. And he's agreed over the phone to meet with us. Let's go guys, this is it." The team of three men trailed by a cameraman walked up the pathway to a small villa. The lead man knocked on the door.

A thin man opened the door. "Yes?"

"Chad Green? I'm Tim Brightwell, from the History Busters Network. This is Roy Mace of US Special Forces, and Harris Conroe, an expert on scientific phenomena. Got some time to talk to the team?"

"Sure," Chad replied.

"Cut!" the director yelled.

"What is it this time?" Chad asked.

"Look, I get it, you're not a professional actor, but you need to be more apprehensive, like you have a lot of reluctance, can we work on that?"

"All right." Chad closed the door as he sighed.

"Oh, uh, Mr. Zalinski?" a young blond woman said as she nudged the director.

"What? Make it quick," the director replied.

"Mr. Hargrove said the network reached an agreement with the UFO Seekers. He wants you to cease production until they come up with a new game plan."

He turned red, and veins bulged out of his face. "Give me the goddamn phone!" Zalinski yanked the phone away from the girl and screamed into it. After a heated exchange, the color from his face disappeared. He handed the phone back to the girl.

"Gotcha!" Tim Brightwell yelled. The entire set erupted in laughter.

"You guys. Why I ought to...." Zalinski shook his fist.

Made in the USA
Coppell, TX
16 May 2023